Dear Reader,

    A word from Roman

MW01139325

    It is always a pleasure to give life to new characters. Bad Before Good & Those In Between is set against the Northwest backdrop and gives you vividly painted images of the metropolitan area known for coffee and rainy days. The journey centers around a young lady with a complex life; a result of events before she was born and her adolescent years colliding with meeting her current world, causing it to spiral in odd directions. She crosses paths with an interesting mix of people, and many of them have self-serving attitudes and goals. Travel along with Zelda as each voyager in her path brings life-changing moments in this novel which offers clever twists and turns.

    Alvin L.A. Horn, a spoken word artist who travels to recite poetry and play standup bass, shares his knack for verse that flows throughout the novel. There is a musical flow intertwined in his art of words.

    As always, thanks for supporting the efforts of Romantic Blues Publishing. We strive to bring you fresh and ground-breaking stories that will help you escape reality when life seems overwhelming, or for when we just want to visit another time and place. We appreciate the love and dedication of our readers.

    Previous works by Alvin L.A. Horn
    The World That Fell Into My Dresser Drawer; a book of poetry, 2001
    BRUSH STROKES; a novel, 2005 PERFECT CIRCLE; a novel published by Zane and Simon and Schuster, 2012
    ONE SAFE PLACE; a novel published by Zane and Simon and Schuster, 2014
    BRUSH STROKES; the re-release, with an added short story, 2016
    All in available in paperback and E-book
    Alvin is also a contributing author in the anthologies: Pillow Talk in The Heat of the Night, and The Soul of a Man 2, as well as a writer for the Inner City News, and a feature writer for Real Life Real Faith Magazine.

    Blessings

SHOUT OUTS FROM THE LITERARY WORLD

Alvin L. Horn is a genius writer. His writings are poetry, a melody intro for a sensual, erotic thriller that leaves you wondering if you were there in the flesh—one of the characters. In One Safe Place, he engages you right away, absorbing you into the secret world of Psalms Black, who fights for liberty and justice for his close friends, using his operative skills as a former secret service agent. The suspense was moving, intoxicating and caused me to search my own vulnerabilities as I watched these characters live their lives on the edge.

Alvin's poetry is just as poignant…tender, emotional, thoughtful, and erotic. I'm a true fan of this brother. I'd read anything he wrote. I'm looking forward to reading Bad Before Good and Those in Between.

Bestselling Suzetta Perkins, Author of Two Down: The Inconvenient Truth and Hollywood Skye.

***

Alvin L.A. Horn's written words and spoken word, have proven to be for me, transforming, infusing, invigorating, replenishing and inspiring, to my mind, body and soul. He gives life and uplifts life, through his words. Alvin's writings transport the reader, to places known and unknown. However, additionally, this cerebral experience and journey, one takes with him, is felt on a positive visceral and cellular level as well. One very personal experience, I have had in reading Alvin's books and becoming, voluntarily enmeshed in Alvin's prolific and incomparable writings is, while experiencing challenging situations, which caused me to physically and emotionally, feel drained, overwhelmed and sometimes, unwomanly, Alvin's words, have literally caused and produced positive thoughts, feelings and reaffirmed sensuality within me, that during those times, I felt were unattainable. This is the POWER in his, beautifully writing. It touches on the tangible and intangible physicality, spirituality and emotions. Alvin's words, metaphorically, can give life to the lifeless!

I whole-heartedly recommend, that one should give themselves the pleasure and exquisite escape of purchasing ALL of Alvin L.A. Horn's books. Alvin's latest book entitled, Bad Before Good & Those In Between," will not disappoint and will take you on a sublime, blissful, intriguing journey! You will be moved and touched in ways, you know and know not! (smile)...

2

I promise you, you won't regret it!
Best Wishes and Pleasurable Reading To ALL!
Author of, Save Your Life, (Not Your Image)
Lovingly, Rashidah Id-Deen

***

There is always anticipation when this author releases a new novel because there are no disappointments in his books. Strong energetic characters placed throughout multi-layered storylines are what you expect, and this writer delivers. Turning pages to this novel, I encountered a mix of characters of mental, physical variations. This novel is a must read!

Alvin L.A. Horn keeps you on the edge of what is going to happen with everything is tied situations laced in of deceit, realistic mayhem and secrets and social commentary through dealings and dialogues. I love the vengeance based on sentimental and moral justice. I highly recommend this book to those who love literature you learn and expand one's reasoning.

The writings in his novels are highly enjoyable and unexpected with descriptive narratives each time with absorbing smells, noise, and silence, makes one feel the potential despair or hopefulness. Alvin L.A. Horn's novels are on par with the best writers of our times with superbly written strengths, and human weaknesses.

Attorney Corey Minor Smith
Canton City Council at Large, Canton, OH

***

"Whenever my guy, Alvin L.A. Horn creates something from the hillsides out there on the West Coast in Seattle, Washington, I always wonder how black folks think out there, while I'm stuck over here like a sardine with the hustle and bustle of the East. Well, Brother Alvin has given us another taste of his uniquely diverse experiences with 'Zelda Harjo' a Black and Native American woman, a go-getter on a quest to find sanity in an insane life of unpredictable circumstances. And hell, ain't that what we're all trying to do? In Bad Before Good & Those In Between, Alvin L.A Horn gives it to us again, real and thoughtful."

Omar Tyree -- New York Times bestselling author and NAACP Image Award Winner

BAD BEFORE GOOD
& THOSE IN BETWEEN
A NOVEL
BY

ALVIN L.A. HORN

Romantic Blues Publishing
www.alvinhorn.com

PUBLISHING

Seattle Washington

Publishing 1-206 240-3468

ISBN-13: 978-1981494705
ISBN-10: 1981494707

Cover layout: Alvin L.A. Horn

For information regarding special discounts for bulk purchases, please contact at: alah57@gmail.com - Alvin L.A. Horn – Romantic Blues Publishing.

ACKNOWLEDGMENTS

God, thank you for giving me the opportunity to write and to be read by many. You have blessed me with gifts that all your children are given for their own; and with my blessings and gifts, I thank you for allowing me to share, help, enrich, inspire, and bring peace. Many don't believe you laugh, but I assume you do, at the foolishness of men. I hope I made you laugh at some of the ill-advised things I have done acting as if I were in control. Through your grace, my aptitudes have been given a chance for all to see.

I give thanks to Big Mama – my grandmother – and to all the elders of women who have taught me the value of the love of a woman, all in their own way. I'm blessed to have had all of you touch me in each of your individual ways. I write about women like you—the textured fabric of life I have been wrapped in.

I love my sisters; as we know, blood doesn't always make someone your family no more than love itself. I have been blessed with women who just made it possible to be friends to share life as sisters and this brother from different mothers and fathers.

To the men who helped shape me in the mode of whom I am without ever knowing the impact you have had on me. Whether you were my bloodline or a mentor, I have watched you for what is right or wrong— allowing me to choose which is best for me as a man. I love the old soul I am in how I dress, talk, and enjoy the music I do, because of my elders creating the Renaissance man I am, so I pen you in layers of storylines.

To those who loved me when it was easy, I'm a good man, but not a perfect man. I walk humbly knowing the mistakes I have made, and the good things in life I have been able to do. All my writings, I pen to bring awareness to the struggles that this world places as burdens on you and me. Every woman and man handles the weight of mankind differently, that creates narratives, and I'm going to write them.

Elissa Gabrielle, a queen of putting penned ink on paper, and publisher at Peace in the Storm Publishing. Thank you is an effortless expression that people say all too often out of simple courtesy; but then there are those times when someone looks you in the eye and you truly know they mean it...I'm looking you in the eye.

The friends and family very dear to me, the song says, "We go a long ways back." Even if it's not true...dealing with me, I'm sure it can feel like it. Thank you. Each one of you somewhere along the way has loved me in your special way, helping me to stay on course or to get back to where I needed to be, and I thank you for that.

I lost some loved ones, as times waits for no one, along the way of writing BAD BEFORE GOOD & THOSE IN BETWEEN. It hurts like hell they are not here to see this book come to print, but I'll be sure to write those feelings I felt and feel for them in every novel to come.

My editor on the project: Mrs. Editor—Lorraine Elzia, you are my friend and a real pro. Besides editing, you make me laugh and feel good about how and what I write. Lorraine Elzia, Senior Editor at, aVeeda Literary Services. Award Winning Author & Ghost Writer. www.LorraineElzia.com, and Award-Winning Author at Peace in the Storm Publishing.

My Seattle family of friends BAD BEFORE GOOD & THOSE IN BETWEEN is you and me in the 206, 425, and 253. I'm writing for the rest of the world to know just how we do it. We are multi-ethnic often in our bloodlines, and diverse in our friendships. We are rain, and the bluest skies, the fresh ocean air, and snow-topped mountains that can and do blow up, and we are rivers and streams in the middle of our neighborhoods, and fresh fish and crab, and shrimp.

We are the posse on Broadway, Beacon Hill, Rainier Valley, and in the CD Renton, Skyway. We are the posse living in Mountlake, Capitol Hill, Mount Baker, Leschi, Madrona, West Seattle, South Park, White Center, Kent, and further south. We are the posse strolling around Seward Park, Alki, Coulon Beach, Lake Washington, Green Lake, the University District

Avenue, Lake City, the Fremont District, and Queen Anne Hill. We are the posse rolling across floating bridges to the Eastside.

We are the posse living in or near Rainier Beach, Duwamish-Tukwila, Burien, Kent, and Federal Way. We are the posse rolling down to T-town—the 253.

We are Jimi Hendrix, Bruce Lee, Quincy Jones, Bill Russell, Marshawn Lynch and Seahawks, and rain and sun mountains and oceans. We are Vikings, Quakers, Bulldogs, and Eagles. We are the Seattle Super Sonics forever!

Alvin L.A. Horn

Chapter 1

I've been turning this ring around my finger like a fan's blades turned on high in the summer heat. Nervous contemplations box me into corners of my mind that I feel unprotected. This ring circles my finger; spinning in directions of confusion, and it feels as if I have no control. My life is spiraling in moon trips that I never make it back. My thoughts are orbits, and go up and down and around like a painted wooden horse on an amusement ride. Currently, my being is a broken down wooden horse; splintered, and the finish is chipped. Anyone who tries to ride me for an advantage is going to get hurt by their own doing, or what I will do to them. Some days I feel like a sad clown in a circus as I sit on this bar stool.

I glance behind me and see other sad clowns with laughter slipping between their lips. They don't know they're sad, but they know they're not happy. We're in this bar almost daily; deflecting sad truths with strong drink, and/or with piss-water liver killer – Budweiser.

I see men and women of different ages; some appear to be broke, and some I know are hiding money. The old white lady in the corner, she's always there playing chess, and never loses. She takes the old men's money when their ego gets to the better part of dick-sized brains, and they think to themselves, Finally, I'm going to beat her. She packs a big gun though. She has put it on the table a few times when a loser hints that they may not want to pay up.

The old Korean man doesn't drink unless it is from his own flask, but his pretty young wife drinks wine from the bar. He packs a little gun to keep the other men from shooting game to his mail-order bride. The young brother looking about twenty-five or so, is a lazy SOB Timberland boot pimp, as he's in here bedding down the older ladies to get paid. They pay his cellphone bill, his car insurance, and other bills; and these old women keep up his collection of Timberland boots in every color they make. Everybody's got a need.

11

My view may be a bit twisted and immovable when it comes to people. We, inmates of the un-incarcerated free society, struggle with finding happiness. We seem almost to embrace hard times which jails our minds. Hard times with love, money, trust, loyalty and losing it, shifts into lack of self-worth, and whatever desires that are left unfulfilled.

I see the embracing of the circus; finding temporary joys of, drugs, liquor, men, women, and covenanting other's possessions and each other; while plotting deceptions, or just walking over someone – taking or stealing someone's happiness. I've done my fair share of spoiling my own possible desires fulfilled.

The jukebox blares, and the conversation level volume rises. Heads bop in the tavern and a few bodies move in sync with Frankie Beverly grooving. He's singing about how he can't get over a woman. I daydream of a man who can't get over me. It hasn't happened.

Spreading my fingers around a plastic cup of red wine, I can see my scared knuckles, but the sight can't distract my mind from my pretty ring. It's the only thing that feels good; that, and driving my old car. What I might have to do with my car and the ring makes me hurt inside as if I am losing my virginity a hundred times to the tenth power.

As a teen, I lost my virginity to the star stud in high school, and three other girls all came up pregnant by him about the same time. I was delusional; just happy to be in his stable. Now, a couple of decades later, I hope I'm not seeing things in a misguided view as I did back when I thought those other girls were the lucky ones to be having his babies. That was a twisted assessment on my part; but now I spiral with other pressures.

I reluctantly wind my ring counterclockwise; faster and harder as if wringing out cold clothes left in moldy water. I do it unconsciously, yet meticulously. It's my life; connecting the past and the present. I don't want to remove this ring out of fear of what I may have to do with it. If I pawn this ring, I have lost my last fight; like an older boxer who can't quit, but can't win anymore. I have given and sold so much of myself. Bit by bit; mostly to the highest bidder. This ring is a one-of-a-kind heirloom, with a thick sterling silver band, and with twenty-two blue Sapphire Trapezoids adding up to two karats. Floating in the center is a one-karat diamond surrounded by six smaller diamonds. There is only one like it, and I have it. An old pawnbroker said it was made in France at the time of the Civil War. This ring could be a ring out of a Cracker Jack box, with no material value, as far as I'm concerned. The ring is about connecting history in my soul and life.

I look at my ring and know every pawnshop has rings – wedding rings, promise rings, please-forgive-me rings, make-up-I'm-trying-to-kiss-your-ass rings, it's-too-late rings, and rings of the dead. I know there are millions of rings in pawnshop showcases; all shining back at potential buyers, wishing that they will be the ring of choice and will find a new home on the other side of the glass. I take a swill of my wine and wash my dry mouth that hasn't laughed for a long while. It's a sad thought, but every pawnshop has rings from a brokenhearted woman, and those rings are ready for another woman's finger. In time, a layaway plan of ninety days same as cash, some other accepting woman will smile, and her heart will flutter with joy and hope when she adorns the unknown memoir of agony. And as she stares at her finger, she may even pray that her ring will be a bridge to her man's heart upon which he will honor and cherish her.

Sadly, the tales of many women who walk into a pawnshop with the blues of a broken heart are waiting for the birth of brighter days as she is broke and in need of money. Too often, a woman rips a ring off her finger and attempts to throw it off a mental bridge. In her dreams, she sees a display piece for sale to the next dream come true.

One day, every ring sadly slides off a finger. I have my dead mother's ring. I'm trying to hold on to a dream and not break my own heart by pawning it. I only have a few things of monetary value besides this ring, but this ring is from my mother. My stepdad gave her this ring. To me he gave unconditional love, and I will love him as, what I believe, a man should be. He married my mother and raised me from the age of five. The emotional value of this ring is adorned with a love that can't be broken or sold, but I don't want it to ever leave my physical existence.

Glasses cling and the dartboard dings as cars and motorcycles roar by. I hear the overhead fans swirl. The music grooves as Chaka soars with a song that speaks of circles; life going around and around. Some kids walk by the bar bouncing a ball and yelling across the street at girls.

Rat-a-tat-tat… rat-a-tat-tat

Bullet sprays are heard; the sound of cement is cracking. Not inside, but it sounds like it is coming from the alley back behind the tavern. The boys walking by the bar scramble away. The girls across the street scream and run. People hit the floor inside the bar; well, most did, a few are too cool to admit death could be flying faster than a speeding bullet. I see a couple of bar patrons pull out, .38s and .32s and .22s, but an AK-47 or Tech 9 against a standard handgun is like rockpaper-scissors vs. a sledgehammer.

Uncle Don grabs a bat and heads to the back entrance through the storage area as if he is wearing bulletproof armor. He dares anyone to force their way in, and keep a head on their shoulders should they get in. Me…I grab the 9mm from the cigar box from behind the bar in a drawer that has a special latch where only a few know it's there, or how to open it. I stay low and ease up the other side of the back storage passage.

After the initial gunfire, silence. Uncle Don cracks the door open and listens. I have the 9mm up and ready. Uncle Don looks out carefully, and then opens the door up all the way. He pulls out his cell phone and dials 911. He reports that there is a body in the alley riddled with bullet holes. I go out and look at a lifeless bullet-riddled body. Flies will be honoring the dead body in a matter of seconds. Dead is dead, and nature is quick to claim us back to the earth from where man was created. The smell of tire rubber and gunfire reek like weed smoke at a medical marijuana shop parking lot.

We stand guard until we hear sirens. One can't help but wonder why a violent crime area is the victim of slow police response. Then again, no one has to wonder about that if you understand the first part of starting the gentrification process: let crime reign, and property values plummet, and then banks don't loan money for property upgrades. From there, people are taxed out and sell sometimes below market before they lose their homes anyway. Then slick, slimy, big money slithers in and buys up everything, rebuilds, and sells to people of non-color; well, some upwardly mobile

African Americans buy the new cookie-cutter houses and condos, but not many.

In a few years' time, we'll see all new stuff; such as stores, schools, a new police station, upgraded parks, dog parks, streets with no potholes, and a whole lot less of people of color. If old Miss Mable Johnson's grandson, Jerome, comes home from college for the weekend, his old car will not fit in on the block anymore. If his car has big shiny wheels, it will be towed for parking on the same block as Mr. Johansson's new Benz. Someone from the new Black Watch group will complain that they think drug dealing is going on.

After the police and the body was carted off as another unsolved gang-related murder, the tavern is back to normal. The seemingly-uneducated accusatory local news tried to slime negativity before they drop their mobile studio antenna and moved on. They always ask the less civil, the less articulate, questions. They only shove a camera in the faces of narcissistic vibe killers, and then edit them to highlight ignorance.

My phone vibrates on the bar. My daytime talk minutes are out. I can only talk after 7:00 p.m. It's Officer CC, a policewoman who hires me to do some private eye stuff for cash. She has a slick side business. I'm often the front of the biz-end. A potential customer will seek unofficial justice through her, but I'm the one who shows up to gather info, or to give info. I gather evidence on cheating spouses and find deadbeat daddies. There are times when a few mothers avoid paying child support to a father. We don't charge the person in need of their money and only go after the deadbeat parent. Maybe charging is the wrong word usage concerning what money, we do to the person who owes. Street lawyering, in a sense, is what we do.

A few times, we have had to put an ass whooping on a man who has beat up on a woman, when the woman has no legal recourse because the system has failed her. A man receiving a beatdown by one or two Black women for beating up on a woman, can change a man's line of thinking the next time he thinks about touching a woman the wrong way again. Once, a father hired us because the mother abused the child support to the point where the children were suffering. We straightened it out without laying a hand on her. We helped a few fathers to share physical custody of their children when the mother was shady in how she cared for the children, and vice versa.

Sometimes, if there is a murder in the Black community and the killer needs to be caught, I ask questions in places where police can't ask. Every killer needs to be caught, but there are some killers who need apprehending more than others. If two or more fools go after each other over some ignorant inanity, who should stand in their way? Now, when regular folks get hurt or die because of some hood-boy gunslinger shit, then removal is necessary by any means. Sadly, when a man kills another man, he has left a child without a daddy. The community is always asking for a feel-good moment, wanting the killer to get caught. That's why Officer CC is texting me now; she wants to see if I have heard anything about a murdered daddy. He may have been cutting through the alley after getting off the bus from working all day. It could be he wasn't the intended victim.

I text back: I know nothing, and I need some money

Chapter 2

I often study the men in the tavern; some still look good for their age, and for some, time has eroded good fertile souls. As I don't know who my birth father is, I often catch myself in a daze when I encounter certain older men. If I believe a man to be a good man, I wish him to be the one who loved my mother and me from the start to the end. I wish.

My mother never talked about my biological daddy. She would say, "It doesn't matter." She told me early on to leave her alone concerning that subject. I figured one day she would talk. I waited all her life for that conversation about the man who was dead to her. She kept him buried to the end.

Eddie, my stepdad, is alive, but dead. He's living, but he doesn't exist in his mind very much anymore, yet his heart still beats strong. Shortly after my mother passed away, Eddie suffered from a broken heart from losing my mom. I believe it led to a brain aneurysm and several strokes. Now he has dementia that may have been brought on from years of boxing well past his prime. I take care of him; sort of. He's in a nursing home and his Social Security is never enough to keep them from kicking him out, and then I have to find another home.

He was a strong fighter that hit men who outweighed him by forty pounds, and he would break them almost in half. That's what others tell me with great description of the pain he inflicted on men for a payday. His body still looks like that of a man in his prime, and that may be the reason his body lives. He just doesn't know, from one minute to the next, whether he's in the ring, or in a Star Trek transporter machine. But I love him for never inflicting heartbreak on my mom whose heart already bore the pain of things I don't understand. Eddie loved my mother. She was not easy to love as her soul was robbed at an early age; a by-product of having me when she was a baby herself.

My stepdad taught me to fight, and he taught me not to be angry about things out of my control. That helped me fight and never lose.

Fighting and winning is a business of mind over emotions. Emotions…no one can totally control them. I'm distracted with emotions now, and I'm losing the fight with my mind, and angry about what to do concerning the business of financial survival. Eddie would be disappointed in me, but he would still love me. Funny, I talk to him and tell him my woes. I do that now knowing I will not get much of a response.

I have my stepdad's 1952 Cadillac and, as I'm sitting on this bar stool, I see the front bumper just outside the door. It makes me feel good for a moment. A few of the people sitting in here at the bar and in booths of cracked vinyl seats, are men and women who roll along in old Buicks, Pontiacs, Chryslers, and Chevys. Most of the folks in here are retired or are greeters at Walmart. Grandsons and great-grandsons are trying to pry the keys out of the old hands to place 24-inch rims of bling-bling on their elder's rides before they change the oil.

Inside the Hob Nob Tavern, it's the land of time stood still. Young folks come in and hangout sometimes, but they know the people in here listen to Chaka Khan, Stevie Wonder, Marvin Gaye, and Aretha, still. The older men will go to war defending Bill Russell and Michael Jordan as the best ever in basketball. The mention of LeBron will draw laughs with the help of a double shot of bourbon. I look around and see caked layers of makeup that can't hide hard times. I see men talking as if they could pull a young woman, but no.

I'm an old soul who feels at home amongst the folks. Sometimes I feel I have lived eight decades, but reality is it's only almost four.

"Zelda, you want another pour of wine? I know your nerves should be back to normal by now, but another shot of wine will still do you good," Uncle Don stands in front of me on the other side of the bar. His baritone is equal to Barry White's on the stereo.

"Yes, Uncle Don."

"I done told you don't call me Uncle, just call me Don."

"Sorry, I forget sometimes."

"What, you're three dimes and a nickel and you forgetting shit I've said a million times?"

"A million, Don? Really? I didn't forget how to pop the latch earlier to get the gun when it counted."

Uncle Don walks away with his tall muscular body that seems to tell the mirror on the other side of him, Don't you dare add a pound. The only thing showing his age is his salt and pepper goatee. He walks back and picks up my stained bar coaster, puts down another, and then pours more wine in my cup. Bells jingle. He looks up to see who is coming through the door; as he does, he spills a bit on his prized, super-polished, wood counter which was cut down from an old-growth oak tree. As Uncle Dons does, he treats it like he intended to.

"Got to send a little back from where it comes from, it was in an oak barrel at one time."

I give him the side-eye and change back to our previous subject. "I'm 38."

Uncle Don smirks and waves me off. With a behind the back pass, he tosses a bar towel and it lands near me. He expects me to wipe up the wine he dripped onto the counter. He is severing another regular before I have a chance to pick up the towel.

I drink free in the Hob Nob. I am broke to the bone. Uncle Don was my mother's sister's ex-husband. Blood runs like beer with him; if you were born, you were family. During my present state of affairs, he slips me small change from his bar tips, but it's not much as the regulars rarely tip. Boeing laid me off two years ago, and unemployment has run out. The rent is past due…again.

Do I pawn my mother's ring or not? Do I sale the '52 Caddy? If I pawn or sell, I know it's a temporary fix. It's not the lotto. Pawning and selling is nose above the flood water money. After my bills are paid, I'll slither into broke hell. Marvin Gaye is playing on the jukebox, "Inner City Blues (Make Me Wanna Holler)."

19

Eddie's nursing home bill is two months' past due, and then there's the cellphone, food, gym dues, and I need to go to the laundromat to wash some drawers. I need money. I'm tripping over the same bills as others; some less and some a whole lot more. Everyone has that one bill pending…And, that damn dentist who messed up my mouth is blowing up my phone wanting ransom money to finish what he should have finished two visits ago.

Marvin Gaye's, "Trouble Man" is starting to play. It reminds me that I'm a troubled woman. I'm trying to keep my tears frozen before they melt and run down my cheeks. I'm not an external crier; but as of late, I have to squeeze my eyes tight to stop my tear ducts' dam from cracking and flooding. Every first of the month, I try to prepare for a dam break.

I could get some purple money. Purple Daddy, is camped on a barstool at the far end of the bar. He looks constipated as if he's sitting on a toilet and he's stuck. His 1950's style gold tooth smile is about the same as someone straining from hemorrhoids. I slept with his old, one-foot-in-the-grave, purple-polyester-pinstriped wearing ass. Slept. I slept in his bed next to him to make him think he had it going-on, and because I needed money.

I let his wrinkled face and hard stubble scratch my inner thighs. He tried to please me; but even if he had been accomplished at going down on me, and he wasn't, my mind locked my stuff up to being dry and un-receiving. I did let him go down on me and dry hump on my ass with his fat, but limp, manhood; but it wasn't long before he snored the night away. His last hard-on might have been when I was fifteen.

At first, I excused my actions. I told myself that my circumstances overrode and allowed me to act comfortable with slithering into repulsive actions, but my soul never gave permission. I'm human. I'm like most folks, I stroke my psyche and force-feed self-serving lies like, I found myself down in the gutter because I wasn't aware I was headed in that direction. Truth be told, I got down in the gutter knowingly, and I dropped my pride.

I laugh at some of the men who come around here. They generate ignorant thoughts that they are getting something nastier from a side chick other than what they get from their wives. Wretchedly, without realizing it, men who brag are only telling of how low they'll go. Men who freak on the side, pay in some form or another. They spend time and money to boost their ego, and they rarely get something tangible out of the deal.

*****

I felt slimy as I sat in Purple Daddy's Benz that night trying to talk myself out of his car. Johnny "Guitar" Watson sang about a real mutha for ya on Purple Daddy's car stereo. I timidly walked through the door of his house. Me, acting timid, is a sure sign that I'm doing something undoubtedly in the wrong lane. The door opened, and the funk hit me like a backhand slap in the mouth. It reeked. The musk of old swarm-like flies on cow manure. Hanging on his walls of faded paint were dusty timeworn photos of his dead wife who had been dead for twenty years; and so was the air. I figured most women who came through his door were paid. He needed to pay a maid. That is how our conversation started; he wanted a house cleaner…with benefits.

I took three showers that night; one after he pawed me, and then again after I found him spooned around my butt in the early morning dawn. As much as I wanted to be held, this was terrible. I cleaned his house. I started at four in the morning, and finished at noon. I took the last shower before I walked out of his house. I didn't want a ride back in his car, but he made out a check to me in his Benz in my name, Zelda Hargo.

I had rent money, food money, and later, I was able to drive my Caddy to Sears and the old man paid for new tires and a tune-up. I know he thought that would bring me back. I have every intent never to do that again…I have every intent.

When I first came to Seattle, Uncle Don told me, "Old men often chase young women using their sizable retirement paychecks as a bargaining chip for young stuff. When a woman turns them down, they laugh it off as if they are just joking, when they are really wishing and hoping."

As far as Black men are concerned here in the Northwest, through the decades, plentiful blue-collar jobs – decent-paying jobs, supported people of color to creep into the middle class; and few even fare better. Seattle has some lower-income neighborhoods, but never low enough to call them a ghetto. Long money from Boeings, the ports and docks, city jobs, and the multiple armed services bases, had helped empty bottles of Crown Royal and E&J in Seattle. If a woman had no desire to better herself, she could keep her lights and water on with an old sugar daddy's bank accounts. If a woman worked one of these old, no-getting-hard-dicks, she could buy a pair of stilettos from a Macy's outlet, or at least a Target store, and still might have something leftover to buy her kids a treat.

Uncle Don didn't want me to fall prey to the purple daddies, but my choices and options narrowed. I'm twisting this ring around my finger faster.

The Ohio Players start playing on the stereo, "Pain." Uncle Don bops his head and I feel the groove, too. Pain. When my mother died, she took secrets to her grave as if she was burying pain. Those secrets, they knife me to bleed like a cracked wine barrel full of communion wine. I swirl the cheap wine in my cup trying to create bubbles to read like tea leaves. I don't see my fortune or future. I see dark scarlet.

Chapter 3

Bells start clinging over Luther Vandross' crooning, "Going In Circles." The Hob Nob door opens; everyone is a bit on edge from earlier. A few folks check to see how far they are from their weapon. Most do it in an effort to let others know they are carrying – although it's strapped to legs or hips and is never on the bottom of a purse. Ain't nobody got time to be searching for your gun if you need it like now.

Auntie Isiwata, my mama's sister, walked in. My focus on my circumstances just dropped into deeper instability. She's walking toward me with eyes dark like the wood of the floor. It sounds as if her heels are on the attack, as if she's mad at the hardwood. In a way she does. When Auntie and Uncle Don divorced, Auntie got the houses, and Uncle Don got the tavern. He has to give Auntie a percentage of the income that's generated over the cost of running the bar every six months for a long time coming. I think he could generate enough to cash her out, but maybe he wants her around for some reason.

He once told me, "Sometimes a woman can do some ugly things to a man, and displace him from the life he had, or knew, unlike nothing else can. And like a fool, he will still love her, and beg her for her love, and remain in pain, waiting for her to come back to him. Giving up on loving her is something women think a man does, but he's held captive forever in ways he can't express, and she can't understand. When a woman thinks that she is long lost to a man's soul, she exists immobile from his mind and soul as he desires what he can't have, even if fifty other women come after that one love."

When Auntie owned the Hob Nob Tavern all by herself, Uncle Don became her manager, bartender, security, and then her lover. Before he started pouring beer and keeping order in the bar, Auntie was robbed several times at gunpoint. She was never scared, as she cussed at the robbers the whole time they had a gun pointed at her.

23

Isiwata is my Auntie's Native American name; converted into English, her name is Panther, and that's what most folks call her. We are Black and Native American from the NatchezWashitaw people, by way of Texas and Louisiana. My mom and Auntie are half NatchezWashitaw. That makes down to a quarter of mixed blood. Only in our family does anyone call Auntie by the name Isiwata; my mother did, and my grandmother did as well.

My Auntie looks like my twin, although she's seventeen years older. She's all ass and has small, but full breasts. My breasts are like hers. My mom, she had large double D shaped like the front bumper tits on my '52 Cadillac. I'm much taller than the both of them, and my breasts are smaller, but that causes fewer problems for my athletic endeavors. We all have the backside inheritances from the Black side of our family. I think whomever my Black father is, that side of the family put in a big dose of butt DNA. I'm built for physical competition with powerful thighs and lean muscles in my upper body.

Auntie's face, mom's face, and my face, are all for sure from the same mold. The difference though, Auntie's eyes hold perplexities. Her eyes are her knives, spears, and guns. My eyes are almond shaped, and I'm told they present a dangerous expression. Men tell me they love looking into my eyes. It's mesmerizing and sexy to them.

Auntie saunters my way with her pendulum clock movement hips. My uncle calls her walk a guillotine drop because her hips sway is a beheading of making you lose your head if you stare too long. I see every man in the place trying to sneak a quick peek. I smirk and feel myself holding back a laugh while picturing men's heads being lopped off. At times, I have worn some tall heels, and I got the same gawking.

Her almost-too-perfect body is a byproduct of a tummy tuck. A soft rounded belly used to be hidden by the right clothes; now a tight, narrow waist is accented by Coke bottle curved fashions. It looks great on her – a woman in her fifties.

My mother, Auntie, and I, all share shades of light brown with a hint of reddish undertones. I'm a slightly darker pinot noir. Another trait we share is a narrow gap in our front teeth. Most say its attractive and not a distraction from our looks. My Auntie shows what money and a dentist can do as she smiles in my direction without what used to be a gap. She's neither happy or not about seeing me. It's a disposition she has concerning me that I sensed ever since I could say her name. I believe it was the ongoing riff between her and my mom; details of which neither shared. Auntie sidles up next to me at the bar. She smells good. She's not cheap; and whatever she is wearing was obtained from behind a locked counter, and not on front display for easy customer contact. Uncle Don passes by and slaps an envelope on the counter; the half-year payment he owes her. Cash…tax free.

My pretend x-ray vision is burning a hole in the thick brown envelope. I look away to the dark wood floors, wood chairs, and wood tables; everything in the bar is wood, and it's all dead. I'm alive with dead-ends wherever I look. I see Purple Daddy – almost dead. The ring on my finger…well, diamonds are not a girl's best friend if you have to peddle them away. There is death, and no resurrection, as you hand your ring over to a pawnbroker. I need money and I need it to keep coming. I don't have a problem working for it. That damn airplane company sent our jobs to non-union states for half the labor cost. Some say it was the union's fault since they were always on strike. I don't care what the reason is. My eyes come back to imaginary x-ray vision burning a hole in the brown envelope.

"Zelda, I know you need money! You know that I know that you need money. We go over this all the time. I'm here to help you, but I'm going to help you in my way. Even if you find a job, with the little skills you have, it will only be a matter of time, and you'll be back to sitting on this stool again looking at my envelope of money."

"Auntie, please don't go there…again. And why the extra drama of coming in here looking all perfect and smelling good while you take Uncle Don's money in front of everyone?"

"Because he stopped loving me."

"He stopped being in love with you having other lovers."

"He promised to love me until I die, even if I had to wear diapers and couldn't feed or toilet myself. He promised to love me through all highs and lows."

"And he still loves you; he just won't touch you as you live, and even you know that he will take care of you if no one else will. As a matter of fact, you know he will not let anyone else take care of you if you need care, but him. I'm sure of it, and you are, too. Nevertheless, Auntie, how do you love someone who seemingly has things going on her mind about how you feel about things, and yet they don't do anything to work them out? Explain how you just don't give clear communication when that's essentially what you want from him?"

"Oh, Zelda, you know so little of life. I didn't give his love away. I let a few men have some good pussy, and in return, they put a good amount of money between my breasts to keep doing the things in life I need to do. I own real estate, a couple of nice cars, and I go to places a young thing like you only sees on TV. I kept this bar going and kept your Uncle Don in nice clothes."

"Auntie, no disrespect, but your life is not complete. You don't have Uncle Don anymore, and he would kill for you."

"I would slap you in your mouth, but then I'd have to shoot you because you would think you had to hit me back. Plus, we're family."

"Yeah…family."

I try to stare my Auntie down, knowing I wouldn't hit her; but I know she would go for her gun thinking I would, and then I'd have to beat her down just enough for her to think twice about pulling a gun on me. Plus, she's family.

Uncle Don walked by to serve a customer, and his face said nothing; no love, no hate, no missing, no smoke to rekindle a fire. He had moved on in image persona, but he misses her, and my Auntie is the loser.

Auntie rolls her lips and her dark eyes became almost translucent. "Despite reasons you don't understand, I'm still offering to help you as I promised your mother I would. You know she didn't have to suffer as she did with cancer if she would have brought her scared behind up here to one of these hospitals. Instead, she stayed in that little ass-backward town. Shit, those rednecks want Black folks to die if you ain't got no medical insurance," Auntie's tone was a haunting snarl toward my mom's chosen choice.

"Here we are in modern times, and your mother let a medicine man concoct some old herbs and smoke an antidote for a cancer."

I wanted to go in my Aunt's purse and shoot her with her own gun, and then hand her a joint of good weed to help her with the pain as she drifts away. Her talking shit is who she is. She'll walk out of here with her life though. She's family.

"Auntie, we Native people never had cancers before Pilgrims brought their nasty asses over here. My mother had the right to believe in the old ways."

She looked at me as if I was a beached whale, and as if she was trying to decide should she kill me for my own good, or kill me for the rare food with no remorse.

"Auntie Isiwata."

"Oh, you call me Isiwata...wanting to remind me I came from a people who believe in mystical folklore. Well, my ass is Black folk, too; and like I said, it's time for modern medicine."

"Well, Auntie Isiwata, there is plenty of history of how modern medicine has not been good for Black folk. Black women die of heart disease at a higher percent than any other race. And, just like our government gave small pox to the Native side of our people, they also fooled hundreds of Black men into living with, and dying with, bad blood – The Tuskegee syphilis experiment from the 30's to the 70's."

My aunt reached over the bar and grabbed a bottle of bourbon. It's her bottle. Uncle Don never moves it. He keeps it filled, and when she comes in, she pours a couple of shots from it. Just as she wears a facade and too much perfume, she drinks too much. Between her smoking weed and constant drinking, she keeps her true feelings anesthetized as she tries to bury her soul in regrets.

She poured two fingers deep and downed it, then poured another two fingers and cut her eyes over at me.

"Yep, as usual since you were a child…you being all 'book-wormish' with facts that don't mean shit if you ain't living life to its fullest before you die. None of your facts saved her life. No matter whose medicine you choose to die from, my sister is gone. My baby sister is dead, and we never…" Auntie lowered her head and I felt her misery and guilt. It is though, the only time I see her soft side. "My sister is gone and my mama is gone."

I'm hearing my auntie feel pain, and her mask is falling off at the moment. I hear a quiver in her voice and a wrinkle of emotion crack through her makeup.

"Zelda, come with me."

She slammed her glass down on the bar as if she was playing dominoes and she scored twenty-five. She picked up her envelope of money, headed out of the bar, and I followed.

Chapter 4

"Guilt is a poisonous river of muddy water that won't turn clear until one makes penances for their transgressions against the ones they did love or should love. Guilt is a footing for the death of the soul. One can function with guilt, but is dead until one makes good to the ones they wounded. Each time the wounded crosses their mind, the guilt rekindles and loosens poisonous mud from the bottom of their soul," those were grandmother's words.

Auntie has this weird guilt complex concerning my mom. I guess when my auntie left from Texas, she failed to persuade my mom to come with her to Seattle, and maybe my auntie feels like my mom's life never had a chance to be on par with hers. On par.

"Too many people think their life is one to be envied; just as long as the shades are conveniently arranged over broken windows to their soul, and are never pulled up, and the ghosts of their issues are never exposed. Denying hurt delivered, is sleeping on soiled sheets. Trappings of materialism and community standing can't bleach away the dirt one has done while appearing to be clean," my grandmother's words again.

Something I noticed about guilty people, they tend to surround themselves with yes people; the ones who will not change them, and their wrong doings. My auntie, she has those kind of friends.

My auntie was like an older twin to my mother, but childhood promises to be forever close rarely last when two lives have different existences.

Right after I was born, Auntie moved away. My mom said she was led away by nightmares of truth about who she was, what she wasn't, and what she should be. Plus, she had a desire to get out of Corpus Christi, Texas; a dead-end naval base town.

Old car appreciation must be part of my heritage. Auntie is driving her 1962 Pontiac Grand Prix Convertible today instead of her new-every-other-year Mercedes. It might seem as if my family is always fighting the current, and always seeking to be in a life before. My Native grandmother and Black grandfather lived on a Native reservation, and old cars sat as if the ground would swallow them up. My grandfather died years before I was born, so the household was all women when I came into the world.

Auntie is driving down Rainier Avenue and is turning to go uphill heading to the north part of Beacon Hill; an area of Asian descendants and black and white peoples. The red-brick-artdeco marine hospital, and what used to be the Amazon.com headquarters, loom over the whole area. It's so tall it blocks out the sun.

Angie Stone is grooving, "Life Story."

"Zelda, sing for me, please."

I smile. No one in the family that I know of was blessed with a singing voice like mine; but I know my gap is fully exposed when I do smile, and I do my best not to let that happen too often. I have sung since I was a child to anything I heard. Many have said I should have pursued a singing career. I couldn't get past the gap between my front teeth, and being on stage in front of people who can turn mean when you expose a flaw made me say, Nah. I developed a style of singing to shield my front teeth from being seen.

My mom always played the music of people like Al Green, Curtis Mayfield, Aretha, Phyllis Hyman, and others like them. She never stopped playing classic soul music; and right before she got sick, she started listening to the likes of Anthony Hamilton, Aggie Stone, Maxwell, and D'Angelo. My auntie is mixing music from Sam Cooke, Bobby Womack, Kem, and Jill Scott.

I sing along for a bit and Auntie cuts me off.

"Zelda, let me do this for you and your mother."

"Do what, and why do you add my mother into this? I mean, I love my mother. I miss her, but I'm torn and conflicted because my mother chose not to tell me about my biological father. I can't let go of this grief. All I want to do is just ask her again and again who my father is. You say you don't know."

"For the millionth time, your mother made that clear, I can't help you like that. You, being angry about life, pissed at me, upset with your mother, and being sad about Eddie, will not change a thing. Period. Now you need money, right? And you need a place to stay, right?"

I didn't answer as we rolled along. Riding in old cars and having rehashed conversations was the same old song on a different day. She drove over to the west side of Beacon Hill to where some parts of downtown can be seen, and which overlooks the Puget Sound water inlet. The redness of sunset burned through the clouds above the Olympic Mountains, making the snowcaps appear to bleed.

She pulled in front of an old house. It appeared dark and lonely. All the other houses on the block were old, but with pretty yards, pretty painted trim, and mainstream looking cars parked in the driveways or on the street. A few porch lights were coming on as the sun dropped below the rooflines.

My auntie looked briefly at the other houses in front and across the street, but stared hard and long in her rearview mirror. "I bought that house," she pointed past my face to right in front of me. The dark and lonely house was two stories with dormer points on the sides. The front porch had Roman coliseum pillars, and a big bay window on each side of the front door. The yard was unkempt. Two side-by-side driveways separated the house from another house that could have been its twin; built and christened the same day. On the other side, a new three-story, narrow, rectangle box of a dwelling, looked out over all the other houses; that's what they did nowadays, be the only jack-ass amongst the horses.

"Here are the keys. It needs lots of fixing up. You can stay here and take your time remolding. I will provide the money for materials, and if you can't remodel or fix something, I'll foot the bill for someone to come in to assist you. I won't be putting it on the market anytime soon. This area is going to be hot in the coming years, so I'll sit on it. My other houses bring in enough rental money to cover. If you can work it out, you can have your stepdad stay here with you. It has a mother-in-law basement potential that, if you fix it up first, you can rent it out to pay for an adult attendant to watch and attend to Eddie."

Auntie turned and faced me as a few cars drove by. I couldn't see her eyes as she had put on huge bumble-bee-lensed sunglasses. She can be weird like that sometimes. Between her expensive weave that looked cheap because it was way over the top – Tina turner over the top, and the sunglasses, Auntie could rob a bank and they would say someone had on one hell of a disguise.

"I can live here rent free if I fix it up?"

"Yeah, and you can take your time."

"I can have Eddie stay here with me if I can arrange help with him, possibly renting out the basement?"

"Yes, and don't ask me why, Zelda. I have told you what my plans are," her voice was tired as if she had already taken an hour to explain.

"Auntie, I am grateful."

It was hard to say that to her. To let my guard down with my auntie who has been a lifetime of forks in the road that keeps me guarded. When I was around five, she took me from my mother, and I don't remember being angry or not wanting to go with her. I loved being with her as well as being with my mother. In fact, I wanted to go with her, I'm sure as much as my memory of being five years-old can summon up. My mom was reserved. She didn't laugh too often, and my auntie was funny and laughed and played and danced, and would spoil me with gifts.

A fork in the road: I watched my mother and Auntie fight verbally and physically while I sat on my grandmother's lap one day on the porch. We watched them scream and pull hair. I didn't cry. I was mesmerized that two women, who beheld the same appearance, were wrestling on the ground. I might have smiled as I felt like I wanted to be in-between them to feel the both of them embracing me. It was then that a man, jogging down our dirt street on the reservation with a bunch of boys jogging behind him, ran over and broke up the fight. It was Eddie. He was training some of the Native boys to box nearby. After he broke up the fight between the two women, my auntie came up on the porch and picked me up. She put me in her car. She yelled at my mom, "I can give her a better life," and then we drove away.

Another fork in the road: the next day, Auntie turned around her 1966 Chevy Impala convertible; she made a U-turn on a two-lane highway. She swung her arm in front of me to act like the seat belt of the day. We drove back to grandmother's house.

With me in her arms, she handed me back to her sister and I got the embrace that I had wanted…to be squeezed between the two of them. It was the most complete love I ever felt. The sisters kissed, and Auntie told my mother, "She's your child and I'm just blood."

Auntie drove away, and I didn't see her again until I was a teenager.

"Auntie, let's go inside and look."

She dropped the keys in my lap, put the car in gear, and pulled away from the curb. "My real estate agent showed me the pictures of every square inch of the place. When you're done, I'll see it then."

She turned the corner almost too fast, and accelerated up a hill as if she was racing. The big engine roared. She caught the last of a yellow light, and the first part of red while going through an intersection. She was driving as if she had seen a ghost behind us.

"What…you bought this place and never went inside or walked around the property? Aren't you trying to play big shot?"

"I have a method to my madness."

"You have some madness alright."

33

"I just solved some of your problems; show me some respect. I'll take you back to the Hob Nob so you can get your car. There is an alley behind the house that has a garage. Maybe you park there, or maybe not. Here…" The envelope of money she got from Uncle Don landed in my lap. "Soon, you'll need your own money to survive, and you can figure that out; but I'll give you a credit card to purchase material and supplies. What's inside the envelope, spend as you please; but once that cash is gone, you're on your own except the credit card for supplies.

I mumbled, "Thank you."

I pulled out my phone and typed. I emailed myself my thoughts, feelings, wishes, and what's going on. Today I wrote:

To God, mom, and my ancestors, you have blessed me to keep the ring, hopefully a lot longer, and I have a place to park the Caddy.

"Who are you texting? That is what you are doing, right? I don't need you telling anybody what I'm doing for you. As a matter of fact, listen…I don't want anyone to know I own the property. Don't discuss it with anyone, even if you have a man. If you have one, don't tell him my name. We from Seattle, that's all folks need to know. People always want to be in somebody's business. If you encounter a realtor or someone who asks you anything, it's none of their biz. The less people know about the buyers and sellers, and what we do, it helps in the end."

"Not even Uncle Don?"

"He knows."

I ponder just how much my auntie and Uncle Don still talk. And, I don't like strangers or many people to know me, so Auntie just said what I do anyway. We are blood for sure when it comes to that. I keep on writing to myself.

It might be possible to have my stepdaddy, Eddie, stay with me and be safe. Thank you for a path. I thank you for wherever the path leads me.

Chapter 5

Auntie drops me off at the Hob Nob Tavern. I walk in the door and Uncle Don nods at me. He played it cool as he always does. I approach the bar.

"Thank you, Uncle...I mean Don, if you helped my auntie to make up her mind to help me out like this."

"Isiwata do what she gonna do."

"Why did she tell you then?"

"It doesn't mean she wouldn't tell me her opinion. She knows to expect a response from me to confer or not," Uncle Don's salt and pepper goatee spread wide as he chuckled. He placed his cigar box on the bar. "Take this to your new place. One never knows when one may need a little help. If you have to use it, and depending on why and how, you take care of the fingerprints first. Never, ever, touch the bullets with your hands, and then scrub your face, neckline, and up to your elbows in hot water and Epson salt, and apple vinegar, then dishwashing detergent. You know about gun residue. Burn your clothes in a safe place, or at least secure them to never be found. The gun is not registered, so no worries there."

Something Uncle Don and my stepdad Eddie had in common with me is that we watch crime shows. We watch them until we know the lines in all the repeats. True crime and madefor-TV crime shows, reality TV crimes, and crime movies...we watch them all. I went even further to read about crimes – old and new, and studied how they were solved. Tearing down and dissecting what was real and what was fake was part of the fun. DNA to solve a crime doesn't happen in a day, week, or sometimes a month or more. Connecting a crime, or finding family members through DNA in an hour show, is one of the biggest fake-outs. Uncle Don told me nothing that I didn't already know about what to do, if I had to do it.

I left the tavern and went to my apartment where my rent is past due by a month. Another notice was waiting for me to pay or vacate. Low-income housing that is rarely low enough. I witness pay or vacate notices on doors in these complexes all too often. I know the manger will be knocking on the door in the early morning. I packed a few things. A few things is all I have. I've sold my furniture and other possessions – piece by piece – over time, and some other things are not worth taking. I carry my clothes down to the car in a couple of trips, and dumped them in the backseat. I carry my milk crates of records, my stereo and speakers, and sparse kitchen items, and put them in the trunk. My Cadillac's trunk could hold ten dead bodies, and I load the rest of my things in it and drive away.

Chapter 6

The key slides in the backdoor lock with ease. I hesitate to enter. I free the short erratic breaths holding me captive. I want my soul to feel comfort, but my emotions are washing overboard. Uncertainty. All because of a sense of is this real, or is this going to be another fork in the road? Is my auntie going to flip the script on me?

The noise is loud in my head. Fear is throwing punches at my mind and boxing me into corners and keeping me from concentrating on the positive. I have a place to stay – rent free, but how do I make money? That problem is still like a clock chiming on the minute, on the hour. Will I be able to bring my stepdad, Eddie, here to live and make it work? What is wrong with this? It can't be…true.

I spoke to my ancestors, bowed my head, and prayed while absorbing the whoosh of cars on the freeway a half-a-mile down the hill. I stood on the back porch; rotting and crumbling wood flexing underneath me. I tried to unruffle my busy mind and let my soul breathe with thoughts of peace be still.

A porch light came on next door, it startled me out of my negativity. The back door opened, and a man looked out. I'm not sure what he saw before he opened the door; he most likely saw me praying at the door. I had left my car headlights on so I could see the darkened porch area at the back of the house. His neck was craning in an effort to see, but he closed the door shortly afterwards. I went inside and found the light switch. I immediately saw trouble, but not a level of trouble that I couldn't handle with hard work. It looked as if someone had been camped out hobo style, instead of living indoors.

As I looked through the kitchen, I saw trash, cabinet doors ajar or off, a rusty sink, and the stove was missing all but one element. The fridge was not worth cleaning, it was in such disrepair. Amongst the ugly was a beautiful classic Formica top kitchen table with chrome legs. All four chairs were there, and strangely, the vinyl padding on the seat and backs were not torn much. I toured the whole house, and it was evident I would be breaking a sweat and taking plenty of showers to wash away grime and funk. Hard work – physical work, is my smoke, my pill, and my drink of choice. I get off on physical exertion.

Green faded paint begged to go away. Pink paint butted up next to the green, and my eyes begged for a paint brush. In other places throughout, dirty white paint yellowed and peeled. But damn, why is there green shag carpet with pink sprinkled fibers in some rooms? I had to rip that out first thing in the morning. Other floors were wood, and curved archways with stained-glass was built-in to book cabinets which gave the filthy house some charm.

On my way here, I stopped at the store and bought a few things, including cleaning supplies; but before I started to do a basic clean up, I set my stereo up, and ran speaker wire upstairs and down. I plugged my phone in to keep a charge, and connected the sound output to my stereo input and tuned in my 80's soul station on Internet radio.

The group, Soul to Soul, changed my mood into being more upbeat as I turned up, "Back to Life (However Do You Want Me)." It helped to move my body and mind. I bleached and scrubbed the bathroom first, burning my eyes and nose, but I made sure I had a clean bathroom. I moved to the room I chose to set up as my bedroom. I mopped the floor and washed the walls. I cleaned the closet, and then I cleaned another room to stage my other things that I did not want in my bedroom. I'll go on Craigslist in the coming days and search the free section and find a bed, dresser, and other things. I can use Uncle Don's truck if it doesn't fit in the Caddy's trunk.

Midnight, and I have my blankets rolled out on top of my sleeping bag. I strip down and let my naked skin be viewed by these old walls. They see the lean muscles of my shoulders, and dampness from my labor. My hurdler thighs, and the small of my back, are damp too from running back and forth from my car, and up and down these stairs.

I haven't been to the gym in a few days, which helps to quell my libido that runs like hot springs forcing me many times to change my panties several times a day. Just the thought of being touched, and I instantly become obsessive with erotic visions and my bodily desires, making my pheromones percolate in the air around me. I often laugh and worry that men, or even some women, can get a whiff of my scent.

I walk the bare wood floors of the hundreds of years they were trees before they became man's walking planks. I feel their medical properties. Earlier, I let the water run in order to clear the rust, and now it runs clear; steaming hot water in an old clawfoot bathtub. I had bought some strawberries and I put some in a blender with olive oil. I pour the mixture in my hot bath. I take a piece of each strawberry and other fruit, and rub them over my face and breasts, to purify and love myself, and to ease stress.

I have to continually wash away thoughts of sexual encounters with Purple Daddy, and then enjoy thoughts of when I had a man whose touch was soft and textured just right. But, as I pull the stopper from the tub to let the dirty water drain, I have to let thoughts of him go down the drain, too. That man – his lips, his mouth – made me submit to his strength and desires. He was a beautiful man, like a morning moon over the mountains. He was physically beyond handsome with a mixture of Black Hispanic and Samoan lineage. He was not a well-endowed man; but the power and the rhythm of his thrusts, and with the right positions, he pleased me into craving.

His tongue was king. With just a thought, I feel a twinge, and moisture makes itself known to my pussy. He could masterfully caress, emolliate, and penetrate every opening of my body with his tongue; lapping, flicking, and butterflying, as if he was rowing for his life out of a storm. I was the sail his exhales blew into.

He was also my supervisor at Boeings. Eyeing flirtations led to, then non-professional, conversations that set into motion the crossing of lines. We'd brush against each other and touch when we thought others weren't looking. Then we found risky places at work to place our lips in compromising situations in the compartments of airplanes, bathrooms, and backrooms; but soon, we needed to rid ourselves of all our clothes. We worked the same graveyard shift, and in the morning, we would go to my place after work, and never…to his place.

I knew he was married. There were no holidays or complete weekends; but impulsively, I was caught up inside the clutches of no harm, no foul to me. I talked myself into believing that lie.

We never talked much after we had sex; but his tongue talked to my body in tones that made me make sounds unknown to humans. He loved placing his nose on the edge of my pubic hair. He would pin me against the wall and take his time kissing me on my neck and collarbone. With me standing with my long legs wide apart, he would get on his knees and sniff my scent for what felt like broken clock minutes. His hardness raged, and he dripped clearness down his shaft and over his balls. My juices seeped down my thighs. He would lick it all the way up to my clit and make me squirt. He didn't just focus on my clit; his tongue performed its nasty dexterity between my toes, between my breasts, and between my ass cheeks. His tongue made my body jerk and tremble.

Unconsciously, I spoke in Spanish, "No puedo tomarlo Poppi, pero no se detienen, por favor no deje de," and chanted a few words in my Native tongue that I learned from my grandmother, "ʔi-hkuʃã-me" meaning, *he drinks me.*

At work, while cutting fiberglass and with dust covering me, all I could do was think about the nearness of him. I was lovesick on his skillfulness and our sexual nonconformity; yet, it was never about a future, a love jones, or what's next. It was only about when would be the next time I'd feel him.

When his wife sat down next to me at the company's summer picnic, her hurt became my wound. I knew then, I had created a poisonous river of mud. To see her up front and just inches away, it slammed an emotional meat cleaver into my face, as if I was separated into a rack of beef ribs; but it was my moralities that were sliced like hot butter. There would be no next time with her husband. While she sat next to me, he hit softball home runs and ran around with his children that he never spoke of, but I knew of. I felt her pain.

He threw a grasping glance my way, and his eyes begged me for my silence; but she knew. When his eyes squinted in the sun the same way they did when I made him cum, I thought about how his tongue made me beg, crawl, and dance for him. In the next moment, I finally felt humiliated by my selfishness.

I had been shoplifting his children's time. I had been swapping fluids with a man who then went home to his wife, where he mixed fluid with the woman who owned the rights. Yeah, I was willing in sharing his hardness and juices, that's what it came down to; but I had been thieving his responsibility to be one with his family. His sexual powers had assassinated my pride. My heart and mind wanted wilted flowers for the grave I had dug for my soul.

Her eyes – looking at her husband, and my eyes – on my lover, I assumed we viewed each other's body on all fours, on our back, on our sides, and him thrusting. I'm sure our open eyes couldn't possibly see anything else near us – no food, no people milling about, and no kids playing – other than each other's naked bodies over and under her man's body reflecting images of entwining flesh. I saw her making love to my lover, and I assumed she saw me having sex with her husband.

She turned and faced me after twenty minutes. "I have sat next to every woman out here that I thought would have a chance to make my husband not make love to me like he used to. I sat down next to you last, because I see a body I can't match anymore after having his children. I see you are in control of your body movements and you have a composure that most women properly think is arrogant, but to a man, it is alluring. You move like a cat as your hips swing in ways that would make a man lose his mind. I have to give it to you as a woman. Every woman out here engaged me in conversation; you turned your back on me as if I don't exist. I don't know if that is arrogance or if it is shame, fear, and hurt. I don't think its fear. You don't act like you have any fear."

She cocked her head to the side and looked over at her husband whose face bore fear as if he'd been caught with his pants down masturbating in full view on the Seahawk stadium's big screen.

She said with her eyes scanning past many of the other women, "I know, I know...I was you before. I became pregnant with his baby while he was with the wife he had before me. I was the side chick. He left her, in part, because child support would cost him more than he wanted to pay, and because they fought all the time. He liked me well enough, and in time, he started to love me.

"But now, with you, he has a certain type of freedom. I have kids; although they carry his surname, you know most women have the responsibility of raising the kids if the man walks. Therefore, I am not free anymore. I still can turn a man's head. I'm not too far-gone, but my body displays curves brought on by children nesting in me for nine months. I have very little freedom to be active like you, so I wear things a woman like you might think is cute, but not sexy. He sees you and he relives his pre-marriage freak days. Every time you are naked with him, you "do-the-do" him like there is no tomorrow. I did that, too. Now, he treats me as if he has to give me some, so-to-speak, and since he's been doing you…he doesn't make love to me, he just gives me some.

"You don't love him; you love his touch, most likely that tongue. But I love him, and so…whatever your name is, could you send him home to his wife and children? Let him raise his kids and let me do the best I can for him. Sistah, I can't compete with you, and maybe it's karma because of how he became mine, but…"

She didn't say any more. Couldn't. Her face was dry, but I know she was crying inside. She confessed her pain to me, the side chick, and asked me to stand-down. She became my shero. I got up, leaned in, and told her I was sorry. I turned to walk away and she grabbed my hand. Her head was down as if she was praying, and a tear hit the ground. In my mind, I saw that tear crawl over to my feet, make a pond, and I was going to sink in a watery grave for doing her wrong.

I turned on the hot water to refresh the warmth, but the old pipes in the house spirts rusty water as it did when I first turned the water on. I guess I need to let the water run for about an hour to clear the pipes. Tomorrow I'll make an assessment of all I need to do. I need sleep.

A crescent moon illuminated the room to help cast a spell of sleep. Some people sleep with the TV on as some comfort; for me, its music that rocks my cradle. I'm drifting off on my cot as Ruben Studdard sings, "The Nearness of You."

Chapter 7

"Stupid Bitch!" I heard from outside my window, as well as a few other articulations laced with aggression as sunlight was turning on the brightness. I hate men who say, "Stupid Bitch!" Stupid used toward a woman is a stupid man, who don't realize he ain't shit without a woman, and Bitch used toward a woman is a man I will kick his mama ass for having him and making sure he never ever addresses a woman as such.

I had slept well. Deep. I don't remember dreaming, but I knew I was hearing someone being cursed at by a man with a high-pitched voice. I sat up and could see, out my upstairs window, a man with a belly the shape of a ski slope, and the end of the slope was hanging over his belt. He should not tuck in his shirt, being tall with sloppy posture. He should make sure his buttons lineup, as they were not. He was a pig of a man.

He was leaning forward and his nose was inches away from a petite Hispanic-looking woman. She was pretty; and for sure way too pretty for an ugly man to be in her face calling her names. Even an unattractive woman becomes attractive when she stands up to an abuser. This pretty, mature-aged woman was standing her ground, and she was already pretty. Her long black hair flowed behind her back as her head was tilted upward. She was speaking. I believe she was speaking slowly as her lips were not moving fast. She was making a point as the man's facial expressions matched the cartoonish contortion.

Whatever she had to say, when she finished, she walked away, and he stood there looking angry. I stood up in the window in my purple cotton camisole and booty shorts as the woman was about to go in the back door to the house. My eyes were on her and not the man. All of a sudden, I looked at him and he was smiling while looking up my way. I felt dirty. My stepdad, Eddie, once punched a man out for catcalling at me and whistling at me as a young teenage girl. I felt dirty from the vulgarity of that man's eyes pawing at me. The man in the driveway was ogling me with no reserve of decency. I moved out of the window view as she looked up at the window. She didn't see me, but I could see her confusion. I need curtains.

I watched the man get in a beaten-down older Mercedes—two tone doors and trunk parts from donor cars—not something the factory shipped out. Even in its worn state, the Mercedes had more class, overshadowing the piece of a man about to pull away from the curb. I'm already thinking I'll have to avoid that man; no good can come from him.

I did a basic cleanup of the kitchen, and cleaned the stovetop with the one element. The kitchen needed to be blow touched in reality to be sterile. I brought in my microwave and coffee maker, then made some oatmeal and coffee while I wrote notes to myself on my phone.

What the world needs now is not more love

It needs old love to last

I see hurt and pain between man and woman

I've heard the verbal jabs staked in hearts of men and women no matter

Handsome and pretty shadows of their past float near the surface, and looks good, feels good for a while, then that lover becomes waterlogged with past issues, and pulls down whatever it can latch on to

Bitter old lovers feel hooked to a ball and chain and sink others who were floating

What the world needs now is not more love; but love, as love was meant to be, not as it turned out to be for too many

I opened all the windows and doors to bring in some new life, and let old dreams and nightmares escape. An old house, as in this house, has stories untold; but shows the pain in cracks, holes, and cigarette burns. An old house's walls have seen pretty, and heard ugly slurs of contempt. Its floors have felt the stomping of anger and tears of, where is my man at this time of the night. As I look at some of the doors in this house, I can assume doors have felt slamming splintering pain because a man wanted sex and a woman said no. I could assume no love lived in that house from time to time, and hate took over and beat on flesh that killed souls. Through years of

45

despise and scorn between souls, some of these doors felt battering rams made of human shoulders—violently casted ajar hinges and latches.

In these bedrooms, maybe a woman wanted love made to her, instead of her always looking up at the ceiling feeling jaded and bored. More of the same, her youth slipped into aged suffering as her body started feeling like it was turning to stone while a man's beer belly slammed against her belly. Her belly, her whole body, was at one time an incubator that children had survived from seed to birth. Maybe a woman cried out in agony inside a bathroom when her incubator failed to hold on to the one thing she could love. Onto the bedroom floor she fell to her knees asking a God to give her peace in any way it could come; even if it meant taking her life away for losing or helping life flush down. Throughout the life of an old house, a woman, a wife, a mother, suffered from her body either stretching, or scarring, from removals of gallbladders, spleens, and appendixes. Maybe someone found they couldn't walk up and down the stairs when a cancer or another ill took over, so they crawled to survive.

At times, moonlight had shown through windows to silhouettes; a man between a woman's thighs, and that man spewed unwanted life into a woman in the direction of the basement, and she cried herself to sleep afterward.

Old age is not the only thing that can bring a house down when pain turns a home back into only being a house with a number above the front door. Coming to grandmother's house is a romantic story on the surface for many as we are told as a child as a threat, "What goes on in this house stays in this house," but if walls could cast out the lies and hurt, we would all choke on the truth and residue.

It was breezy after a Seattle rain, so the air was fresh. I spent the rest of the morning cutting and ripping out carpet throughout the house. I kept a bandanna tied over my nose and mouth to combat dust and mold. I had my old Boeing workshop goggles to protect my eyes. I'll get Uncle Don's truck later, and I'll miss another day at the gym as I was working my ass off. I was grunting, sweating, and cursing.

At a fast pace, my actions turned into a workout. I shadow-boxed each time I went into a room. Throwing jabs and straight rights as Eddie had shown me. I had illusions of beating down Lalah Ali, but in my imagination, she stayed pretty, like her daddy. I wanted to be a winner like her.

Not trusting the back porch, I skipped over certain floorboards and then down the stairs. I had the music up loud as I jumped off the last three steps to the ground, looking at where I was landing with a rolled-up section of carpet thrown over my shoulder. I did not see eyes on me. The sweat dripping in my eyes didn't help.

"Hello."

A faint voice seeped past my concentration, but I was unsure of whom and what angle the voice came from with the music up loud. I dropped the carpet and turned with my body in somewhat of a defensive stance. The pretty Hispanic woman from next door stood to the side of me a few feet away. I came out of my stance, relaxed, and removed my goggles.

"Hi, I mean…hello ma'am," I said. "Is my music too loud?"

"No, not at all. Your music is the kind of music I grew up listening to. None of the hippyhop or very un-soulful noise we see and hear on these award shows - stripper shows," she laughed and I joined her. The S.O.S. Band and the Brothers Johnson…that was some of my nephew's favorites," she extended her hand. "I'm Alanese Delroy."

I looked at my dirty hands. "Sorry, I would shake your hand, but I've been making a mess. I'm Zelda Hargo."

She took her sleeve and attempted to wipe her blinking eyes as the wind was picking up dust. When I dropped the old carpet, there was still plenty of dust orbiting and swarming us. It was making me want to scratch my eyes if I could.

"Sorry about the dust."

It took a moment, but she was able to speak. "You're Native; I can see in your hair and skin tone, but your name for sure says so."

"Yes, Chitto-Harjo is my mother's peoples name from the Natchez tribe; but as you can also see, I'm Black. My mom is half Native and Black."

"Natchez people, proud people."

She stared at me, but had stopped smiling.

"Yes, proud people. Are you Native?" I asked out of curiosity because she was educated enough to know my heritage.

"I'm Mexican, but I knew some Native Americans when I was growing up who were from a few different tribes, so I learned a lot. Anyway, I hope the loud conversation outside my house this morning didn't wake you."

"I'm not sure what you are speaking of."

I hoped my facial expression did not confirm I understood what she was speaking of; it was one of those moments when all parties know what happened, but we declare we don't.

She nodded at me in a way that thanked me for acting as if I didn't hear her family feud early this morning. "So, you renting or buying this old house?"

I skipped over her question. "I'm renovating the place. So, I'll be here."

"I see, huh; well, that house has been in one family's hands for generations. A lot of family hands have lived behind those walls. Maybe you can turn this place and the old history into good."

"Yes."

For a moment I thought to ask her what history, but I was turning whatever had been into a new day for the old house. I didn't need to know. I changed the subject.

"I work better if the music is there as my helpmate. I'll turn it down at night, but I'll still be working; so, if it's still too loud, how about I give you my phone number to text me and I'll adjust accordingly."

"The volume of your music now is not bad, and I'm sure at night you'll be closing the doors and windows as a matter of being safe. I think we'll be fine," her smile was honest. It made me feel at ease.

Had I made a mistake to offer my phone number? That man I heard this morning…I would not want him to have access to my phone number. I assume he is her husband. She did have a ring on her finger, and I don't want to deal with a man who will disrespect the morality property line.

"Zelda, welcome to the neighborhood. You should take some caution around here. At the very northern part of Beacon Hill, there is a homeless camp they set-up along the freeway. Months ago, a few made their way down this way and squatted in the house you're in. The man on the other side of you, he and my husband ran them out of there."

"There is a real mess inside. Thank you for the heads up on potential dangers. I pride myself on being able to take care of myself, but I'll be careful."

"You do throw a perfect straight right, but you drop your left."

Light friendly laughter came with a wide smile. I'm sure my eyes gave away my shock that she understood boxing as she had evidently saw me shadow-boxing. I was tongue-tied.

"My nephew, my husband, and I, raised Aloy Ambrose; he was a great amateur boxer who was on his way to the Olympics, but things got derailed."

I knew that name I thought; I had to think of where from. She went from sounding gleeful in the fact she understood something about boxing, to sounding troubled, as if she was bothered over him no longer being a boxer. It's no stretch of the imagination about what a boxer's life can be at any time or at the end. One could assume a lifestyle of where strong men who break jaws and fight on with broken jaws, often break down in other areas of their life. Sometimes, stronglooking men are characters of weakness when it comes to the women they chase, or the women who chase them attempting to cash in on the beauty and breast influence. Mike Tyson and Robin Givens, each in love with the wrong things; image, money, and sex, instead of loving each other is the story many boxers have lived. A knockout can come from too much of a sweet thing between a woman's thighs, which is a drug in itself. Hell, I was addicted to a man's tongue to sink into playing in the dirt, so I know sex can control a life.

I brought her back to the physical side of boxing. "Well, when I shadow-box, I get lazy and drop my left, but when I spar or fight, I keep it up."

"Oh, a young lady who boxes, well, okay."

"I boxed, and I had a few MMA-Mixed Martial Arts fights."

"So pretty and so tough," her head tilted as if questioning my choices, I assumed.

I laughed.

"I'm going to let you get back to work. I'm cooking and need to get back to it. My husband will be home soon."

"Thank you for coming over and giving me a welcome, I appreciate that."

She nodded and turned and looked at her house and said, "God works in ways no man can understand."

Before she went back over by her driveway, she pulled some weeds, and went back inside. I went back to ripping out old carpet, sending old dust tales into the air.

Chapter 8

I made a call to Uncle Don about his truck, and he brought it by for me to keep at the house as long as I needed it. He had a friend follow him, so I didn't have to stop the work I was doing. I kept tearing out, or tearing down and making assessments, and measurements. My list was long on materials needed, and will have Auntie's credit card tallying to the sky. I met some crafty people at Boeings, and will make some calls to unemployed former co-workers to help with the skilled labor. The economy has reenergized the trade and barter system.

Being nosy, I watched another man pull into the driveway and go to my neighbor's house. He didn't look much different from the man this morning, just not as piggish. Not my business, but it's apparent I need to know what is going on next door to a certain extent. I saw a man leaving in a huff this morning, then the woman of the house makes herself known to me, and now, another man enters the house hours later.

After a long day of physical labor, the sun is dropping over the hill and lowering behind the Olympic Mountains, making the snow tops glow a brunt orange today, and I'm outside throwing trash in the back of the truck. I finally got to the basement and found someone had been living down there. A couple of backpacks with clothes folded and personal stuff were neatly tucked into a corner with boots, but it's all going to the dump now. It was the last stuff I'm piling in.

"Hello pretty lady."

My back was to a male voice that was trying hard to sound charming. He spoke to my butt as my heritage was hanging from the side of the truck as I pushed the load over into the center of the truck bed.

I couldn't move real fast from my position, and the voice asked, "Can I offer you a hand?"

The voice was at some distance, but was moving in as I pulled myself off the truck bed. His voice caught me as a man who might have an alternative lifestyle. I know that could be a poor assumption, but I'm not weird about anyone's sexual preference. Hell, my black side and Native side know all too well about being discriminated against, and stereotypical insults are the norm. I will beat down any person who acts with intent ignorance against a person, or people, if they get out of their lane and insult a person's lifestyle, family, or heritage.

As my feet hit the ground, I turned and saw a short man who resembled George Jefferson from the 70's television show, The Jefferson's.

"Hi, I'm Sadducy Cowen, but call me Duce." He came from the direction of the newly-built house that was an eyesore because it didn't look anything like the rest of the houses nearby. "You're in pretty good shape for a girl. I've been watching you from my balcony, and you know how to work it."

He looked at me as if my clothes were off, and the pathetic tone in his voice had so much flirt in it, I wanted to punch him. He was trying hard to mask something, like I think he's gay; but then again, I wonder how long he had been ogling my ass before he spoke up.

I had not spoken as of yet, and I did not like my encounter so far with Mr. Sadducy - Duce Cowen. "Hello, and thank you, but I don't need any help. I'm just fine; but again, thank you."

"Hey, we all need a little help from time to time."

"Thank you again, Duce, but I'll knock on your door if I need any help."

I know I let my perturbed attitude blow into his George Jefferson face. I was going to cut down the tall, overgrown hedge that was on my side of the property line, but I won't now. "You are from the house next door towering over mine, right?"

"Yeah, that's me. I spent a lot of time planning and spending money, so I get that view over the baseball and football stadium, and to look

53

over the docks and Alki Beach. You can come over sometime and come up to my third-floor bedroom balcony; with my view, you can see over to a few Puget Sound Islands and downtown Seattle. The sunsets are marvelous."

There was no way I wanted to be anywhere near his bedroom. "I like my view just fine. I can see the mountain tops and a little water."

"Ahh, you need to knock this old house down and build something like mine, and help turn this old moldy neighborhood into a place someone likes to live. Although these old houses around here help keep my property taxes down."

I wanted to laugh at what he thought. His house has the character and appeal of a vertical coffin with windows. I kept my mouth closed, but my mind was saying, Get the hell away from me and my house.

"Can you take a break and come over for a drink? I'll show you my house."

"You don't even know my name. I could be a serial killer of men with big houses who don't like smaller older houses. Kind of like a man with a bad hairpiece and he buys a Corvette. Most women run, except for the bimbos of no self-esteem matching the old man's self-loathing behaviors."

He pissed me off and I don't hold my tongue very well when I'm pushed onto that street.

"Oh, you got jokes. I like you, but I'll let you get back to work."

He walked back around into the alley. He left without knowing my name, and I'm cool with that. But damn, he's someone else I'll have to deal with.

I spent a full day of labor to rid this house of old funk and prepare for the new. Early tomorrow I'll get some more done; but I'll stop now and get some relaxation time in, and get some sleep so I can get up early to attend to other's needs. I need money. I need to work out in the gym. I need to see my stepdad.

I need to go pick up some Craigslist freebies; a bed, hopefully still in some plastic or buy a plastic bedcover. I need a dresser and some other furniture pieces. All the things I had when I was working, but it all slipped away as I've been unemployed. I need to talk to Officer CC and see if she has any quick-paying PI work, maybe spying on another cheating spouse. Beating down a spouse batterer pays the best.

I need to get with my warehouse fight club connect and see if I can get a fight. That's some instant cash for whooping some wanna-be-tough chic. I don't often go as I want to be called out and challenged. I have a rep that most avoid me; yet, there is always one who thinks they want to fight me to strengthen their rep by having the courage to fight me. If they last, and maybe give me a good fight before I put their lights out, it will put them higher on the ladder so they can make some money. Unfortunately, at my age in the legal fight game, no one will let me fight in legitimate fights. A promoter told me that I'm not Lalah Ali pretty, nor am I the blonde, blueeyed Sports Illustrated swimsuit model type who could tear your head off. However, he always wanted me to drop my panties. I was fine enough for some pussy.

Bath time before I go to sleep. My apartment only had a shower, so to have a bathtub is something I will be using a lot. This old clawfoot tub has a tall, curved, and leaned-back end that holds my body unlike cheap newer regular tubs with low backs. I can stretch out my long legs, lay back, and relax. I had let the water run for an hour to clear the pipe of rust beforehand. I found a propane camping cooktop stove with several full propane bottles in the basement. I brought it to the bathroom. I also found an oval-shaped, and blue speckled, turkey roasting pan. I filled the roasting pan with water, and let it boil the water to add degrees of heat to the tub so it was full to the brim with hot water. The room was steaming. When I pureed a few strawberries, mixed it with some olive oil, and poured the concoction in the hot water, the scent made me close my eyes and meditate. I wanted a glass of wine, but all I had was a beer that I had no idea why I had it. I turned on Kenny Latimore to croon in my ear. I wanted a man to soak with me.

Never in my life have I taken a bath with a man. I've taken showers, but to relax and be held had never happened. I wanted that. I want to be made love to. Hard, pounding, freaky sex, I'm into that, and that is all I have ever had; but made love to…nah, never. I wouldn't even know what a man did when he made love to me, and I wouldn't know how to start or play my part in making love. Could I have both: physical love and be made love to?

Chapter 9

After my long bath and five minutes into finally laying down on my cot, I heard a high-pitched scream; almost like cats fighting or mating. I laughed that something was getting some. Then a hard crumbling and thudding sound came from under me. The noise was in my house. In a swoop, I was in my jeans and sports bra, and had slipped on my shoes. By the time I was in the hall, I had my gun. Aimed. Eyes trained. Moving lightly, but quickly and silently toward the commotion, I could hear the sounds coming from the basement. I decided not to go down into the basement from the kitchen. I went out the front door and came around to the backyard steps going down to the basement. The door was open. From inside the basement, someone pulled the chain-switch of the light fixture that hung from the ceiling.

"Leave me alone," I heard Sadducy - Duce Cowen, my neighbor, sounding distressed.

"I wasn't bothering you," an angry young voice said. "I ought a knock your teeth out, trying to hit me with that bat."

I came around the corner, gun aimed. Duce was prone on the ground, leaning on his side, bleeding from the nose with a cut above his eye. A young, white, teenage-looking boy had his hand up as if he was still ready to fight and ready to swing, as I can tell he already had.

"Put your fists down."

The kid looked at the gun, then at Duce lying on the ground with his head almost in the fireplace opening. Then he took the safer choice, and lowered his hand slowly and stepped back. A bat was behind the kid's foot.

"Slide the bat away with your foot."

He did.

"Thank God," Duce said, as he sluggishly got up. I aimed my gun at his head. Hell, I didn't know what was what. Two men in my basement, and a fight had gone down. "Hey, don't aim your gun at me. I was trying to save you from this kid breaking in and maybe hurting you."

"Do I look like I need your help? Keep your ass down on the floor."

He opened his mouth and I lifted the gun higher. It made him think, and no words came out of his mouth and he stayed down.

"Lady, I didn't know anyone lived here. I had some stuff in the basement that I left here when no one was living here. I just got out of the youth center. I was locked up, and I just wanted my stuff. I need my things for a job I just got today."

The kid's face was apologetic; but if he was in jail, it could be learned game.

"What's your name?"

"Chevelle Waller."

"Hey, this punk was breaking in and I caught him. Don't let him tell you some bullshit. He attacked me with that bat," Duce whimpered through the pain of the ass whooping he must have taken.

"How did you get in?" I asked the kid. He pointed to a cover plate, about two feet by two feet, hanging open high on the basement wall. I slowly walked over to it with my gun not aimed at either one, but still up and ready to fire. I looked at a rectangular cement tunnel.

"What is this?"

"Lady, it leads to a hatch outside. I used to come in it for months before I was locked up. I took the bat from him. I only beat him with his own bat because he tried to hit me with it with no warning. He came through the basement door. I was crawling back out after I saw all my stuff was gone. Look, I don't need to go back to lockup. I need this job. As of now, I have only the clothes I'm wearing. I'm sorry; maybe I could have knocked on the door, but I didn't."

"Duce, as you call yourself, how did you get in the basement?"

"When we ran off the last squatters here a few weeks ago, I took the basement lock to a locksmith and had a key made just in case we had to go back in here again."

"Ah, you didn't think to tell me that earlier today because your eyes were sucking on my ass. Toss me the key! And go back to your cabin in the sky."

"Oh, you let the white boy…"

I pointed the gun at Duce's nose and I'm sure my eyes narrowed. "You get your narcissistic ass out of my house before I roll your ass up in that fireplace and burn you!"

His face soured and he hobbled out of my basement, leaving my key at my feet. His mouth was still stupid. "I should have let the white boy come in here and do you…as I'm sure that's what he was here for."

"You need to be sure you don't come back here," I let the gun follow him out the door.

I looked at the kid whose shoulders were slumped, seemingly defeated by a cycle of, *How did I get here*. I lowered my gun.

"Kid, I have your stuff out in the truck," I nodded my head toward the door.

Chevelle Waller had on baggy jeans, but he wasn't sagging. From where I stood, I could smell him. He had a rope tied for a belt. He wore a Seahawk sweatshirt and baseball cap with no coat. He put his hands in his pockets, and walked past me as if my gun was not a concern. Sometimes a life has lived on the edge of danger so much that danger is nothing to fear.

I pointed to the backpacks and boots, and told him to follow me. I led him inside the house, and asked him to sit at the kitchen table.

"My name is Zelda. This is my house you broke into, of which, I'm not sure of your intentions; but thanks for beating my punk ass neighbor's ass. So, tell me more about you since I'm not entirely convinced by what you've told me so far. I'm gonna give you the benefit of doubt, but don't lie to me. You hungry?" He nodded as if he was ashamed. "Wait here a sec and I'll feed you, and then you and I can talk."

As I walked out of the kitchen, I wasn't worried about him attacking me or stealing from me. He didn't smell like fear, evil, or desperation. He didn't smell like a liar. A sense passed down from my people. Often, we can smell people when there is some wrongness, or the soul is not in order.

I could see in the light that his skin was cream colored. His face was smallish for his distinctive broad lips and his eyes were dark; he had brownish hair with short loose curls hanging out the sides of his skullcap.

I went upstairs and put my gun away. I had to laugh that the kid took the bat from my Ahole neighbor, and beat him with it, but I had no fear of the kid. I pulled on a sweatshirt to cover my sports bra. I noticed the kid never stared at my sports bar, but Duce tried to steal a long glance even, with his ass hurting from the beatdown that the kid had given him.

Back in the kitchen, the kid was going through his backpacks. On the table was a picture of a Black girl with a pretty round face. I didn't have much to eat; just some oatmeal, eggs, bread and bologna. With only the one eye on the stove, I did the best I could. I fried the bologna, scrambled his eggs in the same skillet, and then cooked the oatmeal in all milk. We didn't talk while I cooked. I wanted him to be okay first. I truly understood what it was to be out here alone, trying to survive.

"You want a shower?" I asked. I got another, I'm ashamed nod. "Chevelle, it says a lot about someone who wants to be clean, and there is no shame in that."

He nodded. He pulled a towel and some soap from one of his backpacks. I walked him to the bathroom just off the first-floor bedroom. Some minutes later, he was dressed in clean clothes and eating at the table. I went into the bathroom after him, and the toilet seat was up. Dark yellow stains from his pee were on the rim. I came back to the kitchen with a twenty-dollar bill in hand and pulled two bottles of water from a cooler; the only place I could store things I needed cold.

"You need to drink water; please drink some now, and take this."

He stared at the money, but slowly reached for it, before the water.

He opened a bottle and gulped as if the water was a cold beer on a summer's day. He glared out the kitchen window and seemed to talk to the darkness outside. "Inside, the water is nasty.

They pee on the water fountain like dogs marking territory; so, if it doesn't come from a container, you don't drink much water."

"Understand, but you need to drink water. Your pee is way too dark."

He looked at me as if he was a child about to be in trouble. He didn't avoid eye contact.

"Who is the girl in the picture, if you don't mind me asking?"

The whole time he was eating, he kept looking at the picture. He gulped the last of the water in the bottle and opened the next one.

"My girlfriend...but she's the reason I got locked up," his facial lines tighten. He stood and looked at me, but his shoulders dropped, and he continued to look out the windows into the darkness.

"Man and woman stuff can lock up hearts, minds, and bodies into situations that we react in ways we regret. It wasn't because you put your hands on her, was it?"

"No!" his voice scraped across jagged rocks and caused me to flinch. "I wasn't black enough!"

I took a long look at him; scanning his features even more.

"Her father came at me with that crap, and his fists, and I knocked him out. Then the police and judge...you know whose side they took. I never mistreated Iman, and she loves me, but her father is a black racist."

He sat back down as the anger expressed by Chevelle Waller was shooting flames. Whoever this boy is, and what's going on in his life, he chose to tell me his story. I felt for him. He was hurting, but some wounds are self-inflicted. I know, as my life is full of contradictions. I was angry at times and blamed others. I'm without knowing what love feels like from a man other than a man wanting me to get him off, and him doing the same for me.

"Chevelle, I have questions, and I know you don't know me, but try to trust me. He kept a blank stare at first as I asked many things and he told me about his life. Along the way of him talking, his stare ventured into the dark outside, and it never changed.

"I lived with my grandmother, a Black woman since birth; but when I turned fourteen, she died, and I entered the foster system. I never really knew my father, he was a criminal and I only seen him a few times. My grandmother had adopted him, and when he became of legal age, she had to disown him for crimes against women. I was told he took advantage of many women. My birth mother was one of them, and when she became pregnant, she could not go through an abortion. My father took advantage of her by stealing a large inheritance she had. My grandmother felt my birthmother might have thought she was punishing my father's family, and gave me to the grandmother when I was born. My grandmother treated me as the best thing that could ever happen and called me her real son until she died.

My father was a light skin brown man born in Louisiana, and my grandmother's people were from there. While she was visiting, she said God sent her to an orphanage and that she saw my father, and it seemed he was more alone than the other babies. She brought him back to Seattle to raise him, but he was trouble from the time he could walk, and his life never changed."

"Do you know where he is nowadays?"

"No. People think I'm white, but I don't pass for white. I understand my father, being the conman that he was or still is, passed for an olive-skinned Italian to rip people off all the time."

"Chevelle, you are what you want to be, not what others deem you to be."

He wants to be known as Black. His dad – although he's not sure, but he thinks – was half black – and his mother is white. His girlfriend, the picture I see, she is a full-figured Black woman. He is what he wants to call himself, until the police pull him over if he's driving. Would he get a break, looking white as he does? Yeah, he stands a better chance of not being tasered or shot; but if your soul says, *I'm Black*, well, you live the life you chose.

"Thank you. I'm a man first, my grandmother made me proud of who I am. I never go around trying to pass," Chevelle laughed. "I have become my own race of the unknown, not the other box you could check as an option. But if someone asks, I'm Black."

"Where you laying your head?"

He looked at me for the first time with, I don't want to answer eyes. "Are you squatting down by the freeway below me?"

He nodded.

"And your new job?" I asked.

"Doing the laundry at a nursing home; its three to four hours and three days a week for cash. I did house remodel work as an assistant to an old guy before I went in, but he has someone else now."

"You have skills?"

He nodded.

"Speak up for yourself. Sell yourself. What skills do you have?"

"I can do carpentry, some plumbing, and I can do basic house wiring."

I told Chevelle what I had to do to the house and all the plans I had. He walked through the house with me and showed me, and told me, how certain things had to be done and some alternatives. He was on good terms with the old timers who had taught him for years how to do house remodel work, and he could ask questions on know-how, and borrow tools, if need be.

I offered him a room in the basement to stay in exchange for work and food. If I had any money, I'd throw some his way when I could, but I made sure to tell him not to count on it, and he was more than happy with the offer.

I then spoke to him in a knowingly tone. I let him know how strongly I felt about drugs and drunkenness in my house, and no girls, and no friends before I meet them shall enter into my house. And, what's goes on in this house shall stay in this house, and no F-ing drama of any kind. I made him laugh for the first time that night.

"I got it, I'm good with all that. You have offered me a place to stay. I'll avoid anything that could mess that up. There are people outside right now, and I have slept with rodents walking by, and men and women crapping nearby. I'll respect your house. I'm not a criminal despite me coming into your house tonight; it was just to get my things. If, by chance, no one was living here…yes, I might have camped out. But I'm not a thief or anything like that."

He smiled. It made him look younger than eighteen. I needed this young man, and he needed me for both of our lives to become better.

He'd have to help make the basement into a complete apartment as the first project. I'm hoping I can make my stepfather move in there. Soon! It was 3:00 AM when we finished talking, but we could have talked a lot more. I let Chevelle sleep on the dining room floor with a spare sleeping bag I had, until we can get him some bedding that had not been outside. I had no fear of him. Maybe I was stupid, but my Native senses told me to let him be, and he and I would both be safe. I made one last trip down the stairs and through to the kitchen, acting as if I was there for some water. I had bottled water upstairs. I noticed his shoes and clothes were aligned, straight, and folded to store display neat. I had noticed earlier that besides his yellow pee stains on the rim of the toilet, he had cleaned the bathroom sink and shower when he was done. He was raised right at some point, and may even be a little OCD. We all got ours about something or someone's.

Chapter 10

A few hours later, daylight and gray skies woke me. Desolate walls made me think of paint, and what colors I would choose. My stepdad, Eddie, was on my mind. As a man, when he wasn't fighting, he painted houses inside and out. Often, I'd assist him on his paint crews, so I learned to mix and match colors and types of paints. I'll be all over Craigslist picking up paint today; but first, I'll visit my stepdad. I know when something comes to mind, move on it.

I strolled into his current nursing home before the administration came in. I had to avoid them. The African men and women there…I went out of my way to be friendly with them. When I made a pie for Eddie, I'd make sure I brought at least two or more to share. I owe them for the extra care they give my stepdad. A few times, if I saw them at the bus stop when I left from the nursing home, I take them home.

Most nursing homes have kept Eddie for quite some time, sucking off his social security. Everything goes just fine until they have others who can pay over the top of their SSI with higher incomes. Then I'd get the notices that he was too far behind. I insisted on him having a room by himself. I adorned the room with pictures of my mother and me, and from when he was in the army, and his boxing pictures. He had pictures from when he sparred with Ali, although he was in another weight class. My stepdad was hard to hit, so Ali used him when he was preparing for a defensive fighter.

When I hold conversations with Eddie, he will respond at times somewhat clearly for a period of time, but his mind will wander. If I speak of my complications, it appears that I confuse him rather quickly; but I share with him anyway. When I enter his room, he's sitting in a chair watching game shows — actually, they are watching him. He always knows it's me, but sometimes he speaks to me as if he's talking to my mother. They drove to many places by car, and the Cadillac was a car they drove to be different while on long road trips. Sometimes Eddie talks to me as if he and mom are planning a trip, and when they pulled over and enjoyed the sights. I enjoy

67

these times with him, as I did when I was a child on many of those trips. I listen to him drift down a road with no centerline, no curb, and with loose gravel spraying when his mind pulls over. His words fall away from his lips. Lost. He starts to make sounds. They don't add up to anything a one-year-old child would utter. His eyes close, my heart breaks. Quietly, I leave. I don't cry. I wail inside. I give an orderly ten dollars to take breaks with Eddie, and I slip out through the service entrance to avoid walking by the administration office. I'll pay them later.

Money. The envelope my auntie gave me that she got from Uncle Don was eight thousand dollars thick. Uncle Don told me he had not paid her in a year, and he was making up for the back money he owed her. I know that money will burn up fast. I'm feeling good about the fact that I kept my credit union account open. It was a struggle, but it paid off as I deposited the money in my account, minus a little cash to have on hand to pick up a few things I can't get for free. The plan is to make my own money and not live off the money my auntie dropped in my lap; if I can help it.

I made my second trip back to the house by mid-afternoon with another truckload of Craigslist finds: mattresses, dressers, a good working stove, a couch and chairs, lots of other needs and comforts, and some paint. Chevelle was back from his job and we were offloading when a black Cadillac SUV pulled in the driveway of my neighbor lady's house. The vehicle sat in the driveway with windshield wipers racing the rain now as it was downpouring. We had to hurry to get things offloaded. A man in one of those too many button-down suit coats, with pinstripes, exited the vehicle with a Seahawk umbrella. He had all the fixings to go along with his suit, with two-tone alligator shoes, and a cowboy-cut Stetson.

He tipped his Stetson my way, and kept on to the house and opened the front door as if he lived there. In two days, I've seen three men come and go who all favored each other, but all very different in their dress and with their approach.

My stepdad told me, most men don't favor other men in their house as a general rule when they ain't home. Crows on the line in front of the neighbor's house squawked and flew over the man's car and dropped poop. The man didn't stay long.

Sticky sweat from my body had dried from hours of labor. As usual, I set my working pace on high to call it a workout. Winding down, I wanted to move the truck from the front yard to the back. I sucked the fruitful blood from a pink grapefruit as I leaned on the seat of the truck with the door open. A Harley rolled by, made a U-turn, and then turned into the driveway next door. A busy driveway it is. The Harley didn't stop in the driveway; it rolled along across the yard. He's a man! He commanded his iron horse to do what he wanted it to do. Some men ride their motorcycle, and some command their mount.

His body – like a warrior in his tight leather, who broke wild horses bareback with the strength of his thighs, his chest pronounced – I could clearly see behind his vest there are oncoming surfing waves of biceps and forearms which could stop waves from hitting the beach. With a skull helmet revealing his face, I almost smiled wide enough to let my gap show, thinking that no man looks that good. Maybe my eyes have become irrational from too much coffee and no man in my life.

He dismounted his horse - his Harley, and he rolled it down the walkway toward the porch of the house next door. His black leather chaps had the straps tucked tight under his ass cheeks. Oh my. Instead of me driving the truck off the front lawn, my eyes stayed parked on him, and he started walking my way.

Why is my heart thumping in my ears? It feels as if I'm feeling a pulse through my eyes. I close my mouth. I was breathing in more air than needed. As I suck air through my gap, I close my mouth. I don't want him to see my tooth gap right away. Now I'm conscious of my thick lips that I know spread wide when I smile. *Am I smiling*? Oh damn. His stride covers rivers and valleys as he approaches me. For some reason, unknown to why, I got in the truck and closed the door.

He stepped close enough for me to swing the truck door open and hit him. If I thought I could knock him down so I can possibly kneel down and give him CPR, I would. His smile said, I won't hurt you. I wanted to feel his fineness against my face. I wished to let my tongue be an ice cream scooper, and lick his brown skin from them deep dimples and swallow him.

My eyes traced his face and stopped to rest on his chin - almost square with a well-groomed goatee and chin-strap bread; short, but thick in blackness.

"Excuse me but...," he said. No words followed. He stood there almost looking lost; standing and staring at me. Maybe I should swing the door at him to wake him up. Awkward!

"My aunt...next door...told me she has...a new neighbor...and you..."

I cut him off rudely because the way he was speaking was peculiar and disturbed me a bit. The tone of voice was manly soft, not overly deep, but sultry when he gets the words out between the stops and starts.

"Hi, my name is Zelda, and I am your aunt's new neighbor. And you are?"

"Aloy Ambrose. Here," he handed me a business-like card with his smiling face and it read:

Hello, I'm Aloy Ambrose. You may notice that when I speak, I may have some hesitancy or delay. I'm sorry if I take up too much of your time. I have a minor brain injury called Apraxia of Speech. Don't worry, I do comprehend quite well. Please be patient with me.

I felt a bit foolish for being so judgmental; maybe thinking he was drugged. I feel simple for whatever was going on in my mind. I wanted him to be as perfect as in what I saw in his physical appearance. There's nothing wrong with him. There is something wrong with me for flopping around like a goldfish out of water.

"Mr. Aloy Ambrose, I will be patient. I'm in no hurry."

"Oh, but your eyes say so much."

A car swooshed by going too fast, and the air and engine were loud. I noticed that many cars on this street go by way too fast.

"I feel foolish is what I feel; and what do my eyes say?"

"Your eyes say…you feel…bad. You should not feel…bad. I have heard recordings of my speech delays. It freaks…me out, too."

His laugh was deep. I assumed he had laughed many times at people's reactions. I'm feeling a funny peculiarity about how he is reading me, when I am the one who reads people. Different felt good; almost like letting someone else drive when I'm always the driver, and they have their route.

"Mr. Aloy Ambrose, are you the boxer your aunt told me about?"

"I did box. I train others and run a fitness gym."

The sun broke through the clouds. I eased out of the truck and stood in front of a coffeecolored warrior. His deep inside eyes, they gleamed like the sun reflecting off bronze. Nervous. I lost my voice as I contemplated if he may be trying to put together his next words. We stared at each other as if we agreed to do just that. An approaching figure disrupted perfect silence.

"Say, nephew, who is my new neighbor? Hello little lady. I'm Sargon Delroy. So, you bought this old outhouse? Well, have fun; the old sticks and stones and ghosts of bones, shake with every toilet flush."

Now just a fight away, I address the man. "My name is Zelda, and it looks like both our houses were built the same day, by the same builder."

"You're right, but your place is in so much disrepair. You have your work cut out for you."

This is the second person, one from each side of me, to tell me to kick this house down the hill. This man is now rubbing me the wrong way just like the A-hole on the other side of me in the fake mansion.

Sargon Delroy might have been good looking at one time, but lack of pushing away from the table distorted his body to look like a four-door Ford Pinto, when they were only made in two-door models. His face was butter greasy with narrow eyes that were nearly crossed-eyed. Unlike a well-trimmed five o'clock shadow, heavy stubble was a mainstay of, I stopped grooming long ago. The thing that saved him from being unattractive was height near the 6'1" range, and how he carried himself when he walked; as if he used to be able to move athletically.

Aloy stood erect, being a little taller than his uncle. I could see he wanted to interject, but trouble lines creased his forehead. I felt for him, not knowing the family dynamics.

"Well, I need to get back to work. Thanks for coming over to meet me. Please keep an eye out for my place as I understand there were problems in the past. I do have a young man rooming here, so it should be just him and I going in and out."

"Yeah, I saw a car's headlights shining while someone was on the porch the other night. I figured it had to be legit, and now I know it was your fine self," he smiled, and his left cheek rose like a dark moon rising behind an erupting volcano. I could tell he wanted to see what my reaction would be.

"Uncle," Aloy called out in a, What the hell is wrong with you, defiance. He moved to the side of me, causing me to look up to his tall profile. There was lava fire in his eyes, rolling downward onto his uncle. Warrior rage. Clouds moved in.

"Hey, it looks like you all are talking and I'm not one to cockblock,' Sargon Delroy smirked with his foul statement and walked away. I think I took my first breath in the last ten seconds.

"I need to get back to work," I said to Aloy, wishing for a little space and time from whatever it was that just happened.

"My uncle can be a foolish man. May I ask you...to accept...an apology for his... rudeness?"

The long pauses that happened between his words added more sentiment to asking me to forgive his uncle.

"All is forgiven, you're not responsible for another man's boorish behavior."

"No, we all are too responsible for the faults of others if we want to make a difference."

I was beginning to like his slow and deliberate speech; and for sure, his train of thought.

"Aloy, I'll be cleaning up and shutting down in an hour or so, it has been a long day. Would you like to come over and have a cold beer in my humble, crumbling sticks and stones?"

Clouds had parted again. He stood facing west with the sun going down in his eyes. The hot lava was gone. I now wanted to wait for a response for as long as it would take.

His lips parted, and I thought he was about to nod yes, but a car horn blew. A clean, white, newer model BMW sports coupe turned into my driveway. It had down poured a couple of hours ago, and the streets were still wet, but this car was bright white, clean, and now idling in my driveway. I think it had gone roaring by earlier. A tinted window came down, and a woman tried to stab me with her eyes with an, *I'm superior to you*, expression. She was fair skinned and pretty. No matter what her color of skin was, she was cute. However, if that makeup eroded under a Seattle cloudburst, I wondered just how pretty she would be. She had on more war paint than a Zulu warrior, or a white man with black shoe polish on, trying to look black. I don't like her, whoever she is.

"Aloy!" she sharply called out, but kept her eyes on me. I, for some reason, looked at how bad my front yard was with overgrowth and unkempt grass.

"Excuse me…I'll be back."

I watched his all solid-man-walk to her car.

I was glad he didn't use the word apologize, and I hope he doesn't. He turned, and if it weren't for his powerful strides that would make a mountain lion run away, I would have jumped in the truck and drove away.

73

As he stood above her car window, her lips moved, but her eyes stay glued to mine; and if that is his woman, I'm enjoying her anguish that she's acting out. As his lips parted, she backed up and drove away. If she looked back, I wouldn't know; she had rolled her window up. Walking in her heels or driving in what has to be expensive heels I figured she wears, I wouldn't give another woman or man that kind of control over me. I would act out in front of another. No man or woman shall ever make me angry over another. I have faults. I have crossed lines, but another man or woman igniting unruly jealousy in me is lightening parting the sky I wish never to feel or to fall from.

Now, as I sat back in the truck, he spoke to me through my window. "Can…I still have that beer? Please don't let her ruin my invite," he smiled. He won.

"Okay, give me an hour or so; but can I assume you'll be honest with me about what that was about? Nice car, and a Barbie doll behind the wheel with an attitude as foul as the manure a cow puts out right after being branded. Beyond that, why did you get straight off your motorcycle and come over to talk to me? And oh, I asked you to have a beer with me and you agree. Arrogant or assertive? Are you just an outgoing nice guy?"

"I'll tell…you later," he smiled, and strangely, everything near my hips—in and out, clinched.

"Aloy Ambrose, Mr. AA, can you give me two hours, please?"

He smiled wide and reached through the truck window and gently touched my upper arm with two fingers. Then he made a peace sign. His fingers had my horny ass thinking of slowmotion penetration. I nodded, but nasty thoughts wouldn't let me make eye contact. I wanted to rip my panties off and put them under his nose, hoping my scent would trap him. My panties, right now, would for sure moisten his chin, and I would gladly kiss away my own sweetness.

I'm getting way ahead of myself. I've gone astray in my lust. Nevertheless, even if we are just having a friendly neighborly conversation, my panties feel as if a river has run wild through them from his touch. Damn, it has been too long, but I don't know anything about this man. I'm getting way ahead of myself. I turn the key, start the motor, and now I feel the rumble under my ass. I chuckle as I drive away from Mr. AA.

Chapter 11

After hitting Craigslist and making runs to go pick up things to make my stay more comfortable, I filled the house with furnishings and other necessities. Chevelle and I worked at cleaning and making the place livable. He had totally bought into the fact that if he helped me, he would have a safe place to lay his head. He wanted to be a part of my project. He was not a lazy kid, and was very intellectual.

He said school had bored him and that he had slept through most of it, but kept almost a 4.0. However, he said he would have dropped out if it wasn't for the fact that he loved being on the wrestling team. He won his weight class in the State tournaments twice, but tested positive for marijuana use in his senior year and was stripped of his past championships. He did not finish the last half of his senior year after wrestling season was over; and when college scholarships went away, he had made some mistakes, and mistakes always change the course of our lives.

After we cleaned up, I gave him some money to go out and eat a good full meal. I wanted some alone time. Chevelle had set himself up in the basement fairly well. He had his own area to chill. I still wanted the house empty for a while. There was a working toilet in the basement, but the sink was busted. We'd fix it soon. He said he'd use the outside hose for water if he needed water. I had found a water cooler on Craigslist and put it down in his living area for drinking wateas a reminder of his needing to drink water more often.

After my shower, the only thought was about Aloy Ambrose. Who is he? The warrior who rides his iron horse as if he makes roads for others to ride smoothly? I Googled his name on my phone…and, oh, wow! My stepdad and I had talked about him way back when.

I'm a bit in awe. I met a man, and he has dealt with a lot, and he intrigues me. My mind is racing into, *What if.* I'm conflicted. I need to focus on this house, my stepdad, and my future earning power.

I don't want him to smell my scent of a womanly lusting and longing for a manly touch. Even while showering, he punched his presence into the bathroom and touched me. I slowly lathered my body with extra body wash, and my hands roamed under thick pillows of suds. Feeling my breasts, I imagine his hands cupping me and squeezing my nipples. His hands…they looked as if he could extract honey from a rock. His touch on my arm was like a warm summer heat. My breasts rise to meet the hot beads of water to kiss my nipples. I imagine his hands immersed in warm baby oil and coating my face, neck, breasts, tummy, and down my legs and up over my ass. If only I could feel him kneeling between my thighs, and his hot tongue licking my honey that's now running down my leg. I pictured him handling my body, and his tongue drying me as if a large beach towel encased my body.

I removed the tethered showerhead and turned it to pulsate. I rinsed the suds from my body; and long after the suds were gone, each bead of water sent a rhythmic beating against my skin. It felt like a hot desert rain. The shower pulsation kissed me around my neck and over my shoulders. In colored daydream. I brush stroked hallucinations of him behind me with his hand outlining my body from my shoulders downward. I let the water pressure massage my spine and drain down between my ass cheeks. My imagination removed all limitations to his fingers. He had free access to all I had.

I parted my legs, and quickly I go up one more level. I put one foot on the edge of the clawfoot tub as I felt the water run down my back. He, I mean, the firm thumping water made its way to dripping off my lips between my inner thighs. A swelling. I felt a wanting of penetration. I throbbed, and my clit tried to sing a song. My sensitivity had me singing in tongues.

The bathroom mirror in front of me, it saw me wet. Somehow it seemed I perceived him there with me, licking my thighs. That's not water slipping down my inner thigh. The steam rises up my nostrils. I wanted to smell Aloy Ambrose as visions of him party behind my eyelids. Even when he walked toward another woman, I saw his back was a weighbridge the world could not break. His walk, he looked as if he could cross the Serengeti

Desert in leaps and bounds. Behind my eyelids, his body danced above me as I lay wide open under his control. I can see him. I can feel him, and his soft voice drugs me into being his puppet.

I placed the showerhead spray directly on my pussy, and one of the shots of spray hits my clit like a warm tongue flicking from side to side. I felt my ass cheeks clamp, and my toes – which are already straight – lifted, but went firmer with tension. I let forth sounds of getting off. I thought of him being behind me as the water runs off my clit. I glide two fingers inside my hotness, stimulating what might be his length and width, and him dancing inside me.

*****

There's a knock on the door and I don't move fast. I know who it is. I sprint to the bathroom and look in the mirror to see if my relived shower feelings show on my face. I laugh thinking what would that look be. My jeans – the ones that show off my backside – and a tank top with a sport bra underneath, met Aloy at the door. He stared at me and I waved him in. I think we have figured out our basic communication.

We sit in the kitchen across from each other. I poured two glasses of Perrier water and dropped two cherries in each glass. I decided against having beer. I had the stove hood light on as opposed to the kitchen overhead bright light. The low glow gave off the aura of a Sunday night prayer service, and he was the preacher man coming to lay hands. There was still enough light to see his beautiful black skin, and his dark copper-tone eyes. The chrome of the legs of the table added star reflections in his eyes. I tuned to Soul Oldies Internet radio on my phone, and had it flow through the stereo. Dang, why did Bootsy's, "I Rather Be With You" have to come on just as we sat down?

We stared. We smiled. We actually spoke at the same time.

"I Googled you, Aloy, you were…"

"Zelda, I understand…you boxed. My aunt said she saw you…shadow-boxing."

We stepped on each other's words. But his words took time to arrive.

"Go ahead, but please start with you. Can I...can I know a little about you," he said.

I told him I was born in Texas, and had moved from place to place as a child, which I had done when Mom met my stepdad, Eddie. Eddie fought in small towns and big cities. He fought the local up-and-coming fighters who wanted to make a name for themselves. My stepdad quite often schooled wanna-be champions, but he still lost the fight in the end due to bribed judges. Those up-and-coming fighters really lost to my stepdad. They were only awarded their wins by judges who knew to award the fight to the local guy if they wanted to get paid to judge future fights. Those fighters got beat up pretty badly on their way to being called the winner.

I found myself relaxed while talking with Aloy. I had not confided in many about my life, and felt the need to stop living in my head. Living alone with my thoughts hurt many times. I told Aloy about my plight in dealing with my stepdad now. I also told him I had a relative who bought the house, and that I was doing the renovation, and doing a little of this and that after being laid-off from Boeings.

In a way, I wish I had kept the house info to myself. Partly though, I don't want to be a liar to someone who has not earned the iniquitous side of me that resides in all souls. Another side of me, I'm a bird with a broken wing, and healing comes...sometimes. I guess I really needed a friend, but my aunt told me to keep our personal stuff personal. My admissions to Aloy make me ask the question of myself, *Can I trust myself*, because I have grown so lonely.

We laughed a lot when we talked, and I answered most of his questions. A few questions I deflected, but I felt comfortable enough to tell him my fights now are off the books, my fights are tough man or should I say tough woman contests. . He understood what it meant, and that felt good. Most of the women with big names in boxing avoided me. He laughed when I told him I was impatient to play the game of Going through the ranks; especially when I could be the champ if ever given a straight shot at the title. He respected my reasoning with a gentle laugh.

I felt relaxed enough to let him see my gap when we laughed, and we laughed a lot, and I hadn't laughed in a long while. I needed a safe zone to let go. Aloy Ambrose was cool people.

"Okay, okay, I told you I Googled you, Aloy. So, I know a little about you; let's talk about you. Like, twenty years ago you won 101 amateur fights and only lost one. I also know you made the Olympic team by knocking out every opponent in the tournament. Then…"

He cut my tongue off. "I never lost, but the other guy was declared the winner," he said that assertively with no hesitation. "After I had a fight stolen, I knocked everyone out after that to leave no doubt," Aloy's tone turned a bit dark, but I liked it in a way. He was clear, for a little, in his speech.

We talked about his boxing career and then we talked about how it ended. I thought he might not want to from the information I had found on the Internet. It was sad. Nonetheless, he told me the story in detail. In various ways, different promoters threatened him to entice him to sign backdoor deals, anticipating on making great returns from him winning after he would turn pro.

After the Olympic trials, local business leaders put on a banquet for him after he made the Olympic team. The world was that he would win the gold medal and go on to be the heavy weight champion one day. He was on the heels of Mike Tyson who was on the top at the time.

As Aloy and some friends were on their way home from the banquet, two trucks rammed their car, and ran them off the street. Men got out with guns, and pulled everyone out of the car and shot his friends in the arms and legs; all except him and Duce, yeah A-hole Duce. The thugs told Aloy he would suffer the same fate and more if he didn't make the right business choices.

With the story I was hearing in my kitchen, an illumination of an interrogation room took form as if an old black & white TV glowed in a dark room. He confessed to a situation that jailed his future; it sealed his fate for life. As a fighter who can't accept defeat and is willing to go down swinging, Aloy went for the knockout that night. He won and lost.

Again, he lost most of his speech impediment as if he was lifting his soul off the canvas to be the fighter he used to be as he voiced his legendary survival.

"I was angry. I…became a wild man with rage. I leaped. I guess I moved so fast, clocking several of the men with guns. I knocked them out with either my fist, or by taking their guns and hitting them in the head. As I went to help one of my friends who was shot in the leg, one of the guys I thought I had knocked out cold awoke groggy, and pulled another gun out and shot me in the back of the head."

We sat in silence. I made coffee and he talked again.

"My skull cracked, and the bullet fragments lodged on a nerve center causing me to talk as if I'm forgetting what I want to say. At times, it gets bad enough that I had to have little cards made to give to people, as you now have one. Anyway, the shot to my head took me down for the first and last time in my life. I got up and the son-of-a-bitch who shot me in the back of the head was trying to get up and run. I picked up a gun and pulled the hammer, but it jammed. I walked faster than my shooter could get off the ground and run. I got my hands around the throat of the man who shot me, and I strangled him to death. I know you read that."

"What was Duce doing all that time?"

"He shit and pissed on himself and fainted, or acted like he fainted."

His words, I had to wait a long time to hear.

I told Aloy about my encounter with Duce after he told me they were not friends, but that they were cordial. He said that they grew up as friends, but Duce was somebody who liked to play bigger than he was, and that he had a short man's syndrome. Duce's father was one of the men who wanted Aloy to sign deals with his business partners.

I had to ask.

"Don't you think Duce's father might have had something to do with you and your friend being hurt; especially seeing that Duce wasn't shot?"

I know my almond eyes had turned to perfect circles in amazement that Duce, or anyone related, still lived.

"Yes," Aloy stood and walked over to the kitchen door and maybe looked over at Duce's high-rise box. I thought he was going to leave, but he leaned on the door, turned, faced me, and stared at me. "But what was there to do? My boxing career…was over, and I'm wounded for life; and in many ways, my friends still suffer. I had no proof, other than my common sense."

"Wow, Aloy…I'm sorry; and I thank you for telling me when you didn't have to."

I wanted to go stand next to him, but what then?

"I have…no problem telling it. Often, I'm sure people don't realize I was a young man who was not all that savvy to evil people. Yeah, you Googled me, but the real story cannot be told when it comes to the pain I felt then, and the pain I will forever feel. The pain seems to ride high no matter the tide. I still have head pain from time to time, and headaches. I talk like a punchdrunk fighter, but I'm not. Many who don't know my story think…I'm brain damaged from boxing. I could have killed Duce's father. I thought about it.

"He had to know who was behind it all. I thought about hurting Duce. I planned it out in my head and heart, but Duce's mother was like a second mother to me.

I noticed that with that sentence, Aloy had no problem completing it without any delay. I asked him what became of those boys, knowing they are out of prison.

"When you hire young punks, you get boys who watched movies and had limits in understanding the magnitude of deeds. One man is dead from the violence of my hands. The others went to prison and lost living a regular life. The ones who put them up to it and should be incarnated...they walked free. All I wanted to do was go to the Olympics. I'm not hateful, but I don't give a damn what happened or what goes on for them now!"

Silence, only his deep sigh entered my ear. I felt fear; not that he would strike out at me, but his anger seemingly made the old wood in the house make unsettling creaks. I waited for him to relax.

"Duce's father owned the house you're in now, and the house next door where Duce knocked down and built his house. Some days, I want to be the big bad wolf and go huff and puff and blow his house down."

He pursed his lips and blew lightly. It brought to my attention for the hundredth time since I met him hours earlier, just how pretty his face is. I wished he was blowing a kiss toward me or placing a kiss on me. His light blow was in the direction of the sticks and stones house in the shape of a Cracker Jack box. The man inside that box was no prize; he was rotten.

Aloy told me of the Cowen family history and behold...some of the pain I imagined this house had felt was true. Mr. Cowen was a short man wielding abusive power, and he beat his wives. He had three different wives who lived in the house over the decades. The first wife bore him a daughter, but that wife left after too many fat lips and black eyes. Many of the neighbors couldn't imagine how she ever got away, as he limited when and where she went. No one has ever heard from that wife or daughter again.

The next wife is Duce's mother, who Aloy loved; but he might have loved her because of the abuse she stood up to in trying to be a good woman in raising Duce and his sister. As a child, Aloy would hear howls and shouts of survival from both her and from old man Cowen as she would fight back. Aloy could tell that sometimes she got the better part of the old man. The next day, she would act as if she was an untouched queen. She was beautiful, and much taller than her husband. She died from cancer, but Aloy abstracted from it that it was her way to beat the beatings; she let cancer lead her away. Her daughter was from a previous marriage, and that girl's father raised her, but she visited often. Aloy reflected that Duce's mother became thin looking, but stayed regal to the end. Before she passed, she made it to his early fights when he was a teenager and brought her daughter.

Old man Cowen married again to a young, beautiful, full-figured woman, and she was gone in a year after looking haggard and depressed. When old man Cowen died, he left no will; and although Duce's sister was his half-sister, the courts gave her the house because their mother was owed half of the estate. Duce got the lot and a sizable life insurance.

Duce's sister rented the house out over the years, but lack of repairs ran the value down. She finally sold the house and it resold a few times after that, and now I'm trying to rid it of its ghostly history. Aloy believes Duce and his half-sister have very little to do with each other.

Aloy sat back down and tilted his head back. His eyes blinked many times before he lowered his head and looked right through me, I felt. The soft glow of the light from the stove hood behind his head gave me a chill I hadn't felt since we had been visiting. A darkness rose over his aura.

"Aloy, I don't know you, but you share so much. But what you haven't shared is why you came over to meet me. And, who, if I may ask…who was that woman in the white car? Is that your woman checkin' you?"

For two hours, our conversation ventured from serious to small talk, with some laughter. I was getting sleepy. I had a long, physical day. I didn't want it to end, but why had he made a beeline to me right after he arrived at his aunt and uncle's house? It can't be that he found me that attractive. He's way too fine for him to be looking at me, as I wish he would, but I will keep letting my daydreams about him be unrestrained, but he's not here for my panties. Fine men only want to cheat with me as their sidepiece. Been there, more than once, more than thrice.

"Zelda, it's timing that brought me over to meet you."

"What?"

"My aunt called me and told me she saw you shadowboxing, and that when she spoke to you, it was apparent you had fighting knowledge.

I'm in a position that I run a gym, and I need a woman on board to work with the women and men, but mostly for the women who come in need of a trainer. I had to fire a guy who was using the gym as his personal dating service, and was trying to do every woman who came in the gym. I can't have that. I want to give the gym a different vibe from the female perspective. It's not a boxing gym per se; we do more fitness training than anything else. I base the physical training and conditioning on boxing workouts, and then we have a few who I train for fights, but they are mostly youngsters. Hopefully, they learn to use their fists instead of guns in the future.

"Can we discuss you being available and your expertise being obtainable? The pay is a decent hourly wage with commission; and if you wanted to train fighters on the side for money, I can work that out. too."

I took it all in as it took a long while for him to finish, or maybe I was in a hurry for him to finish. Now I'm staring at him as if I'm the one with a speech impediment and can't put my words together. Knowing I need income, this fits me; but his girl, I suspect, might not be cool to deal with. It might not be cool to be around his sexy allure…period. My legs have been twitching under the table from being close to his legs.

"Hours? Tell me what kind of hours are we talking about, Mr. AA?"

"If you could, six hours in the in AM; or you could work six hours in the PM, that will work, too. Also, any five out of the seven days will be fine. If you work more hours, that's up to you."

"I need time to work on the house and to tend to my stepdad as often as I can."

"Okay, you choose AM or the PM, or switch it up some days this, and the other days let it be something else. As long as we can have a…predetermined schedule for the clients coming through the door, I'm good with it."

I flipped my head to the side and looked at him with my eyebrows raised.

"How is your girl going to like it? Let's start this off right, no BS. That woman in the white Benz is more than a friend. I'm not wantin' to get caught up in a love triangle; especially when I'm not a part of the triangle, but just imagined to be. I'm sure, if she saw me around all the time, it will be a problem. Can you handle your business? A weak-minded woman thinks any woman near their man, or even her ex-man, is a reason to have a war. I just want to do my thing; so I don't need your woman, or women, trying to smoke my behind in their hot exhaust."

I heard Chevelle come in the basement door, and a moment later, I heard his radio come on. "I want to introduce you to the young man living here before you go, if that's alright."

"Yes, before I go, and I should go soon. I have to open the gym at 5:00 AM for the, *before I-go-to-work* crowd. It's not a crowd, only a handful; but they pay, so I'm there. Zelda, the woman in the white Benz is my friend, Parasol. When I was an up-and-coming amateur fighter on the way to the Olympics trials, she and I dated. It was serious then, but things changed after I was shot and all the recovery time and issues…she couldn't deal with it, and I can't help her in the ways she needs."

His speech impediment, brain freeze, or something else, held his silence a long time.

"She and I go out when one of us has a need to have an escort for a function. My speech problems mean I'm just her arm piece, and I act and be…quiet. There are times I need a woman to be with me for an event, so we trade space and time. Her coming over today was purely by chance. She has a friend who lives nearby. She would have kept going, but when she saw me, she stopped; she had to show her face. She doesn't give a damn about what I do unless she figures it might make her look bad. She, on the other hand, what she does is a different story."

"Yeah, it sounds like you and her have unfinished mental commerce. Complicated relationships often become denial of your circumstances, and that is a bitch. Denial of how your circumstances negatively affect others is a bastard child that no one wants. So, you want me to work with you…I'm more than on board. I thank you for offering me what sounds like a great opportunity, especially since you do not know me. But please…please don't get me caught up in you-all's thing as if I'm stirring a drink that no one wants to consume."

He laughed, and I loved it.

"Zelda, you are direct, but not disrespectful. That works for me. The mean-girl thing makes me repel, and that mean-girl thing has started to happen between Parasol and me. I'll work to keep our workflow a positive thing. I'm looking forward to what you can bring to my gym. Yes, timing is a great thing. I have female Zumba teachers, but I need a woman who understands weight training, boxing, and boot camp conditioning."

I nodded. One of the beautiful things about this man is that, despite the fact that he has a brain injury that affects his speech, he is sharp minded. We continued to sit in my dimly-lit kitchen talking about what I could do to make the gym a better place. Before we knew it, we had been talking again for another hour. I told him he could meet Chevelle another time. Aloy gave me a friendly bear hug at the door. I needed that embrace. No man has held me since a man who should have been holding his wife only was embracing me. I had a job. I have a couple of friends in Aloy and Chevelle. I have a place to stay. I have some blessings around me. I'm thankful.

I sit in the living room bay window and watch him get on his stallion—his Harley, and he slowly roars away. I close my eyes, and the streetlight works its way behind my eyelids. I speak to my elders and God.

Thank you for timing. Thank you for placing people and things in places I can reach. Thank you for the grace you have extended into my life. Thank you for trials and tribulations which bring me to the good and bad and those in-between.

Chapter 12

Up when the sun hit my eyes, I was down in the basement with Chevelle. We are working to fix, make, and build the basement into something nice. During one of the trips from yesterday, we picked up lumber, and all the things needed to do the jobs ahead.

True in fact, Chevelle has skills as he framed walls up quickly to get us going on making a complete basement apartment. He has vision of the possible; he set things in motion. Beyond him leading the way, I'm happy for him to have a place to sleep, eat, and be clean and safe. I feel I can mentor him in ways he too will need in a tough world. We got hours in, and then he headed to his part-time job.

I take off to go see my auntie; we meet for breakfast at a casino restaurant near Sea-Tac Airport. I needed to get the hardware store credit card to buy materials since I used some of the cash yesterday for lumber. I let my auntie know about Chevelle. She didn't say much; just that it's all on me. I tell her I have a job in a gym with flexible hours. I share bits and pieces about how that came about. She had a few questions about who was involved. She sure wanted to know a lot about Aloy: who, where, and how. I didn't tell her a lot, nor did I want to; but actually, I love it when she is at least inquisitive. It feels like she cares about me, as my mother did. Auntie has always had a lot to say to me about men and their bad deeds, their bad lies, and their nomadic ways when it came to women. She, though, grants herself a pass when it comes to her bad deeds with men.

Mid-day, I walk into the 4 Corners Boxing Fitness Club which sits on the Rainier Beach area lakefront that's on the south end of Lake Washington on a park's edge. Boats line the waterfront condo area of the most diverse zip code in the United States. High and low incomes dance in the same streets of drive-by shootings and muggings, along with Starbucks and libraries. Schools and mortuaries could be prisons by the configurations, and you can clearly see it driving in from every direction. It's the urban revitalization that will predictably supplant the occupying demographic in the area.

Old rundown buildings of revolving door businesses from nail shops to barbecue joints, and fast-food, lines the hood. White women push baby strollers and wait for buses right along with boyz in the hood, with their pants well-below their butts. A general street code - a safe zone of, don't mess with regular citizens, works out a psychology line of, I'll stay in my lane, most of the time. Of course, a car is not a person and a house without a security alarm is not a person, so they both are fair game.

In the parking lot of the 4 Corners Boxing Fitness Club, you can see a new Lexus parked next to a lowered teenage Honda, and a Cadillac Escalade on dubs is parked next to a Subaru. It was clean inside, but smelled of sweat mixed with other scents. I had to ask myself why some women put on smell good sprays or lotions before they worked out.

A converted old warehouse type building appeared clean around the outside. Huge windows had been added, allowing lots of light into the inside that I saw as I walked in.

"Hello Zelda."

My eyes opened wide enough that I could feel my forehead skin touch my hairline. She knew my name. At the front desk, a very pretty woman greeted me. Her skin was a creamy light toast in tone, but I don't think she is Black or Native. She had on a pink Seahawk jersey. She looked up from a book as she was sitting at a front counter.

"And you are?" I said pleasantly.

"JoBelle, and I know of you because Aloy told me to look out for you. You're coming to join us. Seeing you in front of me now, I remember seeing you fight at a fight club warehouse. You whooped some Russian chic's ass. You had her drooling on herself. I'm the one who yelled, *Bye Felicia*, and everyone laughed. People still talk about how good you are, and that no one can touch you. And yet, you still come across as a woman; a lady. Some of these fight chics act as if they need to be mannish to be thought of as tough. That's not sexy. Up close, you got those Serena Williams arms. Damn!"

"Thanks for all that. I remember hearing someone say that, and that was you, huh. Nice to meet you, JoBelle. What's a nice girl like you doing at fight club fights?"

"Shoot, don't get it twisted by my short Filipino self, and the pretty face. I'm not on your level in the fight game; but I can scrap when I need to, and I do enjoy contact sports."

We both laughed as a handsome man walked by baring muscles he wanted everyone to see. She had a Seahawk poster on the wall behind her, with these fine brothers called the Legion of Boom.

"Hey, sir, I'm gonna need you to check out towels from the front desk to wipe your sweat off from any machine you use, or are you just here for hot yoga?" JoBelle smiled. The hot body stud just smiled and kept walking, but with an added bounce in his high ass cheeks.

I reached over and we touched fists.

"Aloy had to step out, but I can show you around. We even have a little office space for you, and it has a locker in there for you, and a shower."

"Well alright then."

Right after JoBelle gave me a tour, I actually got a workout in on the heavy bag. Aloy made it back just as I was finishing. We met by the windows overlooking the marina.

"Tell me how this came to be with you owning all this on the lakefront?"

He didn't answer, or he was trying to. His face seemed troubled, so I let it ride for now.

"When can you start?" his tone was impatient, but maybe I was confusing his slow delivery as him being irritated.

His eyes avoided direct connect with mine as I answered him.

"I'll be here from 11:00 AM to 7:00 PM three days a week, and 6:00 AM to 2:00 PM the other two days. That way a noontime crowd can always get me."

"Can I ask…?"

My phone vibrated. "Hold on one second."

I apologized. I turned away because my cell phone was in my bra. Chevelle's name came up. I had purchased a Pre-pay cell phone for him. I thought it would be the right thing to do since he and I were coming and going and needed to connect with each other regularly to get work done.

"Chevelle?"

"Zelda, I'm in trouble," Chevelle's voice was strained and weak. "Help, please come." Agony gored my ear.

Then another voice came through his phone. Hello, is this Zelda Hargo?" a male authoritative voice entered my ear; at the same time, music got loud coming from a Zumba class that was starting in the gym.

"Ah yeah, and who is this?" I said, as I trotted over to my little office. I signaled Aloy to follow.

With my door closed I heard, "I'm Sergeant Martin of the Seattle Police Department. I'm on the phone of a young man, Chevelle. He is in the emergency room of Harborview Hospital. He has been beat up rather badly. I'm trying to sort all this out, but he has not said a lot other than some guys jumped him."

"I'll be there in twenty minutes or less."

I clicked my phone off and repeated to Aloy what I was told.

He grabbed me by my arm firmly. "I'm taking you up there; your car is too big to drive fast through the city."

There was no hesitation in his voice, and his unyielding directness made me submit without even thinking twice. I had never felt that from a man unless we were having sex. In my sense of urgency, his physical and verbal aggression overrode me into almost forgetting what was going on. I had my feelings acting silly all of a sudden. He led me out of the building. JoBelle nodded at me as she must have sensed there was some wrongness going on.

I dismounted off the back of Aloy's Harley, leaving the helmet on my head as I sprinted through the double sliding doors of the hospital. As fast as I could without running into people standing in the way looking for medical services, I made it to the help desk. I don't know Chevelle that well, but whatever happened to him, if he's in trouble, or anyone tried to hurt him, or possibly a gang thing went down, I would try to get him going in the right direction. Yet, all things have limits.

I asked the desk nurse for Chevelle, and she pointed to a gurney in the hallway. Doctors were finished with him, and they weren't going to admit him. He had given permission for the doctors and the front desk to give me information about him. Two police officers stood over Chevelle. They tried introducing themselves to me, but I stopped them by putting my hand up, and gave them a hard stare. They moved aside. I wanted a first look at Chevelle and his condition.

I leaned down and whispered, "Do we talk later or now?"

He shook his head slowly without opening his eyes and whispered, "Later."

His eyes: one was blue-black, the other had a swelling like his lips. His nose was broken. I can identify a broken nose. I've broken a few; not my own nose, but others. Chevelle held a bag of ice on his forehead and one of his hands was bandaged as if it had a cut.

"How can I help you, officers?" I asked.

"Well, apparently he was leaving a job at a nursing home, and in the alley, he says he was jumped by several men," said the officer with too perfect white teeth. His height allowed him to stare down into my eyes. He highlighted his features with daily grooming from what I figured to be a stylist, I imagined. The smug look on his metrosexual face made me think he collected women's panties instead of giving out traffic tickets. He smiled at me as if he would mount me and hump me, and I'd beg for more, if given the chance. He was trying way too hard to be sexy.

I cut my eyes hard at him to let him know I despised his ass as I retorted, "Well, it's not apparently. I dropped him off this morning at his place of work. He earns an honest living."

"Well, it was in broad daylight, and he's seemingly having a problem since he can't identify the thugs – I mean perpetrators; who and how many attacked him. If it was some kind of gang jump-in thing, we don't need to be here. Life will take care of itself sooner or later if they were gangbanging douche bags; and a white boy like him has better options anyway, why he got to be gangbanging?"

The other police officer stood, looking like Gomer Pyle, while his sarcastic partner had a bowel movement out of his mouth.

"So, because you say he's white, he's got better things to do? Sir, I hope you use better English when you write your reports, or did they let you become the police on a lower learning curve? You assume so much on so little knowledge."

His face attempted to go hard. I smiled and cocked my head to side. If he had me alone, he'd beat my ass; but he'd walk away without out being able to generate sperm ever again.

"What other reason...I mean really...why would they have done this to you?"

The dude acted as if his words curved around me to Chevelle, then he spoke back at me. "Is he involved in gang activity?"

I looked at him with searing revulsion. I wished I could hurl a hot spear across his eyebrows and singe off what was left after his last plucking. I didn't respond. I didn't believe Chevelle was involved in gang activity. I believed him to have been honest with me, and when I told him no drama, I meant it. I believe he understood that.

"Is he free to go, or is he being held and charged with anything, like it's a crime to be a victim?"

The police officer squinted at me coldly. He felt harassed. I wasn't cooperating with him, I was being a bit belligerent, and he couldn't do a damn thing about it. He was in a visible place— an ER of a hospital with lots of cameras. They chuckled as they walked away as if they had won a round. Acting as if you're one up when you're not is like toilet paper hanging from under your dress. Everybody knows your shit is hanging, except you.

I helped Chevelle up, and we were walking to the front exit when Aloy walked our way. The police officers, I could tell the Gomer Pyle looking officer knew who Aloy was. They stopped to talk, but his partner walked around him while tugging on his partner's sleeve to signal to keep it moving.

Aloy pointed to taxies, but he let me know he could have a friend come pick us up, if I could wait just a little longer. I looked at Chevelle's abrasions and bruises and thought he needed to be as comfortable as possible, instead of in an unsanitary taxi.

Aloy moved in front of Chevelle, introduced himself, and told him he would be okay no matter what has happened. He was there to support me, and that meant Chevelle had support, too. He pulled out his cell phone, and as difficult as it is for him to get his speech processes together and talk fluently, I listened to him ask someone to come pick us up.

His speech, at times, is so labored. He told me that when he is around some people, he may act mute; yet near me, he had let his guard down. Sometimes, it's odd how we live and never accept our situations; we put ourselves down, and hold ourselves down. I could tell that wasn't the case with Aloy. In my presence, he showed a sense of pride in who he was and what he did. He's lost several things that meant the world to him, but he has kept on going. He runs a gym, he stays involved with youth, and he appears to be a good guy as he has offered me a job without asking many questions. I'm not accustomed to many people in this world who reach into their soul pockets and hand you time and effort.

A Cadillac Escalade pulled up to the outside area where we waited. A friend of Aloy's was helpful as Aloy rode off on his motorcycle. I went to go get a newspaper to put on the seats just in case Chevelle bled, and he smelled awful like dog piss, but the man said not to worry about the leather, it would clean up. I couldn't thank him enough. Sumlin was his name. He walked with a severe limp. The drive to my place was full of history as Sumlin shared.

He was the friend that Aloy was knelt over, helping with a gun wound to his leg, when Aloy was shot in the back of his head. Sumlin lost the normal use of his leg and his football scholarship; yet, he has coached state football championships and track champions. He didn't lose mind and heart. Sumlin made it clear that he would do anything for Aloy. The reason why…at the time of the shooting, he had seen the gunman raise the gun and he shouted for Aloy to duck. Instead of ducking, Aloy moved his whole body in front of Sumlin, and the bullet hit Aloy in the back of the head.

Sumlin helped me get Chevelle in the house and comfortable, and then he dropped me off at the gym to retrieve my car. Four hours later, Chevelle woke from sleeping on the couch. I woke from his stirring and groaning as I was asleep on the floor near him. His sleep was painful. I gave him some Demerol I acquired off the street. I placed ice on his hurts and discomforts.

While in my sleep, dreams sent joy to my worried mind. Aloy played the lead. *Why is this man so nice and giving?* He doesn't know me, but he has given me a job and then jumped in to help me help someone I don't know well.

I turn my attention to Chevelle. "I know you're in pain, but try to tell me what happene and with who and why."

I know my tone sounded assertive, that was not my intent; but it is what it is when I need to be in the know. What was he in, and how deep?

Pain filtered past hurt lips. I listened to Chevelle mumble words. "I told you why I went to juvie. Iman's dad shoved me around and he tried to use a shooting stun gun on me, but didn't quite know what the hell he was doing. Stupid mutha'!" Chevelle opened his eyes the best he could, and lifted his chin to gaze at me. I read it as the young boy part of him that was ashamed he cursed like he did in front of me.

"I knocked the stun gun away and I gave him an ass whoopin to remember. He stored his big payback and unleashed today. I guess. But, as you know, his first vengeance was to report me as his attacker from that ass whoopin' I gave him. They could have charged me as an adult, and I was in regular men's County lockup for a while; but I had not been in trouble before, and I was sentenced on the day I turned eighteen. That's how I served my time in juvie." He sat up and stared at me through his blackened eye, the other one was almost swollen shut.

"Today, as I was leaving work, I stepped into the ally and I was hit on the back with something hard. As I fell trying to run, I saw Iman's dad and three other men, one was huge. They beat me, kicked me, and cursed me; then they spit on me and peed on me as I was laying there. That's why I had no shirt on at the hospital. The medics ripped it off because I was soaked in piss."

"Chevelle, how did they know you worked there and when to meet up with you to hurt you like this?" I already know how.

His head lowered. His chin almost went into his chest. A tear dropped in his lap. His heart might have felt as if it was falling from a bluff. "I emailed Imam and asked her to meet me at a park near where I work. She had met me there the day before. I can only assume her dad cornered her or he read her email."

"You love this girl, right? Does she love you? Is she worth all you've been through, and all you're going through?" I spoke slowly. If a snake could talk with contempt, my tone was slipping toward that direction believing this girl might have set him up.

97

"Although you and I have just met, you offered me a place to stay," he almost whispered his words as if he was checking his thoughts. "You have trusted me, and I have one other person I trust, and that is Iman. I was going to ask you to meet her. I believe she loves me." His swollen eye opened as wide as it could and I can see his truth.

I ran my tongue over the front of my teeth and back, and then tried to slide my tongue through my gap, but it's not that wide. I do that instead of biting my tongue when wanting to speak coldly.

"I know she understands me. She knows I'm going to be something special. One day I want to marry her. One day I want to build her a house. One day I want to give her all I can to make her happy," he said all that while touching his puffy face.

We sat in silence. I envied all he said he wanted to give to someone. He reminded me of my stepdad – a fighter, and someone who gave everything to my mother to make her happy, despite the fact that it might not ever happen. I got up and opened the front door and stood in it. The fresh air after a rain blew inside. I hoped it brought new thoughts or deflected from the old. I left the door opened as I went to go get a book. I lit a candle and I sat down next to Chevelle and read a passage from Cornet's book.

The Soul of Love

"The soul chooses to know what it knows as its realisms and blocks out other realities. That thing called love is not disciplined in the heart; but an art of painted elementary level stick figures, or all the way to the wildness and greatness of a Picasso. Love has its own heaven and hell, and is what we die for in wars of the heart. The mania of love is doing it all for the feeling someone else feels the way we feel about or obsession of them. The most difficult thing on earth, is receiving love as it comes in how it works, plays, lays its body down, and rests near you.

Love makes fools out of us because of the foolish things people simply do. As Adam and Eve shared something they knew was bad for them, and as in every woman who has willingly shared her man, and every man who let a good woman go; all being the foolish things we do.

When we believe we have aged to be mature, the hurting soul fights internally to get over and under the past failures, and love on again, in prayers, and hopes and wishes to be better this time. Some folks reject a love as an injection, as if it would make them pass out like the sight of a hypodermic needle going in their vein. Some inject one bad love after another, putting the needle in themselves, and then blame the serum antibodies inside. Love can make some run like a monster chasing them in a bad movie. To some, love is a drug they become addicted to and will hoe for temporary fixes.

Love is a book that you read, and don't know the end, so you read on. You read on through the hopes, tragedies, and character flaws, wondering if your own imperfections are keeping love from loving you. We read on to the last page wanting to write the end as if it was your own story with a happy-ending. Some treat love as a theater you can walk in and walk out of when you choose, taking one in or leaving one in the dark.

Love cycles and recycles. Love has no equal in the amount of pain and joy we can feel. The love for love never dies in us; it just re-positions or lies dormant in our desire, much like a buried treasure. Then the soul digs deep and feelings are unearthed; we study past loves, and learn to believe in love again, as we must, in order to survive."

I read to Chevelle about what I had no personal knowledge of, as love had not touched my soul. I have never been held by a man who loved me, and I have never loved a man like I never wanted to let him go…yet.

"Chevelle, you got some battles to fight if you want to win this war. Are you really sure that she is down for this? Is she down with you fighting for her? Could it be she is simply thrilled that you'd fight for her? It might be entertainment for her. There is a desire that a man will walk through quicksand and back for us. Many times, men don't make it back in time, and a woman will move on. She may have moved on while you were in juvie."

He lifted his head, and the streetlight filtering through the window made his face handsome again. He turned in a way where his profile looked proud. I moved back down to the floor to let him stretch out. When I did, I slid my palm on the wood floor that used to have carpet, and caught a staple I had missed when pulling the carpet up. The sting told me I might be cut. I sucked my finger and tasted my blood. I needed Chevelle to take control of his life to avoid conflicts in order to keep his life and lifeblood inside of him. He needs more than a roof over his head. I wanted to help him with understanding women at a young age, and try to avoid being a naïve boy. He will be a man in the years to come; but no man, young or old, has got it right when it comes to young women, but sometimes they get close enough. I chuckled at my own thought, as if I know anything.

"When you met her in the park, how was she? Was she happy to see you?"

"Yes. Well… in a way, yes; but her girlfriend had come to visit me when I was in juvie to give messages back and forth between me and Iman. But, I think she said more than I had said. Iman questioned me if I had another woman. She said she heard that I liked another woman and I didn't like her any more. She was surprised to hear from me when I emailed her."

"Chevelle, an elder once told me, "*A woman who likes you, she will make certain sacrifices, and she'll make adjustments. A woman who likes you and loves you, she sees no sacrifices too great or adjustment that she is not willing to make. She'll just love you as it is, as it will be. But the moment she don't think you like her, when she has loved you, she'll regret ever knowing you.*

"I am not passing judgment on you and your girlfriend. I have failed in falling and being in love and relationships; but listen to me…I'm a female - a woman, and sometimes we make decisions to be with someone, and we might not share all we are feeling in trying to protect ourselves. There is good and bad in that for sure.

"There is no shame, or reason to be shamed, by anyone else's mindset. I'm much older than you. I have failed many times in confusing love and lust, and only now understand the times that were lust. What I have

100

come to think…if it was about booty, so be it. If it is about more, it will prove itself. If it's about wanting or hoping for more, well, there is no foolproof way of knowing. I'm going to ask you to meditate and reflect on what you are feeling, and rethink what she might feel about you."

Chevelle lifted his body, which might be 160 pounds, off the coach; but he moved as if he weighed 300 pounds. I almost jumped up to help him, but he was up before I could give assistance. He stood unstudied. He tested his legs and made it to the bathroom.

I needed some water. I went outside to my car to bring in a case and some other things. At Aloy's aunt and uncle's house, I saw his uncle and two other men. Aloy let me know the other men I saw were his uncles; three brothers. He said they were different from each other but often the same in ways. They were leaning against the garage in what appeared to be a jovial conversation while smoking cigars.

Before I could get back inside, "Hey, little lady, why don't you come on over and meet us all," Sargon, the foul man I met along with Aloy, chuckled. I wished Aloy were here to keep him in check again.

"I'd love to, but I'll have to make it some other time. I'm a little busy right now," I kept moving toward the house.

"Well hey, what about Sunday afternoon? I breakout the grill often, and my brother – Pastor Shomer, can burn some meat and make you think its chocolate cake tender. He makes the best Q sauce any man has ever had. My other brother here – Sans, he just eats and plays a mean game of dominos and every card game known to man. We'll have plenty of drink, and even if you like to smoke that medical marijuana, ah weed, or whatever you wanna call it, my pastor brother will go upwind to let you do your thang."

"Thanks for the invite, I'll see if I can make it," I heard my voice carry in the night breeze along with the whoosh sound of vehicles from the freeway down below. I leaped three stairs at a time and heard one of the brothers shout, "Damn, look at that shit." I wasn't trying to impress them, but I wanted to get away from them now.

My phone vibrated on the kitchen table no sooner than I put the water down. I'm a bit annoyed, and it's Aloy on the other end when I answer. I try to soften the tone of my attitude, but I was still quick to tell him his uncles invited me to the barbeque on Sunday, and that I wouldn't go if he's not there to at least give me someone to talk to other than his aunt. He lets me know his uncle, Pastor Shomer, is the decent one out of the bunch as far as manners and respect. The uncle named Sans was an ass on too many levels he said.

Now, I did want to sit down at the game table and beat them at everything while talking plenty of shit. I'm the only one in my family who can play cards and dominos with skill. I hardly lose, and can cover for a bad partner if I have to. Uncle Don and I play on the bar top at the Hob Nob almost every time I'm in there. He can talk some shit, too, so we get along well while playing.

Aloy talking on a phone is the one thing he tries to avoid, and I can see why. He said JoBelle at the gym is his voice most of the time. He had to call me to check on Chevelle and me. Thunder cracked, and lighting flashed twice. Five minutes later, rain was ripping through the night sky. I didn't stay on the phone long with Aloy, but updated him on Chevelle. I let him know that I'll be in tomorrow.

Aloy offered to bring some food by, but I declined. He rides his motorcycle every day, and I was not having him bring food by and get drenched on our account. He owns a truck, but leaves it parked most of t time. I opened a couple of cans of soup, made some Jiffy Mix cornbread, and baked it in my new, but used, stove that I found online. Chevelle sat at the table after he used all the hot water from his shower, but I couldn't blame him. I'm sure his body hurt. When the cornbread was ready, he slurped the soup down and ate half the cornbread. I gathered info on all he could tell me about his girlfriend's dad. I wanted him to drop the girlfriend. Yet, if he loves her, love can be a hurting thing as I look at his black and blue face.

Chapter 13

I'm out of my bed too damn early from my unrestful sleep. I was helping a man understand that love and war can hurt him, too. I jabbed him in the throat. I kicked him in his nuts. He went down. More kicks to his rib cage, and blood came quick and heavily dripped from his mouth. I placed at least twenty or more hard kicks to his thigh bones. He might be out of work for a month. Steel toe hiking runners signed my name on his ass.

In my unrestful sleep I dreamed it would go down just as it is, but it's real. Iman's daddy was about to get into his truck from out behind his house, and I had been waiting for him. I'm getting my workout in today at 6:00 AM. He is feeling the same pain he put down on Chevelle. I didn't say a word as I'm beating down a bully. If he don't understand, I'm leaving him an answer.

Officer CC was down the block monitoring the police band, and would call me on my burner cell phone if I needed to be on my way. To clown this man even more, I had on a mask like the ones the robbers wore in the movie, Dead Presidents.

Questions I had asked of Chevelle last night, he had no idea I was constructing a plan to do what I'm doing. Iman's daddy for sure wouldn't think an attack on his ass would come so quickly.

Iman's daddy groaned like a dog that had been hit by a truck as he grabbed for his thighs; loudness couldn't escape his mouth because of the throat jab. The pain in his legs made him lift his ass up in the air as if a doctor was about to perform a rectal exam on him. To make sure he knew why this was happening to him, I pulled out a box knife and poked him in the base of the back of his neck while pushing his head down for him to know to stay still. I cut a long slit in his pants down the crease of his ass. I ripped them open. I straddled him and lifted up my skirt. Yes, I'm wearing a skirt with crotchless tights. I'll wear a skirt if I have to kick ass; it gives me total freedom with no restriction. I urinated on him like he and his buddies had done to Chevelle. I was even a bit angrier because I drunk damn near a gallon of water, and my bladder was pushing on things inside me, but I wanted to saturate him with piss.

Then I gave him the most horrifying, rude feeling he could ever feel; no, I didn't insert anything in him, I pulled out a stun gun and I zapped his ass and kept zapping his ass. He jerked and kind-of howled, letting me know it was time to go. I'm sure the added effect of urine salt and the voltage went up the crack of his ass. I know I wasn't ladylike; I'm still a lady when done.

Most every woman will do unthinkable deeds to protect a child, right? Besides, he wasn't much of a man by bringing two other full-grown men with him to beat a boy down just to warn him to stay away from his daughter. He got what he deserved; the message to stay clear of Chevelle.

*****

I taught my first classes today. JoBelle does major recruiting, and handles the Internet advertising and other promotions. She's good at what she's does. I have a full class of twenty, and I put the girls, and a few guys, through the paces of a boot camp boxing workout. Although I'm not in the best shape of my life, I'm a lot better than most. I was hard on them and they liked that.

I didn't get a chance to talk to Aloy today at the gym; he is quite a busy guy, involved in a lot of activities. I have to say I'm proud of a self-made prominent black man. He could've folded up his life and blamed everyone for his disappointments, but he's got a warrior spirit.

I saw his cute girlfriend, or his *woman friend*, I guess I should say. She came into the gym and I saw her looking through from the yoga room. She didn't give me a mean look, so maybe she feels secure that I'm just doing a job. I'm sure she quizzed him about me. What woman wouldn't in trying to protect her territory; although he says they are not boyfriend and girlfriend, he says...

I'm headed home to check on Chevelle, but first I need to go see my stepdad, Eddie. I'll pay his rest home bill almost up. I can't spend all the money my auntie gave me, but I do have a job now to keep him in one place and not have to move him into another home.

Chapter 14

Up off my cot again in the early morn, I look out of my bedroom window, again at a side angle so as not to be seen. I see what I saw the first morning I was awakened in this house. Aloy's uncle, the greasy looking one—Sans, once again was in the driveway speaking to Aloy's aunt Alanese. It didn't appear to be as confrontational as the first time I saw them, but her body language said she wished he wasn't there. His message in how he stood was, I don't give a shit. I watched them speak until she walked away from his beaten down old Mercedes with the two-tone doors and trunk parts from donor cars.

Ten minutes later, I'm making coffee and about to scan through Craigslist when there's a knock on my back door. It's 6:30 in the morning. I'm thinking like Mr. Rogers from the children's TV show, *Another beautiful day in the neighborhood.*

"Hello, Zelda," Alanese stood in my doorway with a coffee cup.

"Come in; I have coffee brewing, if you need some."

"A warm up would be nice," she slumped into a seat at the kitchen table.

"Ma'am, come sit in my living room," I said as I poured her cup full. We sat across from each other and looked out the window. I surveyed her gaze; she was distressed. Awkwardly, I waited for her to talk. Why is she visiting me at this time of morning? I caught myself slightly pushing my big lips to the side in thought. Yesterday, at this same time, I was beating the crap out of a man for beating on a child. Now, I have my next door neighbor, in the waking hours, sitting in front of me; for sure she has something going on with the blood brothers. She's married to one brother, and in my opinion, he is a bit slimly. The brother I've seen in the driveway in the morning leaving from her place without sweet goodbyes, he is all the way slimy, with a huge pinch of creep oozing from him.

Her coffee cup was almost empty again as she puts it down. Her lips trembling, I finally take the lead. "Ms. Alanese, I can tell you have something on your mind. I'm a pretty good listener, if you want talk," I nodded to her. "I assume that you are here to talk about…"

She cut me off, spreading her hands out wide in front of her and talking.

"Zelda, I'm sorry to bother you with my current state of affairs. Actually, my current affairs have been going on for a long time, but no one was living next door to observe them, so I'm really coming to apologize." I opened my mouth to talk, and she pushed her palm out to hush me. She continued. "I found myself tangled in something that I could never imagine would happen. I love my husband. He has some flaws; some bad. He has a history; some bad. You know in this world…or maybe you don't, but with some men we just don't walk away from them despite the fact that they have issues. He doesn't beat me, and he doesn't appreciate me. He doesn't love me like a…a woman."

Her voice whispered, but she wanted me to hear. I thought about these walls again hearing the suffering of a woman. I'll need to knock some walls down and put on thick coats of paint to cover over the yells, screams, wails, sobs, and the blues. I'll paint any color in this house except blue, and I love blue; but this house has had enough of the blues.

"Could be another woman, other women. He loves to sleep when he does come home, but instead of sleeping with me, he sleeps in another room." She stood up and walked toward the door not as if she was leaving; just taking a break, she came and sat back down.

"His brother…I…I didn't bring him into my bed because I was lonely. He forced himself there and I didn't resist. I don't resist each time. I don't make love to him. I don't have sex with him. I'm letting him have sex…on me.

"I finally told him to stop some time ago; to leave and don't come back. But he has control now. His brother—my husband, they have done dirt together, but I do fear what my husband would do to me? Yes…no. I'm in a maze feeling that my husband must know his brother creeps in his house and does his two-minute business. I end up escorting him out of the house telling him not to come back each time. I'm not quite sure what to do, or if I should do anything at all.

"Nevertheless, I want to apologize to you for having to see this. I should be stronger, but I'm not. Please don't judge me too harshly."

"My elders taught me to not shame. I'm not going to advise you. I have no advice to give. I can only offer you a seat and ear, and more coffee. I do ask this…I was invited to a barbecue at your place by your husband; should I come?"

"Please come. The food is always good and people tend to be civil. Pastor Shomer, my other brother-in-law, is a decent man; and so is his wife. Shomer and my sister-in-law, Eneta, they adopted a wonderful boy and girl a few years ago and they are well-behaved children. Please come, let me adopt you into the good parts of my life, if you please?"

Chapter 15

I had a long day at the gym and was glad to be coming home. I picked up two kids to train. Their parents brought them in to learn how to box. Great, that will be extra money. The boys' parents want to keep them off the streets, and would rather that they learn how to fight with their fists than with a gun. I agree with them, and pray to the ancestors and God to see if that blessing can happen. Pulling into the alley behind the house after teaching and training at the gym, I see Chevelle looking out the back door window.

As I come to the door, I am greeted with a 'hello' from a stranger before I can really see who's who. There is an extremely beautiful, young, Black girl sitting at the kitchen table with Chevelle. He stands.

"Zelda, this is my girlfriend, Iman."

I'm a bit shocked; actually, I'm a whole lot shocked, but so far from living in this house, I've learned that I shouldn't be shocked over anything.

Iman stands, and she has the body of a grown woman. She's on the thick side; almost full-figured. She walks around the table. She's comfortable in her skin. I can see that by the way she stands in front of me wearing 70's style afro puffs. Her expression is pensive. Her eyes are beautiful as well as all her other features. I don't know what a young man sees when he's thinks a woman is pretty, but I can see Iman would turn heads, even in males who are not into women who are as thick as she is. Her eyes seem to have truth in them; yet I'm wary from knowing what I know so far, and she's here in my house.

Chevelle has no idea what I did to Iman's father. I'll never tell him that and put him in a position as an accomplice; that's the last thing he needs. Nevertheless, I did viciously beat the crap out of her father a couple of days ago, and today she is standing here in my kitchen. I'm wary.

"Zelda - Ms. Zelda, I understand you may have reasons to doubt how I feel about Chevelle," her confidence came through when she looked me in the eyes as she spoke. "The doubt, and maybe confusion, comes from me having fear of my own father. Not that he would beat me or do physical harm to me, but living in his house, I am under his thumb of rule verbally. I am watched. I'm told what to do with no regard. I am nineteen. I am his child, but he's been extremely overbearing; and now, ever since Chevelle and I met, he's a tyrant.

"He hates Chevelle for what I consider to be very ugly reasons. He doesn't like Chevelle because to him, he's white. Whether Chevelle is white or not doesn't matter to me," she smiled at Chevelle and he had that little boy grin that pops up from time to time, even with his swollen face. "I know he is Black anyway, so I'm standing here asking for you to give me a chance. I need your support."

"What kind of support? And let me sit down. I'm tired, it's been a long day."

She waited for me to have a seat. "This morning, I visited my father in the hospital. He is in pretty bad shape. He was jumped by some thugs, he said. With tears in his eyes he told me I'm free to do what I want to do, and he's going to give me money to go get my own apartment. He wants me to move out by next week. He said he will co-sign a lease to help me. I have a job and it won't be a challenge financially. I work at a company as a payroll assistant. I'm really good at math and accounting, and do taxes on the side. But the main thing, I'm going to be on my own to see Chevelle and be his support as he's been mine."

Chevelle interjected. "We're not moving in together. I want to help you with your place, and we know we are not ready to live together."

I noticed Iman didn't smile as she had been. Her eyes seemdc to get lost. A possible want not coming true had deflated her posture and subdued her.

"I have to ask, what are the reasons you two are telling me this? Because the only thing that counts, as far as I'm concerned, is that my house is respected. I don't...I don't want to sound cold, but I just got in this house, and I'm trying to make it livable and nice; that is my first desire. As long as you two don't take away from my time or resources…you do you."

I had no beef with Iman, but I wanted lanes in place and clearly marked. Crossing them is a no-no. I will move the lines farther away from me rather abruptly, and paint anyone into a corner.

Iman sat quiet; her pretty face stayed pretty as she closed her eyes slowly, then flashed open as if scared out of her sleep. She might have felt cornered with Chevelle stating that he was not moving in with her. If they had not talked about it yet, and she had made assumptions, shock had hit. "I'm sorry if I came off hard. I had a long day and really wanted to come home and take a hot bath. I think we'll all be fine; but I want my peace and freedom to choose my battles, and not to be thrown into conflicts and crusades not of my own making or choosing."

Chevelle installed a light dimmer in the kitchen for me. He knew I liked sitting in the kitchen at night, but not with the bright lights. I dimmed the lights and the stove lights glowed. I pulled an ice bag out of the freezer and placed it on the back of my neck. Teaching class, training, moving, and working around the house, all had my neck aching and stiff.

"Ms. Zelda," Iman almost whispered. "I've been freed. My dad, a single father who, up until yesterday, was not letting me move forward with my life, has released the hold he has on me. I may have some tangled thoughts about my new freedom; but I'm a decent woman, much like Chevelle. My father, a couple of days ago, was checking my phone and texts. That got Chevelle beat up. I feel awful, and in no way do I feel good about my father getting the same treatment, but I'm free; and I want to make the best of it."

I nodded.

"Ms. Zelda, Chevelle says you are very resourceful. The one thing that can make my journey to living on my own better, is if I had a car. I have my driver's license, and sometimes I drive a company vehicle; but I would like my own car. It is not a priority, it's a want, so I understand if you think it's foolish, but I ask for your help. Otherwise, I'll be going to some jackleg car dealership and probably drive off with something that will break down a few blocks away. I have money saved, but not enough to buy a new car."

"I'll talk to my uncle. He often knows people who can help. You know you have to have car insurance, money for gas, and upkeep. Even though a car can be in good shape, it might need tires, it might need breaks, oil changes, etc. When those things go wrong, your car is not breaking down, it needs maintenance. You need to understand that. Can you afford that along with paying for an apartment?"

"Managing money is what I do very well. I've already allotted a budget for some of the things that you have mentioned. I will need to check with someone who knows more than I do to make sure of what I need to do, but I have more than enough, and I can save money. I thank you for whatever you choose to do."

"Iman, I will look into it for you; but right now, I've had a long day. I'd like to take a hot bath and do some reading. I'm not sure how you're getting home from here, but I'm ready for a nice quiet easy evening."

I know she lived two miles away. I was in her backyard yesterday shocking her daddy's ass, that has freed her, although unknowingly. I did not know that would happen for her good. I'm pleased that a young woman is no longer being held by her father's hardline control, which was stopping her growth as a woman.

"I'll get back to you about the car." She nodded. "Oh, there is one thing I want to say to you and Chevelle. At eighteen and nineteen, I need you to understand that in your current situation, neither one of you needs a baby. I hope you're being safe. I hope you're being foolproof. I pray you're not taking chances of bringing a child into this world. It is no joke; it's not something you get to play at and put down when you're tired of playing. Too many babies are being raised without one parent or the other, or no parents; and if you look at either one of your stories, that holds true for you. Iman, I don't know why you don't have a mother in your house, but it makes no difference. Don't play! Iman, your young eggs will beg for him to lose control by your pheromones rising into his nostrils; and your voice, your touch, your womanhood, will try him. Chevelle, be mature, control

113

your manhood. Don't let it start thinking as if you can control her eggs calling out to your sperm.

"I'm not talking about the science of sex. I'm talking about the creation of man from the time woman and man were once one, and they have wanted to join back and be one again. The most beautiful purpose on earth is to create a child, and to love that child together as one, and watch them become a man or woman. The other side is ugly when a man and woman create a child and they allow their blessing and responsibility go the way of tears that can't fill a river to survive a life's journey. Use protection systems together."

Chevelle stood up and said he would walk Iman home. After all I said in what I thought was wisdom, neither of them said anything. Was that their age, or was that respect, or was it that I hit a nerve?

My wisdom tells me I need to go to the doctor to have my IUD checked. I'm not having sex, but I want to be ready if I do.

Chapter 16

It only took a couple of days for Uncle Don to come through with a car from one of the barflies wanting to get close to him. Iman now owns and likes her mid-size 2005 Pontiac. It needs some cleanup and a headlight replaced. She paid $1,000 for it. She's driving her car to my place, with me and Chevelle in the car to drop us off so he and I can go to the barbeque next door.

I'm taking Chevelle with me. If I need someone to talk to, I'll have him. I anticipate Aloy being there to talk to, but his *sorta-kinda* woman could show up. I can talk to his aunt, but I want fallback. I can't be un-neighborly and not come by; well, I could, but I'll play it by ear if I ever come next door again afterwards.

I'm walking over with fry bread and Alloy pulls up on his Harley. He walks over to Chevelle and starts talking before I do. Their hands shake firmly. Chevelle thanks him for the help of getting me to the hospital to be by his side so quickly, and then for asking a friend to get the two of us back to the house. They never had a chance to meet prior to Chevelle being jumped.

Early, before many of the guests arrived, the only brother there was Pastor Shomer and his wife, Eneta. They are nice and I'm enjoying my conversation with them. They weren't asking me a lot of questions; some, but no interrogation. Their adopted children—Oceana and Skyler, are sweet, funny and well-mannered. The kids were African; adopted in Greece from an Eritrean ran orphanage. Although they had been in America for more than six years, and now are the ages of thirteen and ten, they both need to eat more. They are so skinny for their age. But then again, the body composition from the region of the world that they came from, I knew nothing of. I was a thin child with a big booty. The Native kids on the reservation had plenty of childhood teasing labels for me, such as fiddle booty. I was all stringy except for my ample backside.

Pastor Shomer went to go grill with the help of his brothers who had shown up with the food. Eneta and I headed to the park on a walk with the kids. I felt at ease with her, and that is not something I feel with many women. I don't have any women friends that I hang out with. I wish I did. I tell myself I'm too odd of a woman to be around other women. Then there is my perceptive sense that lets me know when someone is not fond of me, or speaks ill of me. That is not so bad; but when they then speak to my face as if I don't know their lips have parted and spat evil, I have no understanding of someone who is at ease with being fake with me.

I don't trust myself. I could finger jab a woman in the throat just as they say my name, and smile in my face. Sometimes, my ex-coworkers and I go have drinks, but not often. I find too many women think in competition, or compare their version of right and wrong and tell others; yet, I wish I had sisters. I wish I had brothers.

On the way to the park along a wilderness trek, I played with the kids—Oceania and Skyler, and had great fun with them. Big cousin Aloy, as they called him, was their hero. He had shown them how to use their hands well in self-defense. The two of them and I shadow and slap-boxed, then we wrestled in the grass, swung high on the swings, and jumped off.

Eneta, walking well behind us, spent most of her time on her cell phone some distance from me and the kids. When we got to the park, she stayed on her phone; and for some time, she sat on a park bench well away from me and the kids as we were playing on the swings. As we walked back to the house, Eneta and I connected in conversation. She told me about being a First Lady and said, "Many times, I'm an ear to bend to hear about children problems or money issues; but most of the time, I'm responding to women who have problems with men. Being a First Lady at a church – helping women with their marriages and their situations with men – is a full-time job."

She shared that she used as much wisdom as her Bible taught her; but most of the time, women had problems beyond a verse and chapter according to her.

"Zelda, sadly, as much as we are a sexual society, many women are left unfulfilled, and that is my number one consultation. The sisterhood lives in discontent in their sexual love lives. Many women are held down by men who use their mentally ordained control to keep women in a place. Their bodies and souls are needing. Often a woman is led to believe there is something wrong with her for having needs.

Want to see a men wilt? Let his ego get bruised when his woman wants sex more than him and he can't keep up."

She and I both laughed. I know in my life I had made a few men call me out that I was wrong for wanting more than he could give.

"Zelda, why of course, there is more to life than sex; but sex controls everything we do. We women must stop fighting a lost battle to change that, and change who runs the sex game. We have power that we give away so that we can be thought of as loving queens and princesses, and wholesome mothers and daughters. We have to gain control of how, when, and what, to say to men who have natural born egos to reject hearing and responding to the needs of their women. As men chase sex, women also want sex; whether they are single, in a relationship, or married…there is fulfillment in being served satisfaction. It's crazy that men don't realize what they're missing out on when they chase a passionate woman, and are getting hardcore sex. How much more fulfilling it could be if they would first realize that women are the stronger sex.

"The overriding bewilderment I try to help women understand and deal with and heal, if any healing can be had," she chuckled and continued, "Women do sex better than men. Why? Because she controls everything, and a man will submit to her when she turns him out with that control. A man will place her on a sexual pedestal and never know what hit him. Women have the same rights as a man to seek pleasure, and that is…have other lovers in their head or bed. Every man has crossed that line, women should, too. All men cross the line with another woman; we have the same right, but we don't."

"Eneta, are you saying women need to have other lovers, even if they are married?"

"No! However, if men understood they make women live with that threat of being played. So consequently, if we put them on the same sensitive conceptual bed of, *We can go there and we will get down there*, men will start to think about keeping mama happy in many more arenas, and the bedroom for sure."

"Men can get ugly if their ego is stood up, too."

Eneta stopped and looked at me, or through me. Cars, I noticed, drove too fast down these narrow streets and one whizzed by. I called for the kids not to get too far out in front of us. At that point she seemed to regain her thoughts.

"Thank you for being so nice to the kids, they seem to really like you."

"Thank you, they are sweet kids. If you need someone to take them to the park, I have no problem doing that."

She smiled and nodded. "Zelda, men will be ugly no matter what we do as women. Even a righteous man can fall down before God. An ugly acting man is just ugly; nothing we can do about that man. Even more so, we women must grab and hold on to what we can do, despite ugly men attitudes. As we know, men can take longer to grow up. Maybe if we are right as women, when a man is ready to be righteous, we might be the one who has helped them treat us right."

She stopped walking and laughed hard for a moment. The kids played tag at a slight distance. Eneta and I observed an elderly man across the street wearing ovealls with a cane. He was bending down in his garden pulling weeds. His old house stood out in all the new construction built around his old single-family abode. He lived in a home, and all else were dwellings. With her voice lowered, and maybe humbled, she continued.

"Okay, maybe only ninety percent of the men have crossed the line. Many women think their dad was a saint that had to be in the other ten percent."

I had no understanding of much of what she said; but, as far as I knew while with my mother, my step-dad was a saint. But was my biological father? Was he a good man or a bad guy? And which is he now?

"Zelda, it is no fairytale for us women. Men have dropped their drawls mentally at some time for less desirable women than the woman he has in his life supporting him. We women want to believe in the fairytale of *Never, Never Land*, shall my man stray. Somehow, we say things like, *Just don't let me hear about it*, and *He bet not make some baby out there*, or even, *Don't bring anything home.*

"We have been thinking and saying those types of things for a very long time, to which men feel it's a license to spread his seed just as long as it doesn't sprout, and just as long as we don't find out what other fields he tends to."

We watched the elderly man pull some weeds out of the ground and toss to the side. We started to walk again as the kids kept playing tag.

"Zelda, what is your relationship status, if you don't mind me asking."

"I'm focused right now on my stepdad, the house, and earning and saving money. If a man were to enter into my life, I'm not so sure I know how to do that."

She laughed, "When love comes dear, it don't knock, it don't call, it don't fall on you...it just appears. Then, for many, it un-magically disappears, but the relationship stays. It can be deemed advantageous, and possibly nourishing, for the lonely or needy. The other side of a no in-love relationship, is that it can be the pursuing of lust, replacement, standby, or stand-in. Maybe all of it can be just what the doctor ordered to survive."

She sounded like a woman who had a street common sense Ph.D. Prior to talking with her, I had it in my mind that a First Lady – a pastor's wife, would tell hurting women to just pray away their problems.

I'm smiling and thinking of how I want sex anyway I can get it, and I had gotten it in ways I'm not proud of, but I wouldn't share that with her.

A stranger, she is right now in my life. I couldn't tell her that I was the other woman several times in my life. Hell, I knew some of the wives of the husbands I've slept with, had lovers, too. But I wouldn't mind finding out what love and sex felt like as one entity. I also wouldn't share that with her.

"Eneta, you tell women to do whatever they need to do to keep their marriages or relationships, and to find other outlets as a way to cope or thrive in their relationships?"

"Kings and men of power had concubines in the Bible, and there were ruling queens of the land who had men to service them in whatever pleasure they desired. Whether it was a eunuch to hold them in the night or wash their bodies sensually and more, they had men to do whatever they needed and desired. Mary Magdalene in the Bible was a woman who needed to put food on her table and take care of her physical needs. Jesus did not shun her. He embraced her, and she kissed Him on the mouth, and was His companion, and washed His feet. You know, if you have had anyone wash your feet, it can be a sensual feeling. Are we to say because He was the son of God, He didn't feel a thing? He was on this earth as a man. He felt everything you and I feel. He avoided sin, yes, but He couldn't avoid human feelings physically and emotionally. That is why He died for our sins. He understood what we felt on our skin and underneath.

"We had African queens who ruled great lands and tribes; so, what…we think they sat in a hutch on a throne with their clits throbbing and their insides wanting that penetration feeling? Do we think they just sat there, or maybe the best warriors came to their beds and kissed their whole bodies and sired more warriors and more queens—like bees in nature? We have to keep in mind that the Bible is not based on European or Western thinking. Think about what that really means, and try to twist in those two worlds into the Word of God written between the book covers of the Bible. And, we know Europeans rewrote much of the Bible in their limited intellects, comprehensions, and self-serving reasons. This is why faith is our guiding light instead of man's rules and demands.

"Accordingly, yes, I tell women to think outside the norms of the morals of the controls of man. The stereotypical responses of buying and wearing something skimpy and sexy, and having candlelight dinners and baths, are nights to remember; but rarely a game changer," her voiced lowered to almost a whisper as we got closer to being back at the barbeque. "Speaking symbolically, too many women think of what is between their legs as if it is gold; but if it were gold, it would be cold and hard. If a woman's body were gold, men and women would sell it all the same as they do now.

"Our power as women, is to have a man on notice that you will do as he does, and take no shame from any man who tries to heave it upon us. I'm not advocating cheating; just putting it out there. We can make the same damn mistakes a man can and will. To the man who wants to tell a woman she is thinking crazy, he is a man with no moral standing when, as I said, every man has crossed that line before, or had thoughts of doing it. He can rationalize crossing that line in his head, although he wrongly justifies his reasoning.

"So, there are two things I tell woman as a First Lady: one, is to know yourself, grow yourself, and put no limits on your passion and drive; and two, be no less than a man, and we all can still stay on our side of the line as lovers, and ladies, and gents. Women have to learn that they have to treat themselves as fully passionate creatures; knowing how and what unlocks their passion. We have to rid ourselves of feeling and saying, *I don't need all that*. We can't let society paint us into a corner of what is taboo. We can't live by the standards set by men as to their version of what sin is for us.

"Why do we call some men good and others we don't? Is it as simple as a man who works hard and brings home a good pay? Is it his standing in the church, or is it when he cares about our passions and we care about his? And can we all respond to each other's passions? Ask yourself that if you want to fall in love and stay in love. That piece right there, is never-ending; and if it does end on any part, you better open your mind to no limits for yourself."

We stood at the driveway of my house about to go back to the backyard where the food was smelling good. I saw Sans standing, looking greasy and evil.

"Eneta, there is evil out here and users."

She smiled and took her time responding. "Some will twist being open to all options as to leading to the weird, the immoral, or the freakiest addictions of un-wellness that man and woman can fathom. The truth is, people are already what they are, no matter the path. People will go to any depths they want to go, and drown or burn in hellish pursuits. Even when they know they're biting into the serpent's forbidden fruit, hell is their home before they start to burn."

I had been around Christian-religious type folks before, and never heard the frankness I heard from Eneta. It sat me back in my mental chair a bit, but I very much appreciated her openness and had no judgement of my own as to whether she was right or wrong.

Home after the barbeque, it was nice with plenty of great food. Everyone loved my fry bread and had requests. I met people, and Aloy's uncles stayed in their lane. Aloy's woman-lady-exgirlfriend came and introduced herself coolly, but she wasn't rude. The other person I did not know if he was welcome and would show up, was Duce. He had a function going on at his place with a mix of races, but mostly white, and his music – island soul reggae –was blasting. On the other side of my house, I had Aloy's people with classic R&B soul music bumping. Now back home, Chevelle – who had left earlier than me from the barbeque – is in the basement bumping NWA and Public Enemy.

I head upstairs to my bathtub with my headphones to listen to my thoughts.

Chapter 17

I have fallen into a routine over the last month. I get up and with coffee in hand and join Chevelle working on projects all over the house, with the basement being nearly finished. Often, we work some more around the house in the evening on finished work to make things look nice. I have invited my aunt over a few times to get her approval, or just so she can see how her money is being spent. She never comes. That would be her in most things I have done. My mom always came to my school events and sporting endeavors, but I always wanted my aunt to come when she was around. She never did; she wouldn't even ask, and that's the way it still is.

Every day I head into the gym and teach and train. Twice a week I go see my stepdad, and stop by the Hob Nob Tavern and now can pay for my beer. It's always funny to see that old white lady keep taking the old men's money from them as they think, time and time again, that they can beat her in chess. I don't think I want to play her. I watched her moves, she's good, and always four moves ahead when most are two moves at best. She had to put her gun on the table the last time I was there to let a college boy know he had to pay up and it wasn't a joke.

I'm adding more income starting this weekend. I will babysit Pastor Shomer and Eneta's children. As parents, they have busy schedules with church ministry duties and finding free time for themselves. They lost the service of an elderly lady from their church who moved down South to take care of a sickly sister.

I planned on more than just watching the kids; their parents are so busy it seems they are not doing much with the kids. I noticed they can be rather quiet and withdrawn at times, and other times they appear to be normal children. I'm going to take them places for youthful adventures and outings they will like. I was blessed to travel a lot as child, and I know it expanded my mind. They seem overly protected and isolated from the world. If it's not a church function, or the private school they attend, the kids have told me they are at home doing much of nothing. I have picked them up when I had free time. I take them down to Lake Washington, and we walk and talk as we go around the Seward Park loop and enjoy the water and the ducks.

Aloy and I have small talk times when I'm at the gym, but he and I keep it moving as he is busy running a gym and other civic duties he's involved in. I've gotten to know JoBelle. She is a computer nerd as well as a great promotions and gym manager. We meet for drinks. She kind of brings out the feminine side of me since she is girly. I've bought a few clothes; she knows where to shop on a budget. She has taken me to places where men are, and I have enjoyed some attention. Nice fitting clothes on my figure, and simple eyeliner and simple lip gloss…and my number has been asked for. I haven't given it out as I'm on a mission, but I have wanted the animalistic desire of men.

One of the things that I appreciate when I come to the gym is, I see Aloy. He always dresses well; color-coordinated and pressed. Although he's in the sports business, he's rarely seen walking around in sweats. He wears casual slacks and a polo-shirt, and sometimes he sports a coat while riding his Harley. When not riding, he dons a Kango hat color-coordinated to his clothing. I enjoy looking at him from the standpoint of how he carries himself. The men that I see him with—his friends or associates, they tend to dress the same way.

Unlike the corporate gyms, this gym is not a booty call center for a hookup. People tend to come here and act professional to get in shape or stay in shape. You can see the motivation. I enjoy that. Even the young men, some of them played sports for the local high school, Rainier Beach High, and they come in without their pants sagging or loose baggy clothing. The atmosphere makes it easy for me to work.

I stayed late last week to write my workouts down for the coming week. Only Aloy and I, and few others, were in the gym. He has two guys working the gym for the late nighters, the can't sleep folks or odd work hours few, and the workout night owls or police folks who want less people around when they workout.

Aloy and I sat down and we are chilling and talking. I figured after so much time had passed, he has avoided too much interaction with me

125

because of his girl-ex-woman. I still don't know what to call her. It's none of my business anyway. I haven't seen her around for about a month as far as I can recall. The machines and grunts of exertion mixed with the old soul music playing in the background. I had put my imprint on the gym by making a point that people worked harder to older music. It was evident people could zone in on what they were doing and connect physically, much more than being distracted by single beat, non-flowing, Hip Hop that was annoying after a while.

Aloy hands me a beer from a little refrigerator in his office. He has two offices; one to impress people who might want to join the gym, and this office tucked away atop some stairs away from view, but he could see all.

Pictures of Ali, Lalah Ali, and other great boxers, hung on the walls in frames and some were tattered posters. Then there are the female athletes, and he had a lot of them; from track runners in tight outfits, women basketball players—not on the court playing, but in modeled sexy sports fashions, and a lady golfer in a tight cat-woman suit swinging a golf club. I wasn't sure how I felt about seeing women seen more for their sexiness and mixed with sports. I took a moment to think about it. I loved seeing men. I loved men wearing sports tights and tank tops almost falling off of their muscles. And, my inner thighs sweated from seeing muscled thighs, thinking I want thick quad muscles draped over my ass or to have them in-between my thighs. I loved seeing the nude sports jocks in magazines, calendars, and on posters. I needed to check myself, I guess.

I worked with a sister at Boeings; she was *pretty-big-gurl sexy*, or thick, as they say. She was always with a dude that every woman had to look at. These dudes were built with chiseled chests, six-pack tummies and athletic legs. The running joke was, she sent each piece of a man to work out by itself, while she was working the other pieces, or they were working her. Whatever that big-gurl had, she was putting it down on these perfect gym specimens. The constant knowing smile that waved like victory - the rest of us women didn't understand, and I'm sure she didn't care if we did. Was it the desire those studs had for her big-gurl sexy appeal, or was it some things impressively she could do?

Aloy is a man whom women lust for in the fact that his body was God's better work when it came to each section of him being breathtaking. I see how women look at him. Then sadly, I've seen the expressions on women's faces after they walk away, after they then listen to hesitantconversation. He and I are laughing and talking with our feet up on his desk.

"Zelda, have you thought about being a foot model - very pretty feet, nice arch, and…and…and your toes."

I had on my gym slides, and quickly I was self-conscious and removed my feet from his desk. I'm sure my face couldn't hide the scarlet tones peeking past my brown skin. I had grown at ease to let him see my gap while I smiled. I was feeling good, at the same time I was flustered. He complimented me, and his speech impediment was absent for the moment.

The stereo in the gym jammed Shelia E, The Time, and Prince. I looked down to the gym floor and saw two guys lifting bench weight reps in rhythm. A woman across the way from the men was stretching. I watched her as her Seahawk baseball cap hung low in an effort to hide her intense scanning of the two weightlifters. Maybe she didn't know, but she was stretching in rhythm to the music, and maybe booty chasing does happen here.

After a short conversation about my feet, our conversation moved on.

"I'm having a good time babysitting your little cousins. I have a trip planned to take them out of town for the weekend. I haven't decided exactly where, but I want to expose them to the world."

"Ah…yeah…they need a wider view of the world other than being in church 24/7," his tone was a bit dark, and went silent for a moment, and I could tell it wasn't tied to his speech issue. "My Uncle Shomer and Eneta are good people, but I talk more with my other uncles, even though they are crude at times." I cocked my head to the side. He got the message and continued. "Okay, yes…they are tasteless and act rude all the time.

"My Uncle Shomer and my Aunt Eneta, they have always been deep with their church. What they don't see, it's another type of disrespect to the kids they adopted who already lived in hell," he went into his quiet mode as Aloy does. I let my mind reflect on what I had learned from Oceania. She's thirteen in real age, but her used body and survival life skills are retired hooker absorption. She plays like a child of eight, maybe to deflect from long-lived horrors in her short life. She was sold in her country to a warlord at the age of seven, and experienced all the ills that come with ugly men. She was able to run away and make it back to her village and find her brother, and they made it across to Greece. She paid her way with her body. She and her brother Skyler, both had names that can be hard to pronounce, so they were renamed in the orphanage to attract Americans.

Pastor Shomer and Eneta were there on vacation and to adopt children. I have wanted to ask if they could ever have had kids. They are in the early fifties now, so what's the use in asking? My mother told me, asking most women who don't have children if they can have kids, can cause hearts to beat poorly due to a sadness only they can feel, and no one can ever understand.

Pastoral influence - linked to political clout, and Oceania and Skyler were children living in America ninety days later. They will never be American kids due to the ills the world has made them carry as the flag of a survivor's nation; a locating in their souls keeps them enslaved to a residence called Earth. This Earth is a place that spins out of control because man can be spiritless with no rudder.

Aloy came out of his silence and broke me from a revolting awareness. "My uncle and aunt travel a lot going to church conferences for ministers, and she goes to women conferences twice a month, it seems. The kids are shipped around to church members for care."

I could hear his displeasure even through his fragmented dialog. He looked through me and what came across was controlled anger as he fought with words. "I don't want to think that they adopted the kids for the gold card standard of being able and looking leader-ish. The kids…it comes to mind that they are a low-interest expense. A way to look good amongst the church pew seat warmers."

I felt my eyebrows put wrinkles in my forehead. I was a bit shocked at his tough perception as his words took breaks. He knew what he wanted to say.

His gold, brazing eyes seem to turn dark, lost in the distance somewhere. I would have to go mining deep to see down inside of him. But could I climb out, or would I feel trapped? What is really down there inside of him? Aloy's voice – always with a rich timbre and hesitant speech – at the moment had a calm fierceness that made something in me tremble igniting biology between my thighs.

Silence came again as Prince had the weightlifter sweating to *Sign of the Times*.

I wanted to change the subject, so I started to laugh.

"What's so funny, pretty toes?" he asked, as I felt it better for him to come out of his understandable mood.

"Leave my feet alone. I was laughing because I've been able to avoid your uncles, but I want to whoop them again in Spades."

I wondered if he knew about his Uncle Sans' ugly soul exploiting and enslaving his aunt Alanese into a deep well that she can't see a way out of. I watch him leave once or twice a week from his brother's house in the AM, acting smug.

I know I want to knock good ole Uncle Sans out for keeping her in a carnal hell of having to lay on her stomach while his foulness humped her ass. Why do men take what is so easily given by so many other women?

Aloy broke into my thought with his deep laugh. "You will get your chance to play them again, there is a barbeque next weekend, so I can watch you beat them down."

When Aloy is laughing, he hardly has a problem talking. We mocked his uncles' attitude from the last time I was talking smack while I had beaten them down at the card table.

"I've played your Uncle Shomer in speed chess when he and Eneta come home after I watched the kids. Shomer won most of time. It was rare in my past for me to lose at speed chess, but your uncle had a trans-like focus. I thought he was having an outer body invade his innerbody and it took over for him when we played."

"All three of my uncles were golden glove boxers in different weight classes. All three were champions at one time. That got me started at an early age. My Uncle Shomer fought in the Navy and was an armed services champ. The two of us lightly sparred when I was a young teenager. I recognize your description of the trans-like focus. He was like that when we sparred. I was much faster than him, but he fought like he was playing chess, always trying to set up his punches, and it taught me to do the same.

"What's going on with your house?" Aloy asked.

I got into a conversation with him about Chevelle and the progress in the basement, which was almost done, with a complete bathroom. I felt okay speaking about Chevelle as it wasn't negative. "It's been two months. After he was jumped by his girlfriend's father and she ended up getting an apartment, he no longer went to his girlfriend's house as often. The last couple weeks, he's home when I come home.

"He goes to work, as he got hired back at that one place that he was working at when he got attacked. They pay him cash under the table, but I have told him he needs to pay into his social security. Hustling is what we all have to do; but sadly, we all need government paper to live later on. I want him to be his own boss.

"I have had discussions with him about his future. He's got great skills building and problem-solving aptitudes. I want him to think about the carpenters' union. They have an apprentice program which I told him about, and he is eligible due to the fact that he has been incarcerated, and it wasn't a felony."

"I invited Chevelle to come to the gym and workout whenever he wants to, and he has been in," Aloy said.

"What?" I was shocked knowing Chevelle and I talked often and yet, he hadn't mentioned it. Maybe since he is living in my house, and he is around me all the time, maybe he just wanted his own whatever time to claim for himself since he has not been staying at his girlfriend's house as of late. I had not asked him about it in trying to give him his privacy.

"He, and a couple of mixed martial arts wannabes, have connected and workout and wrestle. He's good; great balance and quickness when he boxes, but he needs training on the science of it all. He makes the wannabes look like the beginners they are."

After I told Alloy about all the things going on with the house, he asked me to wait a moment, and he left the office and headed down the stairs. Shortly after, I saw why. His exgirlfriend, or lady friend, was at the entrance desk. I had not seen her come in in a while, and never this late. They talked, and in less than three minutes, she walked out. She didn't appear to stomp or be pissed, she smiled at him like it was business; or was it my mind seeing what I wanted to see, and what was that? He didn't walk her to her car, he made quick passes by all that was in the gym, and kept it moving. He was almost sitting back down in his office when his cell beeped. He checked it. He texted back.

I got up to leave and Aloy said, "No, don't go unless you're in a hurry." An hour later, we are still talking about everything from world affairs to the upcoming Olympics. We discuss boxing and Floyd Mayweather; how good he was. We both agreed that his funky attitude which people see, and the struggles he's had with the law, might be overshadowing his boxing greatness. We both knew that many boxers, like many policemen and politicians, preachers and any Joe, John, or Jeff, all had a long list of domestic abuse issues or philandering issues; but they get up and go to work, and no one can do anything about it in most cases.

I finally told him that I needed some sleep - the morning light would be knocking in five hours. He and I kept talking as we both headed out the door. He gave me a hug at the door of my Cadillac. It was warm, but not enticing to be anything more than friendly. Nevertheless, I realized I still needed to be held and more. Thoughts of saying I wanted more, played chess in my head; but I turned the key, let my engine roar, and drove off.

Chapter 18

I went for a run under the cloudy skies and the drizzle of the Seattle liquid sunshine. It might have helped me run faster and farther than usual. I had to sit down at my kitchen table and relax before taking a shower. My cellphone vibrated on the hardwood floor. Officer CC.

I sit up and answer and I see that beat-up Benz in the next door driveway.

Officer CC has a job for me to go collect some back child support from a dad who is rolling in money, but won't help the mother of his children. It has been a while since I've put in that kind of work, but I'm down. She said it would be easy. She had my back when I asked her to lookout for me when I beatdown Chelleve's girlfriend's dad. There's no way I'm going to tell her I wouldn't or couldn't. I got off the phone letting her know I would do what she needed me to do.

Dear old piggish Uncle Sans walked out of his brother's house with his shirt buttoned crooked, and his belt undone. I'm seething. I imagine Alanese Delroy is laying there still on her stomach, with her faced buried in her pillow. I assume she'll be out in her garden later with coffee in hand as she pulls weeds, while her soul is awash in a dust bowl of torment. Her husband won't touch her, and her brother-in-law violates her with madness. I might have to step in. One dead beat dad, and a punk-ass pig of a man going down for a beatdown.

On my second cup of coffee, Chevelle and I are working away from nearing the completion of the basement. He worked in silence. He's been doing that. The radio, screw gun, and hammer, blast as the wood and other building materials screamed they were straight, tight, and ready for the next phase. I painted trim as Chevelle put the finishing touches on the basement door. I need to have the fireplace inspected, but I'm in no hurry for that. I had a completed two-bedroom, one-bath, with kitchen and living quarter's basement apartment.

"Chevelle, are we okay? We cool?"

133

He stopped and turned my way. "Iman and I are hardly talking, we are different in ways. I'm different. She says she loves me."

Tears fell to the new tan-colored carpet like blood staining white silk. His tears had pain soaking through. This house, once again, heard wailing and captured hard reality feelings. He wept as he sat down on the floor. My thought…he didn't care that I saw him weak and hurting. He was in love, and nothing else mattered. To me, he is a strong man to let it show how much he hurt.

I wished a man loved me like that. To where he would cry over me, for me. In need of me, he would shed tears and wouldn't care who knew or who saw his liquefied pain. I see this young man in love, and I feel I would lay my life on the line for a man who will cry for me and cry next to me. I feel my eyes start to seep. I'd labor the hardest life with any man to make a life with him if he felt the way I see Chevelle feels. The radio has a bad way of playing *that* song at the wrong time and it did; "Love is Stronger Than Pride."

I was seeing a man willing to let his emotions be known. His expression of love was stronger than any weight that muscles can lift. His raw pain for me to see, is an experience for me to see and use as a guide if ever a man were to profess to love me.

With his head lowered and legs crossed, wearing white painter's clothing, Chevelle resembled a monk praying. He seemed to be praying to the floor, and I sat next to him in support of his prayer. I'm just barely old enough to have been his birth mother. I have very little I can tell him at my stage in this life.

"Chevelle, I've been told a man would happily do anything for a woman, and she would never ask him to do anything that would tear them apart…so I have been told. When you hear a single person tell a married person or someone in a relationship what to do, it may be well intentioned, but most likely, I would be out of my league. I'm going to let you talk instead of trying to say just the right thing."

The walls in the basement are all new with fresh paint, but are becoming the junior walls to the senior wall upstairs of bad tales. New bigger windows shed light in the middle of gloom.

Chevelle's voice enters my ears in low volume. "She says she has to work it out on her own, and learn to do things her way. I have a hard time with being around her when there are things she does, or doesn't do, and I'm not used to how it feels to live like her. I try to present how I feel to her as non-threatening as possible, but I guess it comes out wrong. My grandmother raised me a certain way and it's hard to see anything less. So, she and I end up not talking at all, and it makes no sense."

The saddest part of it all is that I had no experienced wisdom to offer. I was in his emotional sphere, learning something more in life as to what I wanted in a man.

"If you feel that way, then you have to understand that you can't put anyone on your balances in life. You can never know the weight they carry, or where the weight is laden. If you do more than is really within you, it affects you; how you are able to love, and is a set-up for you to be disappointed in yourself. She fell in love with the man you are, not some other dude you're not. The same goes for you. You loved her when she lived under her father's roof, and now she's a woman on her own. She may actually be how she appears to be living life, or she may be growing, or not growing fast enough for you. Any, or all of that could be reality. Are you the man to grow with her? Only time will tell.

"You two have only dated before, and now you've spent time being under the same roof; that's something you have to learn to do, and it will present problems, and you will have no choice but to compromise. When a problem arises, it's time to talk about it; whether you have a compromise or not, and sometimes a concession is not readily available, but is on its way.

"You have to have faith in your soul to crawl deep enough to find a path to having your heart be heard, and not harden against anyone who seems not to hear you. Are you ready to move on? Do you want it to be over?"

"No."

"Then go be yourself, and let her be her. Keep in mind, it's her place, her first apartment; she's the woman of the house. Even if you bought her a million-dollar house, a woman is still the one who makes it a home. She is the lady of the house, and you are there to be her aide. She will, or should, make a kingdom for you."

The doorbell rang, and I used Chevelle's shoulder to help myself get up. He took my hand and squeezed.

"Uncle Don, come in. You paying me a visit, or did my auntie send you to come see the work done or lack thereof?"

"Both," he ducked his head under my doorway. I had a little head room to spare if he didn't duck, but I'm sure he did it out of habit. "Show me around, and I know you have a beer."

"9:00 in the morning, huh?"

His notorious smirk held his words at first, as if I had the nerve to check him. "Grown man. I do what I want; but put some tomato juice in my beer if it would make you feel better."

I had more coffee and he had a beer as I showed him around. Chevelle had left by the time we reached the basement. I could tell Uncle Don was impressed as he left the house, headed to go open the tavern up for the day.

Glass windows at the gym gave way to a lake view of a gloomy day as winds added a chop to water rising. Gray skies fought the mind as to who was in control of the psyche. I lifted weights before my mid-morning class of boot camp exercise. It helps to fight off my high-heat and lustful feelings along the gloom from the outside.

I ran harder this morning trying to quell my desires; to no good though. I'm dreaming as I'm teaching. Wanting my hands to pull a man's thick ass muscles down, while feeling him go inside me. I love to control how deep, how soft, or how hard, a man strokes inside me while my hands hold the meat of his firm ass. Sweat and moisture permeated and saturated my body with the thought of hardness. I could smell my own fragrance. I enjoyed my working daydream.

I'm sitting in my bay window and the streetlights gleam off my finished wood floors. I have a candle assisting the streetlights s I read. I have a book, Quotes and Thoughts from a poet Alexandré Cornet. Reading his words on the thought of words, makes me reflect on whatever I have heard, and what I may have said to anyone.

Writing: Ode To Words

Words can be never enough, and often too many
Words can assist and tear down
Words can fall and words can lift Words can be loud or soft
Words hurt and heal Words can be meaningful or meaningless Words can be owned and words can get unchained
Words can cause tears and bring smiles or pain
Words can birth love, words can bring the feeling of dying
Words can be truth or lies
Words can bring respect and words can disrespect
Words can wake you and words can keep you awake
Words can speak of emotions or no feelings
Words can speak of actions or no actions
Words can come up short, and words can come at the right time to save one from using the wrong words that can back
Words are precious

I close the book and break out my planner – my Google calendar on my phone. I'm planning a trip for Oceania and Skyler the weekend after next. It's their winter break from school, and I have suspended my classes for a week as some families have planned family time for the week. Aloy said he would pay me for the week since I'm on salary, and not paid by the hour. It helps that my classes are bringing in money. JoBelle has hinted the money the gym makes is falling short, and that's why she promotes so hard. It makes me reflect on hustling to make ends meet.

I'm taking the kids to Portland, by train. Their mom and dad, Pastor Shomer and Eneta, are going to be out of town for two separate conferences, so it all works out well.

Chapter 19

"And gentlemen – and I use that term lightly – we have just run a Boston on you; that's ten books, and you are set again."

Playing Spades against these men, JoBelle and I have had a great time beating Sargon Delroy and his brother, Sans. It's the last game and time for dessert; more of my fry bread.

If it's odd for me to sit at the table with Sargon and Sans as Alanese watched from a corner of the room, the fact that I know that the men sitting at the table with me shared the same woman – one as a husband who didn't sleep with her, and the other his blackmailing brother – lets me know that Alanese is suffering inside as she laughs at them losing to two women.

The barbeque had moved inside to the basement rec room to host our game for the evening. It had turned too cold to be outside. The smaller inside quarters did not have access to the beer and wine coolers that were in the garage without having to go outside, but that's where we had to go to quench our thirst. I needed another beer after spanking these grown ass boys and taking a dump on their egos.

The milder weather doesn't deter the kids from wanting to play outside with other children from their church. Earlier, we had bundled them all up to deal with the cold, and Enenta and I took them up to the park. As was the case before, she was on her phone. This time, Eneta kept more of a calculated distance; but when she was close enough, I saw and heard the game. She talked in code to a man; too many ah-huhs for it to be anything other than foreplay. The look of her blushing expression was promoted by whoever was delighting her ears and mental libido. He was talking to her clit and everything near as she was walking in the park having phone sex. I'm almost jealous. I miss having a man in my ear talking nasty. As she walked by to hand me some tissues for the kids, I knew the game, and game recognizes game.

To whom she was speaking to, if he was associated with church, his tithes are liquid seed going into her offering bowl as he or she called out to God...and the devil smiled. I've been the other woman enough to know when one is playing in the dirt. A hot shower can wash the dirt off, but an armpit of stain remains, and it's funky.

Our original conversation about the power of woman to achieve goals - as one of them being her sexual power - well, I'm starting to feel it was a ruse. Her conclusions of women's sexual powers…is that she's a hypocrite.

If a cheating man is all the worse and wrong things in life, is a cheating woman any better? Funny, well not really, but every woman knows of, or knew of, the transgressions of a woman doing the nasty behind a man's back. Most likely, it was ignored as not any of our business, and we kept on having a trusting relationship with that woman. If a man used good dick, money, or being super cool, to control a woman, then we see him as an asshole. When a woman does the same, what does that make her? What did that make me when I crossed that line with another woman's husband? What does that mean for me now, as I know Eneta is getting her body satisfied outside of her marriage? A Pastor's wife, no less.

Glad I chose not to get too close to her. I take care of the kids, and that is a good thing. I have noticed she and the kids don't talk all that much. In a sense, I think the kids have a great life because they have a roof over their heads and plenty of food. In their short time on Earth, before now, those things were sporadic.

I walk JoBelle out to her car; she is leaving for a hot date. I let her know I'm jealous and remind her to tell me the sexy details later. I have a few short conversations with others at the indoor barbeque as I wait to get into the basement's bathroom. I could run home quickly and use my own toilet. Squatting over anyone else's toilet is always an undesirable preference most women take. My turn, I dry my hands and unlock the door to go back out. Before I turn the handle, the door opens and it's Sans. He is almost in the bathroom with me before he acknowledges I'm standing in front of him. At least he had not whipped it out in advance of getting in front of the toilet, and missing and pee painting on and around the toilet.

He grins. He's nasty. I see foulness in his eyes. I move past him in the tight space. If he had exhaled, his breath and belly would have assaulted me. Glad his ego sucked in his over-the-belt gut.

I need another beer. I asked if anyone else wanted one. Aloy walks over and almost whispers in my ear that he wants another beer. I let him know I'm going to run over to my place first and bring over some more fry bread. I head toward my place, but I change my mind and decide to take him his beer first. The garage is Aloy's first boxing ring; the place where he learned the basics. It is kept as a shrine to all he accomplished as a pre-teen amateur fighter. Pictures, trophies, and old workout equipment hang from the walls. The garage is what they call a man cave with a wet bar anda refrigerator behind the bar.

From the lower cooler, I moved up some beers and wine coolers to the almost empty upper part of the fridge. There is only one left of the kind of beer I will drink; I had to reach to the back. My eyes freeze on that beer as I feel breath on the small of my back; my tank top had lifted up when I bent over. I held still and felt closeness to my backside. I turn my head slightly and let my eyes try to scan back. I wanted it to be Aloy, but it wasn't. His crotch was on my ass…Sans. I backed my ass up forcibly trying to assault Sans by pushing him into the bar behind him. The rack inside the fridge caught my hair and that pissed me off as I had to do two things at once. I only wanted to concentrate on kicking ass.

He belched and grunted as my foot kicked him in his fat gut. The bar might have gotten him across his back. I ripped the rack out of the fridge with my hair attached and faced Sans. I lifted my left hand to jab him under his fat jowls; directly in his throat. He put his hands on his belly and leaned back, possibly indicating, "*Hey*," and "*Don't hit me.*"

I pulled the rack apart from my hair.

"Hey, relax. I just came to get a beer," he smiled.

Maybe he did…*nawh, he didn't.* The way he looked at me when I came out of the bathroom, and now his coming up behind me and hovering over my ass…nawh. His voice sounded contrite; but he was full of crap.

"Move your ass away from me," I say it like I have hot grits in a pot about to throw it in his face.

"I didn't mean…"

I think about him blackmailing Alanese for humping rights. "You meant to be the asshole you are, you fat ugly punk."

141

He put a surprised look on his face and put his hands up in the air as if I were the police pointing a gun at him; then he turned and stepped away. I let my guard down. He turned quickly and punched me with a hard, glancing, blow to my temple. It was a good straight right hand with his weight behind it. It hurt. I was stunned and off balance in the tight space between the bar and the refrigerator. He threw a left hook that snapped my head. I saw it coming, but I was already stunned. My reactions were seeing in slow motion and freezing. The blow propelled me into a murky awareness.

Head hurt and blurred vision, I felt my body go limp. The room is almost dark. I've been stunned and out once before from sparring with a man in the ring, so I remember this feeling. How long had I been knocked out? A few seconds? A minute? It couldn't have been more.

My ass felt the cold floor. Sans had only gotten as far as pulling my lose sweat pants down to the middle of my thighs. I hadn't worn undies, but even when I was knocked out, I guess my body said there was no way was it going to be easy. My legs stayed clamped together and fought him back, resisting his attempts at pulling them apart. His face was trying to shove its sandpaper surface into in my pubic hair. He was sniffing me.

Sans was so caught up in his lust that he didn't notice the wine bottle I am crashing down on his head. The thud, the shattering of glass…I nailed his ass good. His head jerked down and popped up of my thigh from the impact. I grabbed his hair and slammed his head down between my now parted thighs. I lifted his head to slam it again, and his face was covered in blood.

"Get the fuck off of me!" I yelled in a hushed voice. For what, I don't know. My head throbbed.

I repositioned myself with extreme difficulty quickly away from this wannabe raping asshole, with him being knocked out. I stood. I seethed. I dribbled uncontrolled pee down my leg. I wanted to stab him…kill him…and dig his grave and leave it open for buzzards and wolves to tear at his dead flesh. I pulled my sweat pants up. Blood was all over them; his blood. Although his face is all I felt between my thighs, just the thought of other parts of him that close to me made me vomit on his ass as I stood over him. No, he didn't penetrate me; but his effort in any manner was rape. I started kicking him in the balls from behind. The pain woke him up and he rolled over in agony. It would never be enough to satisfy me.

I grabbed the broken wine bottle and put it against his face; letting him feel me slowly cutting him.

I hissed as I set out to pronounce every word, "If you go near Alanese anymore, or make any trouble for her, or if you get near me or any woman breathing, I will slice your balls off and make you chew on them."

I sliced his face in slow motion. Blood slithered like a snake. He trembled as I assumed a woman would if she was conscious throughout her attack. I sliced a frown under his bottom lip.

I stood up erect for over him and spat. Then I took a beer bottle – the one I wanted to drink, the last one – and I came down hard on his nose. The beer bottle didn't break, but his nose – if it wasn't broken before – it was now. With the broken wine bottle still in my other hand, and holding it like a knife, aiming the jagged edge at his throat I start to lift up in order to give me the force I will need to cut his juggler.

"Zelda...Zelda!"

With the beer bottle and broken wine bottle in hand, I turned, and Aloy stood there with his hand extended to calm me, or stop me, or help me. I'm not sure which one, and at the moment, it could have been all in the same. His face was stone cold with his eyes piercing at the waste of a man laying out cold between the bar floor and the coolers and at my legs.

"Come, Zelda, come now, please."

"He tried to rape me. He tried..."

Aloy's eyes moved to my bloody sweat pants.

"That's his blood; he didn't get in me. If he had, you wouldn't have been able to stop me from killing his ass."

"Zelda, let me take you to your house," his voice is begging me.

I reached back to him for his hand with the broken wine bottle, and he releases it from my hand with some prying. I don't know why I trusted any man at that point in time, but I did. I left out of the garage with Aloy, and he led me to my back door while holding the tips of my fingers. Inside, I slumped into a kitchen chair. Aloy gave me a bottle of water from my fridge. I still held the bottle of beer in my other hand, the one that did not crack over Sans' face. I opened the beer with my bloodied hand. Sans' blood. Aloy grabbed it from me. I submitted. He pulled another beer from my fridge and poured the contents into a glass.

"Zelda, I'll be back in fifteen or twenty minutes. If I'm longer than that, please stay right here. Please let me in when I come back."

He turned and went out the door. I stood and watched him leap off my back porch as if he had wings. He went back into his uncle's garage. He did all that before I might have taken two breaths as he was closing the door to garage.

I locked the door between the kitchen and the basement. I did not want Chevelle to come up for any reason, and the locked door was my signal to him when I wanted privacy. I hear him moving about down there. He's been cleaning out the furnace air ducts and replacing the ones that are too far gone. He came over to the barbeque for a while; the kid is a workaholic. It's his therapy, I guess.

I feel ugly. I turned on the stereo.

So beautiful, the lyrics flowed from Musiq Soulchild. It was a love song, but all I heard was, *So beautiful... So beautiful...*the smooth groove confronted my ugly feelings.

Then I ripped off my sweats and tank top. I wanted to be naked. I wanted to be pure and scratch off the ugly and be beautiful. I wanted to rid my horrid feelings and rage. My step-dad reminded me often that an angry fighter is an out of control fighter; not allowing for a game plan to take place to win or survive.

144

I wanted a long bath, but I wanted to be waiting for Aloy when he came back, so I took a quick shower. I unlocked the back door. I put my .38 under the pillow on the couch.

I lit a candle and curled up on my couch under a warm blanket. The small light in the dark gave me a focal point to go away and get lost.

Chapter 20

"Zelda."

I heard Aloy's voice call my name three times as if he were trying to wake me gently. I heard him when he came in. I peeked to make sure I didn't have to grab my gun for that fool Sans coming through my door. I had been playing a movie behind my eyelids of unloading every bullet in my gun and reloading into the heart of my would-be rapist.

"Zelda, it's me."

I was naked under my blanket, and it wasn't for any man to see. "Turn, don't look at me."

He sat in the chair across from me and turned it away from me.

"What is up with your family?" I lowered my voice. "What did you do with your uncle? What are you going to do? What the hell?" my voice raised with each question. "Sure, you may have stopped me from killing a man, and I may still kill that fat asshole, but I can't sit here after what has happened and speak to you as if I were okay."

"The Way of The World" by Earth Wind and Fire ended, and Maze featuring Frankie Beverly started in with, "Joy and Pain."

The room had my favorite light shining in – the streetlight that came through the front window. The light illuminated Aloy's broad shoulders and head. I got up with my blanket slightly draped over of my body. I'm not the modest type. I walked past him and headed upstairs. Once I reached the top, I told him I would be back down in a few. I changed into jeans and a tank top. When I came back downstairs, Aloy sat in the bay window. My emotions twist and I'm so angry. How do I call him a friend when his family—his uncle, tried to rape me. I found my mouth wide open searching for words.

I sat down on the couch. I'd let him talk if he wanted to. Ten minutes later, the only sound heard was still music. He finally came and sat down across from me on the couch as, "Back At One," by Brian McKnight eased me, and maybe Aloy as well.

"We all have ghosts and heartless souls in our families. I'm sorry you have encountered mine. I failed you. I should have been there to protect you. As your friend, I am so sorry. I did not know he, Sans, was that mutha-fa…"

"I can defend myself. I now know there is a huge difference if a man wants to hurt a woman. He punched me as if I was a punching bag, he didn't pull his punches. Then…he tries to take my pussy while I'm knocked out. I guess I was out less than a minute. Oh, my temple," I reached to touch my head. "Shit!"

Aloy jumped up and looked around. He was trying to see what he could do.

"I need ice. I need ice before I look like I have been beaten. I'll be back."

I went to the kitchen to get some ice. Aloy came up behind me and took the ice out of the fridge and put it in a glass.

"Here, roll the glass back and forth over it."

I don't want him to get too close me. Any man right now needs to steer clear of me; and then for him to be related to the foulness. I take the glass and test his fix, it works; but I move away from him and want him to notice. I go back to the couch. He sits on the far end; away from me.

"What did you do with your wannabe-raping-my-ass uncle?"

"He was still out when I went back to the garage. I went and got help from Shomer. I didn't give him many details." I looked at him hard, questioning him. "I didn't tell him much, Zelda. I just said that Sans tried to come on to you, and you took offense and kicked his ass. But I assume he can put one plus one together. We took him home and threw him on his garage floor. Shomer got a water hose and brought him back to life, then he told him he had stop this madness. I left Shomer there with him."

"What...he has rep for doing what he did to me? And his brothers give him a good talking to?"

"Sans had a wife; a nice woman, but she was terrified of him. She became scared of her shadow when he was near, and she left him one day while at one of the family's barbeques. She drove to the store to pick up some paper plates and she never came back. She didn't take a stick of clothing or anything, just drove his new Benz until she must have run out of gas money. She left the car along the roadside in Nevada. It was recovered slightly stripped, and that is the Benz he drives now, years later. So, I'm going to assume Shomer was reflecting on that history of bringing damage to a woman. Zelda, my family is a closet full of skeletons."

As usual, it takes a long time for Aloy to get it all out, but I tuned in and let him know I really wanted to know what I'm dealing with, and that I shouldn't have to deal with any of it.

"Now I'm bones in your family's closet."

We're sitting in the shadows of my living room with the streetlight coming through as our interrogation light. It started to rain hard, and the sound was soothing to my still trembling soul. Aloy is sitting at the end of my couch. I think he is trying to give me personal space, but wanting to be close enough to not feel distant. I test myself to see if I can relax. I turn my body in his direction, and put my feet up on the couch. Then I extended my legs. I wasn't touching him. Aloy, in his usual speech pattern, begins to tell me his family's secrets.

"My mother died shortly after my birth."

"From what, may I ask?"

He shrugged his shoulders and I let it be. "My mother was raised by who I call my greataunt which is Sargon, Sans and Shomer's mother. My mothers' mother, my grandmother, was not even blood. My mother is a niece of her second husband's family. All in all, I am not related by blood, but they are my family. I was raised as if the three brothers were my uncles, but in reality, they're not. I was passed around at birth because my mom was a child herself. She died young though. She had a thing for dressing and fighting like a man, and she had male and female lovers. That got her killed, so I'm told.

"My real father...who knows? I was told my mother was a very good athlete. Some say that in many ways in how I move, and how hard I trained, that I got my relentless drive from my mother."

"Aloy, conceivably, you may have some ability from your father. I often wonder if I am anything like whoever my father is."

Aloy went wordless for a while before he went over to the door and opened it halfway. I heard the sky crying, it was almost louder than the music. I reached for the volume knob and turned the music lower. Rain played as a drummer. It hit the sidewalks like cymbals being caressed softly. As if water was pouring from a bucket from high above, the deluge hit the soft ground, throbbing like the pounding of a bass drum. The rain hit the windows like the slap of a snare drum. The downpour was like jazz; its natural rhythm soothed some of my anger.

As much as I hated that Aloy was related in spirit to a man I despised, I desperately needed to be close to someone I could trust. I didn't want the lingering effects of how bad a man can be. I needed to be held, and to be able to know that the world was not an awful place. To have a man try to take what I would give to the right man...I just need to find trust now.

I didn't have a woman to turn to in my need. A woman being sympathetic of what had happened to me is what I wished for. I wished I could turn to my aunt, but I couldn't. She'd tell me to pull my big gurl panties up. She'd tell me that women go through what I just experienced all the time. Women go through it on the Native reservation like broken down cars spewed as waste in front of homes of doom. The female body gets pitched from side to side like rag dolls. Too many women are torn from their souls with the frequency rate equal to boys who throw rocks. My aunt would minimize my hurt, my anger, my rage.

I hang out with JoBelle for fun, but had not established that kind of relationship to burden her with my pain. It turns out the ones closest to me are Aloy and Chevelle. No way would I share with Chevelle. He's a kid in a sense, and he might try to avenge as I avenged for him. Although he and I have not talked about it, I might assume he has an idea what happened to his girlfriend's father.

I wanted comfort. Aloy is here. I have pretty-much learned to separate my crush on him and felt he was a man I could turn to and trust. Trust him…problematical complexity; the soft petals of a rose and the thorns it grows. Could this be me and him - the beautiful rose that dies, and the thorns that still prick?

Aloy took a deep breath and blew air. "I don't know who my father is or anything about him. No one in my family knows…apparently," his head lowered, and in the shadows of my dark living room, he and I shared an endless tale of neither one of us may ever know daddy. I felt for him.

"My early years…when my great-aunt and great-uncle raised me, we lived near Houston, Texas. I can still remember the smell of the oil refineries as we lived across the ship canal. My great-uncle was mean and drunk is what I remember of him. He took me fishing, but he and I didn't have much of a relationship. He yelled a lot and made my grandmother cry all the time. I lay in my bed at night scared because I heard my very loving great-aunt seemingly almost howl, or groan loudly, like a wounded dog. My great-uncle would yell. 'Bitch, I do what I want to you, and you're gonna take it.' My great-aunt would hold me so tightly and sing and talk to me when my great-uncle wasn't at home; but when he was home, she was timid and quiet. She was always bleeding. Her dresses and slips were always blood stained and soaking in the bathtub in cold water. She would swallow Bayer aspirin all day like it was candy. You know those red rubber hot water bottles women used to hang on the back door of the bathroom door or shower, well, she had that in use almost every day.

"When I was eight, I came home from school and the police were outside the house and wouldn't let me in. The next week, I was staying with another of my great-aunt's sisters, and attending my first funeral; a double funeral. I was told then that the both of them got sick and died. I never thought anything different until my Aunt Alanese sat me down when I was twentyfive and told me the truth. My great-uncle had a thing for rough sex and accidently killed my great-aunt, and he then took his own life with a .45 colt revolver.

"My uncles all were in the Navy at that time. My Uncle Sargon came home from the service with a new wife—my Aunt Alanese when my uncles buried their parents. My Aunt Alanese has been the best blessing God could have sent me, even though it was through her anguish of having a miscarriage right before I met her. She always says, 'God works in ways no man can understand.' He made a way for me to be raised by her. Right after her miscarriage, she would tell me she was appointed by God to look after me. Aunt Alanese brought me into her and my Uncle Sargon's home, and for the most part, I have been blessed.

"Now for my Uncle Sargon...I'll never be sure, but as I grew up, I felt like I was the pet he allowed my aunt to have. Why? My uncle was never like a dad to me or anything like that. She raised me, and he ran the streets and was often gone for a week at a time. He took an interest in me when I started fighting, as all three of my uncles trained me as a project. Sargon and Sans are the principal investors of the gym. It may be one of the reasons the gym makes no money. They seem to have a perpetual high loan payment. If not for my side work, I would not get paid."

"Wait...how is that? Who pays me and JoBelle, and the few others who work at the gym?"

"I don't know. A payroll firm does the paperwork."

"If you don't mind, I'd like to help you find out what all that is about. I know someone who is good at accounting."

"There is lots of paper and tax work that they keep at the gym in files. I'm kind of settled on it is what it is. I have gotten used to being behind the eight ball of life. If there is no struggle, I almost think there is something wrong."

"Aloy, struggle is life, and life is a struggle that we need to lessen the load of, if we can. Let me see what I can do; if nothing is there, then nothing from nothing is nothing."

"You're willing to help after…"

"I work at the gym, right?"

He nodded, and his head shadow beamed across the room. He stood up. "You want a beer?"

"Yeah, please."

He handed me a beer, and stood back over by the door. His draw from his beer was long and strong. He talked to the rain and me. "I know about my Uncle Sans and my Aunt Alanese. I haven't known what to do. She is my rock, but if she chooses to see him…who am I to question her choice?"

"She didn't have a choice. She's been blackmailed by Sans and your Uncle Sargon, and her own husband has abused her heart with no love. If you love her, you'll help her. No woman would choose the life she is now living. What the hell are you thinking, Aloy? You have known! You said she has been your rock, yet you didn't think you needed to look deeper and have a conversation with her?" my voice drowned the rain out.

He turned his eyes toward me and an intense stare was meant for me to see. "I have spoken to her and asked her what I can do," I heard bass in his voice that rumbled. "She said she didn't want me to do a thing, she had choices. I took that to mean she was doing what she wanted to do. Her words were, 'Just don't be like the men I have known.' You say things I don't know about, 'Blackmailed' by Sans and my Uncle Sargon."

I looked at the rain over his shoulder. It was coming down hard. His voice came at me heated like hot lava. It was not roaring loud, but his tone was searing. I felt my body and head lean away. I didn't like that. I didn't need to feel that…not today; but I did accuse him of something that sounds like he didn't know anything about, and it involves the one woman he loves, and trusts.

Am I taking my anger out on him? Am I?

He sat down on the couch and looked down at the floor. "I have spoken to my aunt several times, but she says she fears more for me. I have cried trying to understand why and how, but she shuts me down and sends me away whenever I bring it up. You say blackmail...it's the first I have heard of it."

Now his voice was apologetic.

"She was trying to break free from him. She is sad and hurting and feels trapped. This is why I told Sans ...if he comes near Alanese or me again, I will kill him. And I will, Aloy, I will."

"I believe you. He does, too. He mumbled several times that he thought you wanted to kill him. He assaulted you like no man ever. You tore him a new asshole of hurt. When we got him to his house, he had passed out again. And when he came to, he was scared and hurt. Out of all my uncles, Sans hit the hardest when I sparred with them. He has a punch. I'm sorry he hit you. I'm sorry he did anything to you, but please don't hold it against me. Please. And please, help me save my aunt; although you may have already. However, I can help you, please let me help you."

"Can we change the subject?" I pushed my feet into his hip. My toes touched his thigh. He looked at me. "Aloy, what's up with you and your gurl? Your woman? Your status with her? Are you sleeping with her?"

"Why? And why ask now, Ms. Pretty toes?"

I tilted my head back and rolled my eyes being silly; but in the dark, I doubted he saw that. "I need to be comforted. I need to be held tonight...held," my eyes fell into my lap. Embarrassed. My feelings erupting out of control – spewing need. My heart bled suffering and needed any love as a bandage. As close as he was to my wounding perpetrator, I needed a man to embrace me and let my soul cocoon. At this moment, even for a moment, I wanted to be in his arms.

He scanned my face. "Let's take a walk," he asked, or decreed, and I liked that more.

"In the rain?"

He walked back to the open door and opened it wider. "Listen, it stopped. My great-aunt would be happiest after a rain. She said that's what God did to the Earth once. He made it rain to save a few and start all over fresh."

It had. I stood and went to the door and stood under his arm that held the door open. The air was fresh. I looked up at his face. He was emotionless in his expression. I walked back under his arm and went to the hall closet and pulled out a jacket and an umbrella and handed him the umbrella for just in case.

Chapter 21

We walked two miles along Beacon Hill Avenue and on down to China Town according to the mile-step keeper on my phone. Silence traveled along with a light mist; it felt good - renewing. The sounds of the city talked to us until I'm sure my awkward question settled in enough for us to talk.

"Aloy, I could have left the personal question alone, but if by chance you will hold me in an embrace, hold me through the night, I don't want you to if you and her are doing you-alls' thing."

As we walked, I was surer I wanted to be in his arms, just to be held.

"I know some men hate that, if they ain't getting some. But...don't judge me, but I have had married men hold me before, but I'm not there anymore," I looked at his face to read him and he didn't flinch.

"I'm sorry I was ever that selfish, and my request to be held tonight is another kind of selfishness that I feel is merited. Your uncle tried to violate me, and I know from my time around you that you would never cross that line."

My face was still sore and I have a slight headache to remind me of the foulness of earlier. I need to be held, just held. I wanted closeness.

Four corners of buildings of Chinese architecture surrounded us when we finally stopped walking. Aloy leaned on a streetlamp. I'm standing in his night shadow. He's looking at me as always before he speaks, as if searching for words.

"Zelda, my last relationship... sheee...she felt people...her girlfriends were embarrassed by my speech. I'm not dumb, and she knew that...but you know, I just talk slow...and sometimes it takes...time for me to respond. In my head, I know what...I want to say, but it won't come out...fast, as you know."

157

He was really struggling to talk more than any time before. Pain was coming with each word. I reached for his hand and squeezed his forefinger. My question is causing him anguish that is intensifying his speech pauses.

"Aloy, take your time, take your time."

"We dated as teenagers before the incident, and while it looked like I was headed to the Olympics. But after the incident, she never let me make love to her the way I needed to, and wanted to, after that bullet entered my head and affected so many different things. I needed passion, foreplay, and to be able to see her in the midst of it all. She just wanted hard pounding sex, nothing more, and I needed more. I wanted to kiss and touch, and be held and be able to go slow with more foreplay. I'm having a hard time saying all this."

"I think I get the picture; it's okay. You two were young then."

I'm blinking my eyes trying to quell my breathing from becoming like a car horn going off warning that I wanted what she had denied.

"I just don't know about certain things anymore when it comes to a woman being there for a man."

His speech was bad. He was aching inside.

"Please don't look at me strange, but I've…well, another woman other than her has been rare. I dated here and there, but things didn't work out. Yeah, I'm forty…forty."

I looked in his eyes, and even then, the streetlights could not hide the golden hues of having the blues in them. The sky cried on his chiseled face. I wanted to wipe away the moisture. I didn't. A bus went by and the inside lights highlighted us against the streetlight pole.

"Aloy, why have you chosen to tell me this? Why me? Why should I know? I want to be clear, if I haven't been, I'm not wanting to have sex with you. I may have asked too much in asking you to hold me."

"Zelda, I'm telling you my story…it has nothing to do with me not wanting to hold you. You asked about my status concerning me and Parasol. Then, what my uncle put you through earlier, I want you to know I'm not them. I'm not that part of my family in that sense. You deserve to know that much after what you went through."

I could tell I exasperated him a bit. I kind of liked it when a man tells me where he stands and what he tolerates. I appreciated his reasoning and concern.

"Were you two ever in love?"

He looked away, and the yellow light from a restaurant depicting the sun glowed off the tip of his pretty nose. I think his nose was running a bit. I wanted to take my finger and wipe away the drip. I did. He didn't jump or look at me crazy. "That's what friends are for," I said.

He nodded. "I believe we loved each other, but that was a long time ago. As I told you, Parasol and I had been together since we were teenagers, but what she needs and wants…" he shrugged his shoulders. "Why she hasn't moved on and found her Mr. Right, I don't ask. So now, all these years later, we still go to social events and other couples-like things, but we are not a couple as many assume. We look the part, as she dresses in credit card limit busting dresses, and me in a tux, or suit and tie.

"My closet is full of stylish clothes that she has bought because I don't have the income. She…at times, she tells me I am the most handsome man in town…but…when in public, she speaks for me as if she's trying to keep me from speaking; as I might embarrass her. If someone asks me a question, she'll jab her way out in front of me…so I avoid talking. If I'm with the men at a function, many know about my speech and how it came about. They still call me champ and will listen to me, but once we are back in mixed company…things change."

I noticed that he speaks with no hesitation when he gives instructions in the gym; but away from the boxing or weight training or circuit training, he speaks with a delay. Knowing him as I do, I would never avoid him or cut him in half because of his speech.

159

"Listen Aloy, my grandmother said, 'It's not what others think of your bond with someone, it's what you think of the union you have with someone.' If you base who you are on what others think, it will bring insecurities in what you are as a person, and tear down what is already hard to build.

"We can't let mouths, ears, and the eyes of others, run us down and run over our relationships when those others don't feed us, clothe us, or shelter us. If Parasol had insecurities established by the outlooks of others, she should have only pursued her Creator's opinions through prayer and meditation."

He nodded, and the bright yellow sign across the street glowed off his cheeks.

"Aloy, it might be that she only wanted you for your good looks, your past recognition and possible fame, and she couldn't find a way to say how she actually felt about you after your incident. Instead, she clowned herself and put it on how she thinks others will, or do, feel as an excuse to hold her feelings about you at the end of a long stick. Judgments from her narrowversion friends has cast fears into her soul and has made her a coward.

"I hate to say it, Aloy, but you letting her play pretend relationship may be keeping you from possibly having love. Your play-husband thing with her may have held you back with those other women."

"I want to be loved for who and what I am, but yeah, how it is for me now, that's on me."

He put his hand on my back and steered me to cross the street. We headed back. He kept his hand on my back, almost seemly keeping me from looking at him. But I had more to say.

"One day, Parasol will come to the conclusion that she never gave you enough of what you needed and deserved. We are allowed to make mistakes in life and not be judged by others who have as many, if not more, failures and faults. We must be strong going through any door, and we should be just as strong when we walk back out that door, if that is what we have to do. When someone comes in your life, they should not leave you in any shape or form that is worse off than when they met you. If they do, a disgrace on them will be there forever."

I stopped and turned and looked at him as we stood on the corner of 12th and Jackson. Misting rain dotted our faces like a busy musical overture. I looked into his eyes and saw a long melody of a heartbreak. Ironic, we stood near where Charlie Parker, Billie Holiday, Ray Charles, and John Coltrane had once blown, sang, or tinkled keys in a 1950's club called the Black & Tan. It was a place where jazz and blues spawned and fashioned itself with threads of misfortune leading to sometimes tragedy. I looked into the eyes of a man who had killed another man in order to survive, and honored friends who believed in him. However though, somehow, the love of a woman had made him a near virgin to being loved by a woman as he was nearing forty years of age, and making him my twin in never knowing love. Love was a vagabond on the run from us. I looked at him knowing I knew nothing myself about having a relationship, other than what I saw in my mother and my step-dad, Eddie. My eyes ventured past his melancholy irises and fixated on something deeper in him.

Then I flinched. My skin crawled remembering that just hours ago, I could have been a complete tragic ending; and he, as I know him, would have killed one of his family. And it would have nothing to do with love, just the honor in him.

"Zelda, could I hold you tonight? Can we make haste and get back to your place? Can we forget for a moment what has been, and what has happened? Can…"

I put my finger across his lips. "That's what friends are for."

We started walking fast across a bridge span and above and ahead of where the old art deco former hospital from the forties stood. I looked at the lighted building as the place a superhero lived. Tonight, I was going to have a superhero hold me.

Chapter 22

I was lying on my mattress on the floor. I had upgraded from my cot, but I did not want a bed frame, so the mattress was on the floor. Because the window was so low to the floor, I loved sleeping near it. I had fabricated some almost sheer curtains. The man standing above me now in his boxer shorts was concealed. His legs, God only made some men to stand on sculpted black mahogany, and one was near me. His chest, I had seen in the gym, but now standing above me - his pecks where framed art.

I wanted to trust myself, but I didn't. I put on sweat pants and a sports bra as if anything would stop my body from wanting and stopping at a line. If I were to jump across though, I know I was betraying what I needed the most. I know he can only do so much to help me by being close.

Aloy slipped in behind me and I spoon into him. His arm feels like a huge padlock from an army of invaders. His warm breath was like the tick-tock of a clock, and a warm summer breeze on my neck. I was falling under a spell of being safe and I could feel sleep coming over me.

The radio alarm; Ledisi, "In The Morning." I set it to that song on purpose. He should leave before anyone from next door, or any door elsewhere for that matter, should see him leave. When the song asked, Will you be here, he was holding me, and no heater in the world could warm me like the blanket he was. I was on my stomach and his hard leg was over mine, and his arm was around my waist. I feel the outline of his manhood on my thigh. It's not hard, but I feel the length and thickness. I know he just felt the deepest breath I may have ever taken.

I turn over to my back, and I feel wetness damping my womanhood. I slip my hand ever so slowly under me and into my sweatpants. I'm damp and getting damper. My scent is rising. I jump up and startle him.

"I'll be back," I say to him as I'm almost out the bedroom door. I move to the bathroom quickly. I close the door and lean on it. My lungs need air. I open the window and reach over and turn the shower on. I place cold water on my face. My face is sore, but there is no swelling, just a little coloring as I look in the mirror. I wait until the water runs hot and get in and hold still before washing myself.

Knock on the door.

I respond with a nervous loud, "What?"

I hear his voice through the door and over the shower water. "I'll see you later."

"Okay…okay, I'll see you later," I hesitate, and then jump out of the shower and crack the door. "Aloy, thank you."

I see him reaching the steps. He doesn't turn, but I hear him, "Zelda, I'll see you later," his voice was soft and it sounded like he meant what he said. I close the door and lean on it again. I start crying. Why…all kinds of reasons.

Chapter 23

Reflections are on each baby hair on my body and on my every brain cell. After being in Aloy's arms, I'm okay. It did help, but I'm not fine, as if nothing had happened between a counter, a cooler, and a floor. It's been a week and most of the soreness in my face is gone. I'm drinking coffee and making the last of the plans for the trip with the kids, and about to go pick them up.

I called my aunt. I wanted to have a heart-to-heart talk with her about anything. It does happen sometimes. I told her I had someone try to hurt me, she asked for more information. She got mad and raised her voice because I couldn't get it out. I hardly told her anything, and nothing close to what actually happened. I ended up letting her know the house is coming along and I wish she would come by. She said Uncle Don had told her everything is going well as far as he saw. She said she would come by, but her voice said not anytime soon. That's her. It's been a few months now since I last saw her.

My Cadillac glides in front of Pastor and Eneta's house. Pastor is out gardening alongside their house. It's one of his hobbies. Given the fact that all three of the brothers look alike with slightly different bodies because of how they have carried themselves, it's hard looking at any of the brothers.

I know he knew what his brother Sans had tried to do to me. He had to know. I knew he knew. He gave me the usual greeting, and then we shared an awkward moment of what to say. He has always been a bit dry and reserved, unlike his brothers. While he was on his knees, he acted like he couldn't find a tool, and I handed it to him. We avoided eye contact. The murky ground from all the rain had him muddy, and he came in and took a shower before we all sat down at the kitchen table.

With the kids hovered next to me, I told the family what I had planned. Eneta gave me a credit card for all the expenses. I had thought a few times about how much a church pays a pastor. They seem to live without any money woes. She wanted me to take the kids to Vancouver, but with them being immigrant adoptees, I did not want to have any problems at the boarder when I was not their adoptive parent. Portland is going to be our destination. Pastor Shomer is headed out of town to Detroit for the week as a guest preacher, and Eneta is going to be gone for a few days driving to Southwest Washington to a place called Ocean Shores. She's a guest speaker at a women's marriage retreat. The getaway for me couldn't come at a better time.

The kids and I enjoyed the train ride. It was my first, as well as a first for the kids. To see the world from different views where cars can't travel, you see rivers, valleys, backlands, and small towns that would usually be passed by without a thought. The small towns almost have a romantic feel; yet, all places have its blues and bad spirits to go along with the picture perfect.

Eneta booked us into a Hilton Hotel by the airport, and we took a taxi from the train station to the hotel to check in. Later, we got dressed and I took the kids to a nice restaurant. I don't get to do that too often. We went to the movies, but I soon realize that being out by the airport, we needed to be downtown to see more of Portland and special places like the Rose Garden and fountains and bridges.

The kids are sleeping, actually snoring, when I head down to the front desk to find out how to get around to the malls and all the sights by buses or Uber. I need to know the cost. The front desk person, a beautiful woman from Somalia, had checked me in yesterday; she sure worked some long hours. I'm telling her my wants for the day, and she suggests that she can transfer me and the kids to the downtown Hilton, and that would help greatly with all the things I want to do while in Portland with the kids. She was pleased to know someone was helping the kids have a good time since they were from her continent. Another thing that she let me know was that the downtown Hilton had certified babysitting services, and her sister was one of the babysitters there. I'm going out tonight for a drink, and maybe hear some live music. Maybe I'll do some karaoke. I could use some me time.

A shuttle transferred us downtown, and we even got the airport Hilton lower price at the pricier downtown hotel. I was singing in Ice-Cube's voice, *Today was a good day.*

Downtown worked me and the kids over. We had done so much in one day. We took pictures all day as we sightsaw and played. Portland had so many parks, gardens, waterfronts, and huge beautiful bridge spans with great backgrounds. Now back at the downtown hotel at 6:00 PM, we all needed a nap. The kids didn't even turn on the TV. I showered after I took an hour nap, and ordered delivery pizza for the kids. I went to check in on my reserved babysitting. I met my airport desk clerk's sister, and I took the kids down to meet her. I see they connected. I was set to go out at 9:00.

A taxi dropped me off at a place called Jammys. I was told by several street musicians that this is the place to go.

I'm sitting at a table by the bar in the back. It's crowded in here and I'm sharing the table with two people; a brother and a white girl. They knew each other as friends, but weren't dating or anything, as far as I could tell. They invited me to sit down out of friendly hospitality. They were musicians; he—James, is a drummer; and she—Carlie, is a blues singer and guitar player. It's open mic night and the house band is playing some good tunes. People are drinking, and I'm relaxed.

The band is playing an instrumental version of "Knock on Wood"; a classic 60's R&B song. Carlie is singing along. White girl got some soul in her bones as a little Janis Joplin style entered my ears. It caught me off guard, but I join in with her. We are jamming. James looks on in amazement. People around us are egging us on and we keep belting the tune out. The end of the song has a call and answer response, and Carlie and I are doing it. The band finished and people around us are clapping and telling us to go to the stage. I think Carlie is a regular, as people know her name. She asks if I know the Sam and Dave song, "If Something Is Wrong with My Baby, Something Is Wrong With Me." I tell her I know the song. I know the song very well. She says, "Let's go do it."

On the stage, I'm a bit nervous, but I can do this. Carlie tells the crowd that she normally does this song by herself, but she is happy to have me up on the stage with her, and she then introduces me. The piano starts in, and Carlie has borrowed a guitar, and she adds a southern soul sound. I get into the song from the first note. "When something is wrong with my baby," I put my soul into the song, holding and bending notes. She joined me on the chorus in harmony. She sings a verse and I come back, and we finish with groans and chants, and pleading, calling, and answering lines. Done, and the standing room place is chanting, *"Carlie...Zelda"* for minutes after we left the stage.

I'm downing a shot of tequila with a beer that someone gave to me as a gift for my singing. I'm feeling good. I'm offered another shot, and I decline as I am taking care of two kids and need to be getting back in a reasonable time. I look to the left for my bag; nothing is in it of value, so I left it there on the bench while I was singing. As I look back, I see, and I freeze. I see him. I see her. I see them hugged up tight as they walk in the door. She looks up in his eyes and smiles. He puts his hand in the middle of her back and leads her toward the middle of the seating area near the stage.

My eyes are on his back looming over her, but she is the star; she is doing the talking. She keeps putting her finger over his lips – shutting him up. He just smiles. If they turned in my direction, they wouldn't see me because my bench is low, and too many people are in between.

I had overheard her in the park and figured out she had something going on, but to see her in the same city I'm vacationing in with her kids... Eneta is here with another man. She said she was headed to a women's marriage retreat, I believe at Oceans Shores, an hour away, now that I think about it. She is dressed unlike any First Lady of a church, I would think, should dress. Her dress, it is near the bottom of her butt checks. Her cleavage was out near the darks of her nipples. Her makeup is flawless, if I were painting a house in rainbow colors. Her hair – I've never seen her in a wig before. Some horse is skinned. It is Eneta; the wife of Pastor Shomer, and if she is trying to hide from possible exposure, she's doing a poor job in my eyes.

Aloy's family. I sigh. I have to remember he's not really related to them through blood.

I watch her, and whoever the man is, having a good time. He is at least 6'6". He carried himself as if he might have played basketball. He's much younger than her. I watch as a few people seem to know him, but he hurries folks away. I watch them as she is oblivious to me.

Eneta is sucking the liquor down. Something dark, mixed in with OJ. She stirs with her finger and then slides her finger between his lips. One hour later, I'm still watching. Now she has gulped four drinks, and another just came to their table. He, the *other* man, is drinking straight dark bourbon on the rocks.

She pays the bill and they head to the door. I say my goodbyes. I'm going to follow Eneta. I wait a minute, peek past the people coming in, and I don't see them at first. I walk out the door and catch them a half a block away as they get into her Benz. *What should I do? What can I do?* They're in her car kissing. I decide to run past with my bag on my shoulder. I get to the corner and taxis are there. A united nation of cabbies are standing by their cars. I get in the first one and state, as if I'm in a movie, "I need you to follow a car."

The man shrugs and says, "It's all money."

A moment later, Eneta passes and I tell the cabbie, "It's that car," and he pulls out.

"I won't get shot at or anything like that, will I?" my Hispanic driver asks.

"No, nada como eso, solo tener algo de espacio space."

"Okay, I'll keep space. That driver appears to be drunk."

"Well, that would be a good reason to keep some distance."

Ten minutes later, of all the hotels, they pull up to the downtown Hilton; but it makes sense that she booked me and the kids at the airport Hilton, and she's at the downtown Hilton. They get out and she hands the keys to the valet. I'm at the entrance of the driveway and pay my taxi. I'm thinking on the fly, *Do I need to know what room she is in?* Well, I don't want the kids to cross paths with her, so I come in a side door with my pass key, come down a hallway, and stand over by the conference rooms. I'm angled to see them, but she can't see me. From a distance, I try to watch what floor button gets pushed; 8. The kids and I are on 6. Eneta and the other man…they're almost humping while waiting for the elevator.

While they wait for the elevator, and Eneta has a tongue where her tonsils might be or were, I slip into the stairwell and run flights of stairs. I'm glad I wore flats with rubber soles. My lungs hurt a bit, but I pass the sixth floor. I can do the distance, no problem, but at the speed I'm running, I feel it. I actually see a cute Black guy walking down as I'm flying up. We smile at each other in passing.

"You're too much for me," I hear him say.

"Nah, I'm not; maybe I'll see ya later."

I get to the eighth floor hoping I saw the man hit 8. Looking in the hallway, the floor plan is a U shape of long hallways. *Did they get to the floor already?* The elevator opens, I see through the stairwell door I have cracked open…Eneta and the *other* man. They turn in the direction of the rooms by the stairwell. I let the door almost close. I hear an electronic key beep as they are laughing. I hear the *other* man say he's going to eat her pussy until she needs a new one. I hear her say, "Don't forget to put that hard dick in, too, but let me suck it first."

The door closes. I come into the hallway. *Why?* Then I think that there has to be cameras in the hallways. I should leave.

Back in my room, I'm glad I prepaid the babysitter. I was to be back by midnight and it's after one, so I tip her well with cash. The kids are asleep. I think of the world they have traveled from and I know there are bad spirits everywhere.

The train ride home, the kids read and slept. My eyes were wide open, but I didn't see rivers, valleys, backlands, and small towns. Eneta's transgression doesn't sink or float me. I needed a few days of calm and joy. I'm okay. I get a text from Eneta asking if I can keep the kids another day because the conference had asked her to stay for more relationship meetings.

My response, "Yeah, sure. Do you…I got you. Enjoy yourself."

I had put my mom's ring back on to give me some comfort after what had happened with Sans. I hadn't worn it in a while, but I wore it while on the train trip; and now, as I used to do, I'm spinning it in spiraling confusion.

Chapter 24

Two weeks have passed. I'm back to how I was living; working on the house, and going to the gym to run my boot camp training. The first week back, I had to put in place a way to protect myself 24/7. No way am I going to give Sans another shot at what he wanted to do, and that is, penetrate my spirit, which would be worse than my body.

Seattle is going through days of cold and wind. People hunker down and ignore each other. I have not seen Sans' beat up Benz next door in the mornings. I'm feeling good for that, and hoping Alanese Delroy is free from sexual blackmail. The other side of being free, she is still lonely and only has Aloy as her heart and soul. He has been over there more spending time with her.

He brought over the business papers I had asked for. He spent time with me at the house a few times, but leaves after an hour of us talking. I guess we both know to leave our friendship where it is. He did put me on the back of his motorcycle last Sunday midmorning; it was cool, and we rode along Lake Washington. I got a high with the two-wheel freedom. We stopped at Seward Park and walked the back-trail along the lake. Many others were walking, jogging, and biking. We didn't talk much. I asked him to drive us over to the Blue Water Grill for some oysters and fresh smoked salmon for brunch. He was hesitant. He said his finances were tight. He had a hard time with me wanting to treat him, but he gave in. He kept saying while we there that he had somewhere to go and he didn't want to be late.

When we got back to my place, I invited him in, but he left. Maybe he's upset that I paid for our meal. Hell, he is one of the reasons I could afford to pay. We said a short goodbye with a long hug though.

Alanese came over for coffee, and she told me that she knew that Sans had come on to me as she put it. I said, "Yeah, but I'm alright." We changed subjects and enjoyed an hour of coffee. She was going down to Pike Place Market to shop, and I offered to drop her off downtown. She only let me drop her off by the light rail station on Beacon Hill. Chevelle needed a ride, too; he was headed south to a friend's house. I dropped them both off at the light rail station.

I stop in at the Hop Nob Tavern and had a beer with a few regulars. Uncle Don wasn't there; the other bartender, Slick Rick, was holding it down by himself and struggling to keep up. When I asked, he said that Don would be back later. It's rare for my Uncle Don not to be working his bar on a football day. A few hours later at home, Chevelle had started work on the main floor bathroom. He was carrying out the sink.

"Chevelle, I need to get a hold of Iman and have her do some accounting; can I have her number?"

He called out her number and kept on moving. He seemed angry. I put a twenty on the table for him to go out later if he wanted. When he walked back to the bathroom, I told him about the money. It looks like his lip was cut.

"What's up with your lip?"

"I cut it while under the sink disconnecting the plumbing."

"Well, keep that clean. Stop now and put some Peroxide on it. I don't mean to sound like a parent, but you should be careful with infections around the face."

He didn't respond, but I see him over the kitchen sink with the Peroxide.

I call Iman right away to see if I can get her these files and have her expertise check and double check to see why the gym seems not to be making more money. Aloy could only get me the membership and attendance figures, building, maintenance, salaries, and the cost agreements such as towels, water, vending, and other related items. Iman answered right away, and I explained what I needed. She said to come right over. She sounded like she was more than happy to take a look.

I found her apartment complex pretty easily. It's rundown, lacking care, and needs maintenance. The parking area has trash all over the ground, and more so by the dumpster. The cars parked – many had been used up as far as appearance was concerned. Other cars were too high-end to be parked in the old, scarcely maintained apartment. Instead of investing in property, folks bought cars from jack-leg high interest loan car lots where no one is turned down (your job is your loan guarantee). I see the license plate frames of free advertisement of where people bought their rolling buckets. I'm sure a repo man came like the bills in the mail to collect Chryslers 300's, Chevy Camaro's, and used Audi's and BMW's; unfortunately, they won't get their oversized rims and tires back when their cars get repossessed.

The door to apartment 222 opened, and the same outside dilapidated look was inside Iman's apartment.

"Come on in, Zelda. I am glad that I can offer assistance after you helped find me a good running car at a great price. It starts and purrs perfect. Here…let me clear this table."

"I'm glad the car is working out for you," my eyes picked up what she should have. Her place was a mess. My eyes were watering from the wind blowing outside and I asked for some tissue. She pointed me to the bathroom. Foulness. Dirty toilet, dirty sink, and I dare not pull back the shower curtain as the floor ain't seen a mop or any cleaning products recently. The last insult, the toilet paper was on top of the roll dispenser. A lazy ten seconds out of her life topped my bathroom adventure with the title of tacky.

No one should have their privates near funky filth when washing themselves or relieving themselves. She had my papers spread out when I came back.

"Iman, I'll come back when you have a chance to go over the papers."

"No, no…stay. I can give you a baseline of what is going on in about forty minutes. You want something to eat or drink?"

"Do you have anything in a bottle?"

"There is beer in the fridge. The last time Chevelle was here, he brought some, but he doesn't drink much unless it's water, now days."

I went into the kitchen and I had hopes; but no luck. The kitchen…I don't think a spot was clean. I now understand what Chevelle is talking about. He wasn't raised like this. I stayed uncomfortable while she wrote, scanned, and did work on the computer. I saw a woman that was clean looking and dressed clean, but her abode was left in shambles, as if wild people lived there, and there are smells of I can't put a food label to.

"Zelda, my initial findings are, your gym is bringing in plenty of money to cover overhead and salaries and still make a profit. There is something going on with monies being siphoned off. Maybe there is a loan payment, or some type of agreement that someone is paying themselves first, and then covering business expenses. Whatever is going on, it is leaving the gym only able to keep its head above sinking into the lake."

I looked at Iman's pretty face and was not hearing her completely as I was stuck in her trash. "What? Can you repeat that?"

She did.

"Loans or something is taking money off of the top? Can you give me a better understanding?"

Outside of Iman's door, people were walking by. They stopped before they went down the stairs; they spoke loudly.

"Man, she's pimping a bunch of dudes for her rent. I just come here to get my rocks off and to watch her big screen. Dude, for real, you brought me to this female's house just to watch the game, and you and her got some freaky shit going on. What's that saying about you? Don't ask for me to come over in the ghetto doghouse again."

My phone, a text from Aloy said, *There is a problem, can you get back to my house soon?*

I wonder what that's about. I text back, *What's going on?*

175

He texted back, *How long will it be before you get back?*

About 15 – 20.

"I'm sorry Iman, I need to go; can you put all of what you found and write it up for the average person to understand?"

"Yes, I can, and I can go over it more thoroughly and get a more detailed idea of what is going on. I'll try to figure out the who, what, and where that other money is going."

"Great, Iman. I need to have a few words with you before I go, and I have to make it quick, so it may come out wrong. Please don't hold it against my heart-felt intensions."

Her head cocked to the side and I just let her have it. "You are a very beautiful woman and your housekeeping is not becoming of you. I know we all can have long days of too much to do, but what I see is a lifestyle that can, and will, hold you back." Her face was stone with shock and shame. "No man or woman wants to use your bathroom like it is. Worse yet, intimately, a man would think twice, and maybe not want a physical relationship with you knowing your bathtub, toilet, and face bowl, are not spic and span clean sanitized. Frankly, I wouldn't expect a man to put his mouth on any of my body parts after being in any of these rooms."

Her face almost reverted back to being a child waiting for a spanking to begin. "I advise you to hang clean towels nicely and have a guest towel. Wash your walls down regularly. I, as a woman, will not let any part of my womanhood be near anything in your bathroom. Getting out of the shower, and stepping on a floor that is not clean, is almost a waste of showering. How long does it take to put toilet paper on the roll dispenser? And oh, by the way, it should roll off the front. Why? If rolled off the back, your fingers can touch the wall, and how many people will be touching that wall after wiping their privates? Just visualize for a moment. I watched on YouTube tests that were done, and fecal matter and urine were on the walls of toilet dispensers where the paper rolled off on the wall side.

"Now, for your house, a kitchen is where you make your food; enough said. Dirty plates and pots grow mold and smell. The rest of your house...well, I see you come by to see him— Chevelle, but does he come over here? He is a very clean young man, and if he wasn't, he wouldn't be in my house. If another man came into your life, he will not stay with you long if he thinks about how you are living; unless he has the same issues of not caring.

"I know you're young and was raised by a single dad, and maybe things were not required or taught. Well, just like I was able to help you with a car, please accept my directness as an offering for you and others, as it is being given in your best interest."

I didn't wait for a response. I let it soak in her shocked soul. If any good judgment was in her, she wouldn't come back at me with an, *I'll do, and live, like I want to* attitude.

She nodded and responded, "I'll have your accounting done by Sunday night."

With her head down, faking as if she was looking at the paperwork, I left. I walked to my Cadillac that took up two parking spaces. Young dudes standing nearby were on the prowl. They knew by how I exposed an attitude toward them, it was not the day to try me.

Chapter 25

I'm pulling in the back of my house, and Aloy runs over from his aunt and uncle's house. I see a lot of people over at their house. I see someone I had not seen in a while – Sadducy - Duce, my punk ass other neighbor.

Aloy opens my door and stares.

"What?"

Aloy stares. I know words are coming. "Sans is dead."

"Dead?" Aloy stared at me too long. "How?"

I see Alanese pacing her driveway with tissues in hand. Chevelle comes out the back door and is walking toward me. He and Aloy stare at each other. I see Pastor Shomer holding his wife tenderly on the back porch as she appears to be crying.

"Sans was found tied and beaten in his garage by a neighbor who has the code to open the garage. He came over to borrow tools."

Chevelle moved back. I'm standing now. I'm thinking, *I'm sorry, if Aloy is hurting over this man. I'm not the one to aid and comfort him.* Aloy doesn't appear distraught. He's seen death. He's taken the life of a man, even if it was that of the man who tried to kill him.

"The police say he was beaten for a while by more than one person, or by a very powerful person."

"Take me over to Alanese."

We start to walk over and Chevelle goes back in the house. He hardly knew or had spoken much to Sans.

"Wait," I grab Aloy's forearm. It is rock hard with tension. "Let me run in the house real quick."

He glares at me...I think. I turn and run up the stairs. I trot all the way to my room. I unload my gun from my waistband. The same one I gave a glimpse to the thug boys at Iman's apartment complex when they were near my car. It's the new gun; a .22. I bought it because it's easier to conceal than the .38 I had. I bought it just in case I ran into Sans again.

I meet Aloy in my driveway, and we walk over to Alanese. I know her emotions were like she was losing and winning. A convolution only a victim and abuser relationship can understand; along the lines of how a kidnap victim has twisted sensitivities for their kidnapper.

As I get to her, I see a face fraught and wrought. Her eyes are broken scorched pieces of glass, and cracking more. My hard ass feeling about Sans fell to the ground, as well as my own tears, as I grabbed her and held her. She feels as if she is fainting, going limp in my arms. Alanese and I had grown somewhat close through her pain, confusion, and her loneliness. I had been a stranger that walked into her life, and a catcher of her agony as she is wilting in my arms.

"Did he ask for this?" Alanese whined each word in my ear.

I didn't respond, I just held her. Where was her husband? I didn't see him. I do see Sadducy standing next to a woman I didn't know, but she seems awfully upset. I sway my head in her direction for Aloy to see. The woman started walking our way.

"Hi Auntie Trice," Aloy said to her. She rubbed her hand along his back and then patted his cheek. She left her palm there for a moment.

Alanese lifts her head off my shoulder, and the two women connected eye-to-eye. Alanese slips away from my arms, and the two women embraced tightly. I moved back a step, and Aloy places his hand on my shoulder to kind of lead me away. Rain drops started pecking my face. Aloy and I walk past Sadducy who was now talking to someone else. We walk to the front yard where other people were gathered. Many of the people I had met at the cookouts.

I didn't know what to say. I put my hand on his bicep. The tension was cement, but he seemed to absorb my touch. I looked through the bay window and inside the house, and I now see Sargon and Eneta; she is leaning on Sargon's shoulder, not her husband's. I wonder should I go to the kids. I wonder how this might affect them.

"Aloy, do I go in and pay my respects?"

"No, no worries there. I'm glad you're here for Alanese...and...me."

"Aloy, I want to go home. Could you go check with Eneta whether I should go and be with the kids? Come over and tell me if the need is there, or come over later. I would like some more details as to what has happened when you're ready."

"Don't matter...he hurt too many people. That is Auntie Trice over there, the one who left Sans after he beat on her for years. He, like my grandfather who did that to my grandmother... Sans would have rough sex with Aunt Trice and then beat her. Aunt Alanese and I helped her get away, and we kept to ourselves. Only Auntie Eneta and Shomer have known. Sans and my Uncle Sargon were too close, so they were kept out of the loop. I will be over in a while."

"I'm so sorry for you and your family, and the others he caused pain and sorrow to. He was not a feather in the desert blowing and landing softly wherever he went. He was the cactus whose thorns impelled poison whenever women came close enough." Aloy nodded, and I felt bad for the truth I delivered, but no man should get a pass for hurting women.

I hate when I read or hear in the news of men we think of as great because of how they represent some high-profile persona, but then we find out about crimes many want to ignore. However, peeing on an underage girl, or drugging or beating a woman, is a crime, and needs justice applied to the lowest offender as well as the highest. Nevertheless, parts of society give these men a pass because of who they are perceived to be. God wants men to protect their mothers, daughters, and sisters. Period!

Damn this Seattle rain pouring on miserable circumstances. I tell Chevelle when I came in, "The horror of how people die freaks people out. Murder, cancer, old age, a car accident...they all weigh differently, when in the end, someone is no longer here, but the dirt on the grave weighs the same."

I fixed some dinner for Chevelle and I, but make enough in case Aloy comes over. I know he needs to eat with so much happening. For most of the dinner, Chevelle is quiet. Then he looks at me with anger or fear; they both fly in the same wind.

"Zelda, he hurt you; didn't he?"

"Who?"

"That man that is dead."

"Why do you ask? Just what makes you think such a thing?"

"He hurt you," he makes a clear-cut statement.

"I'm not good with talking about anything like that."

"I hate any man who would do that."

"Chevelle, do you think they need to die?"

"Men like him can bring so much sadness and damage. I'm an unwanted living legacy spewed from a man's loins."

I'm hearing Chevelle's slow drip of blood from a wound. I hear the splash of each drop of an old wound in Chevelle, but it's still fresh for him, it's what his birth father did to his mother, and then what she did in giving up on raising him.

"Stop, just stop," I raised my voice, wanting him to stop, and for me to stop. His eyes widened, and I lowered my voice to just above a whisper. "You are a wonderful person, and if you know anything about me, I don't send up BS smoke signals to appease my pain, and you shouldn't either. Leave and live a new legacy here with me, and in this house as you have been.

181

"When you talk like you are, you are telling yourself you don't believe in yourself. If you don't believe in you, you'll let someone walk all over you. You'll be blind to it all until after you realize you lost what you can't get back very easily, if ever. You'll let someone steal your river of life. Don't let your self-esteem float away. God expects better of you, even when others don't. Don't give your power away to what others did to you. They will wake up one day, or not, and they may die without ever knowing how bad their judgment and deed was, but God will handle it on His end. But you...you have to live for another day in believing in yourself."

I wondered why he thought something happened between Sans and me. With all the high emotions thundering right now, I still chose to talk to him about Iman and the conversation I had with her.

"I went to your girlfriend's place today. She's good with her accounting skills." I felt myself getting tight in the throat. I took a long gulp of the hot water in my coffee cup. I got up and sliced a lemon and started to heat some more hot water. "I think I understand how you're feeling concerning being over at Iman's place. I saw her place and I got it."

"Yep, now you know."

"I spoke to her about housekeeping. Not from what might be your standpoint, but as a woman to another woman. I believe she heard me." I watched Chevelle close his eyes as if he was seeing something; maybe seeing her place and wondering if it could it be any different. "I want you to think about how you can support her. You can't put her down in any way. Maybe she's insecure about a number of things. You can properly assume her father did not praise her a whole lot. She's a pretty young lady with a full figure, and sometimes people act pretty ugly toward a woman for any number of reasons, and body shaming is one of the top ones. Maybe her father did that, and it might reflect on other parts of her life. Some people climb up and their pride in themselves shines, despite the opinions of others; and some people become depressed and act certain ways; ways that aren't as positive or productive. You love her, Chevelle. I believe that. You have told me as much. And if that is the case, then show her as her man that you've got her back as she climbs from whatever depths she's been in.

"You can't come across as another man telling her what to do as her dad has done all her life. She may have problems with how people see her, and instead of doing something positive, she is doing the opposite. Go over there and ask her if you can you help her, or say to her, 'Let me do this for you.' Clean her bathroom from top to bottom and encourage her to work on the kitchen as you clean the bathroom. Buy some rugs, some new towels, and a new matching shower curtain. Then you two can maybe cook a meal together and clean. Then take time to help her do other rooms. She might be overwhelmed with thinking about all that needs to be done, so help her, and then see if she can maintain it on her own. Watch carefully afterward; she has to want to be that woman, but help her get started. She may not know what super clean and organized is. Pull together your money, and go on Groupon and get a 5 star hotel for a weekend. You know her father never treated her to anything nice. You be the man to show her." I went upstairs and brought back $200 dollars. "Give me your hand." He looked at me funny, but extended his hand, and I slipped the folded money into his palm.

He smiled, and nodded. I went into the living room and sat looking out my bay window. People had left from next door, and just a few cars were parked. I had purchased an iPad from a pawn store. I went on the Internet and searched local news. There it is. Man found beat to death in his garage, two blocks from the Beacon Hill light rail station. My first thought as I stared out into darkness and the wetness is, who, followed by what was their reason. Over the top of that, is the thought of all the people I know today that were near the Beacon Hill light rail station — two blocks from Sans Delroy's house — Chevelle, Alanese, my Uncle Don, and me. Not to mention, where was Aloy? He had to run out of here earlier after our motorcycle ride.

183

Chapter 26

10:00 PM, I'm in the bed listening to the radio, and dreaming; without sleeping. I hear Aloy's Harley. I get up and open the door to wait for him to come. He is standing on my porch. He never came back earlier, so I guess the kids were taken care of. He's wearing different clothes than earlier. Leather, and more leather. He looks at me strangely. I'm in a tank top that looks more like a pencil dress given how it fits me. It goes down in length to my thighs, and hugs my body. I just don't have time for the modest thing.

I take his hand and lead him upstairs. We can talk in my room. He sits on the floor next to my mattress. I lay back down. "You ride your motorcycle 24/7 no matter what the weather?"

"Yeah."

"I've never been to your place. Why?"

"My place is above the gym, and you have never noticed."

"Oh."

"Zelda…"

"No, Aloy, I did not kill your uncle, if that is on your mind."

I knew you didn't."

How?"

"You would have killed at the time he tried to hurt you in the garage. I would not have been able to stop you."

"Then what was your question?" Why was I being defensive?

"Can I lay next to you tonight?"

"Go back down and push your motorcycle in the back. And lock the door when you come back in."

I'm lying on my side when he slides in behind me. His arm pulled me tight. I still feel the tension in his arms. I feel his heart beat on my back. Slow, but a strong pulse sends shock waves. It feels like it is pounding through me. I place my feet on his. I feel his warm breath stroking my neck. Now, my heart is pounding. In a short time, his breathing has a light snore; it's so calming. I'm drifting off; feeling safe, and feeling like I'm allowing him to be safe from a world that destroys.

*****

Wakening and not sure what time it is because the sky was still dark, I see a plane's light cutting through the sky. I feel him and I turn my head his way. I see Aloy's lips. I'm on my back, and his face is even with my nipple. My tank top had slipped away. His warm breath is brush stroking my breasts and centered on my nipple that is now gum drop firm, and slightly aching. My room is hot. Or is it the perfect body next to me turning my internals up?

His deep breath flowing across my nipple is making me squeeze my thighs tightly. His leg is over mine. His arm is over my navel. I close my eyes and wish his hand would slip down and pull on my tank top and play with me. I want him to play in my wetness and stir me into craziness. I want his huge hands to spread my thighs and deliver his tongue and baptize it in my well of sweetness. Damn his warm breath is like nibbling on my nipples. I want his thick lips to suck me. Kiss me. I want to feel and see him naked, standing over me, drippin` clear like wine from his hardness and fire raging to be in me. I want him to land in me and go to the end of me. Why is it so hot in here? His kisses have a feel unlike any other. I want wet kisses down my spine. I want to lift my ass high and feel him going in me, inch by inch. I want his legs pushing, and I hearing him going in and out of me. I want his strong hands turning me, and making love to me from the front, the side, and then from the back. Then I want him to turn me again to touch all my senses.

I see me. I'm standing over his muscled darkness. He is still drippin' down from his shaft the thick clearness of life. I slowly squat over him and downward grind at the angle that makes me cum. Our eyes lock as I've recovered from my orgasm, and I start going up and down on his hardness. Our mouths are open with heavy breathing and strong lungs talking to each other.

I see him between my legs. I place my feet on his chest and my toes stroke his pecks. He uses my legs to hold him from going too deep inside me and he is going in me about two inches deep. Over and over. My G-spot is on fire, and the head of his dick throbs with pleasure. His down stroke is so intense inside me. He changes up and grinds in a circle. He has a smiling sneer like he knows I like it. He starts working up to going hard with long strokes, and then back to his hips circling. He's controlling me. Just the way I like. He spreads my legs wide and back; leaning over to kiss me. His tongue goes deep in my mouth. I feel his hardness pounding me while his tongue is probing my mouth.

I engage his length. It hurts, and I want more. He lifts his chest off me and I admire his body. I lift my legs, spreading wide and extending my hands to grab my feet. Damn! He takes one and sucks and licks between my toes. His dick is stroking in me as if he is dancing inside my fire. He hears me scream, but it's not about pain. I can't help myself from saying nasty things. I have no control. I don't want any control.

I open my eyes from what I want to see, and feel my early morning fantasy dream super wet between my thighs. It is the crack of dawn. Coming in my window, a plane's lights are flashing. I don't look over at his peaceful face; I keep on feeling his breath caressing my nipple. I smell my scent. I slide one leg away. I'm sticky. I lie there and watch the break of dawn, the parting of the sky, wanting him to part me.

"Are you okay?" his voice penetrated. I jerk, not knowing if he had his eyes on me for a while. I've been biting my lip.

"Yes," I say, trying to be seductive.

"Zelda, at times tonight I watched you sleep, and my eyes have been open for a while. Your face has been going through many expressions. It's nice how you curl your lip up and your nose flairs and your cheeks expand. You've had a smile for a while."

"I want to know do we have morning breath."

"What, huh?"

"You heard me. Kiss me, Aloy. I need to be kissed and you need to be kissed."

He didn't hesitate. He straddled me, lowering his chest close to my breasts. His lips brush lightly over mine. Our noses kiss for a while as our lips crack encryptions and write our code. Our lips part at the same time. We didn't play shy; we tongue each other with no limitation. He's cupping my face and I suck on his tongue. My hands roam his back and reach past his waistband. I squeeze. We groan into each other. He is over me, keeping his pelvis from touching me. I push on his hard ass. I can't help myself, and I try to lift mine to meet his. His strong legs keep me in place, keeping me in-check.

We're having coffee twenty minutes later. If either one of us had morning breath it sure didn't matter. He's on his phone getting coverage at the gym for both of us. I know he has family business to tend to, and I needed the day off with all that is going on. It's well past time for a visit to see my step-dad. I'm going to take him for a ride. I need to talk to him even though I know he won't identify with much of what I have to say. Still, I want to talk to him.

I pour more coffee in Aloy's cup and sit down and look at him as he hangs up. "We okay after I've held your lips hostage?"

His eyes smile, and we smile. "Zelda, that is not what I came over for, but I've needed to be touched. I'm not good with us doing much more though. I'm just not there yet."

"Okay. I won't push, and I won't let it change our friendship."

I felt a sting, he said he's needed to be touched, but I was not mentioned in that need it seemed, it was just the intimacy he needed. I'm trying to keep a smile on my face. He prepares to leave and puts on all his leathers. I watch. I open the door for him and we embrace. He kisses my forehead and leaves.

Before he left, we talked about the questions the police asked the family. The family sat down last night and talked and prayed. He admitted the family felt a certain way about Sans and his well-known behavior, and wondered had his own need to freak cost him his life. Aloy said Sargon would have no part of the conversation, and was pissed that Sans' ex-wife was there, but Pastor Shomer said she needed to be with the family, too. I'll call officer CC to see if she knows anything.

*****

I had a good time with my step-dad, Eddie. I drove him to Tacoma to a soul food restaurant. I told him a man tried to harm me and that now he's not here anymore. His blank stare didn't bother me. I know somewhere down inside him, I have to believe he hears me, and he is always concerned.

Tonight, I'm going to have a quiet night with a glass of wine and a long hot bath to help relieve the tension of Aloy kissing me. I'll have to put the shower jet to work. I've been wet all day. Aching. I'm still feeling his lips. I still taste his morning breath; it was sweet.

Chapter 27

It's Friday night, a week after the demise of Sans. I had the kids and we were traveling to Ocean Shores. That's the place where Eneta was supposed to be instead of being in Portland with her lover when I saw her. The funeral is tomorrow, and I was asked by Pastor Shomer and Eneta to take the kids away from all the doom and gloom. They didn't believe it would be healthy for them to be near people who were upset. The kids can go into shut down mode. They are playful at times, but other times they're almost robotic and their batteries are low. I can't fathom what they have been through. Oceania has a sad demeanor in general, and I know the poor girl has lived in a hell. You don't one day turn that off and be the joy of the world. I'm glad I have them with me.

Back to my routine and, as if nothing has happened a month later, the weather is changing in Seattle. Days are a bit longer and the sun has graced us for a few days. I'm sitting down with Aloy and showing him the results of looking into the accounting records of the gym. I have to give praise to Iman, she was so complete in how she arranged the results so that it was clear what is going on with the gym money.

Dells LTD is a company that has a large loan debt holding over the gym. So, a loan payment is paid to them before all other money is allocated to other debts and salaries. The loan using the gym as collateral is leaving Aloy on the short end, and limiting gym growth. The loan goes back to when the gym first opened, which is strange since it's still in place twenty years later. Who is this company? I went to Seattle legal records and found that Sargon Delroy, and the now dead Sans Delroy, own Dells LTD.

I went to the Hob Nob last week and met with a man my Uncle Don knew and asked about the Seattle underground history from back when Aloy was on his way to the Olympics and was shot. Aloy told me people, most likely some form of organized crime, wanted him to sign a pro contract before the Olympics, and he would not. He thought Sadducy's dad was behind the ambush when Aloy took a bullet in the brain.

My uncle's friend, Mr. Magoo, was able to give some deeper knowledge. He used to own several night clubs over the decades and ran a numbers racket back in the day. He, as they say, *knew where the dead bodies were buried.* Aloy never knew the complete sources of his troubles; like Sadducy's father going along with two of Aloy's uncles who had pre-signed a deal with some longtime Seattle gangsters. Aloy, all this time, thought it was just Sadducy's father who had connections to the people responsible for his ambush. They all tried to get Aloy to sign what would look like a legitimate deal, post dated for after the Olympics. Aloy told me he'd be thrown out of the Olympics, or have his medal revoked, if he won and it came to light that he had turned pro early. Word is Sadducy's father alone put in play the thug boys to scare Aloy.

Maybe his uncles didn't know about that part, but they knew they owed the mob and that the mob never lets you forget. So, after Aloy got well from the bullet in his head, the mob fronted the money to the brothers and Sadducy's father to open the gym, and used Aloy as a pawn to get people to come in. It was a way to have a constant source for the money the brothers owed. It appears the gangsters set up the brothers' LTD as a shield, and they would take the fall if anything happened. The loan will never be paid off, it looks like.

Mr. Magoo resembles the cartoon character Mr. Magoo. His real name is not given to me. He was, or is, real gangster in his own right, even at his age. His words, "The money the gym brought in was chump change compared to the unions that got pimped. I doubt anyone is collecting that money. The Delroy brothers are living off that money most likely. You know the people who were getting paid all these years are dead, and the Seattle gangster scene has changed and is handled by no-business sense kids. If there is someone collecting, they can be got rather easy. Your Uncle Don over there, I owe him for a few favors. Back in the day, he took care of some people for me when they didn't act right, so if I can help you, let me know. No charge."

Mr. Magoo let me know that Sargon Delroy runs a gambling house. I thought he worked all this time and he doesn't. I never gave any thought to anything about Sans and where he worked.

"Sir, would you mind just finding who is still in play or not. If you can trace where the money is going, that would be the favor you can pay my uncle back for.

A week later, I'm eyeing Aloy, and he has an intense glare on his face. It's after hours on Sunday night; the gym closes at 8:00 PM. It's the only day it closes. He and I are over by the ring at a table. I presented all I had obtained.

"I'm tired from everything. It feels like a mountain that keeps getting bigger the higher I climb," Aloy sounds like he's almost ready to collapse down a mountain. Maybe I told him too much.

I pull some food out from a paper bag. "I have fry bread and tuna sandwiches. I'm sharing if you want. I brought enough for two."

He nods.

I'm here on most Sunday evenings to help clean. JoBelle left earlier after cleaning her area. Everyone kicks in added cost savings when the gym should really have a custodian. I like the quiet after everyone leaves, and I turn the music up and shadow-box in the ring. A few times, Aloy and I shadow box at each other. He has taught me how to anticipate and slip a blindside right hand, like the one his deceased uncle hit me with.

"I don't want to talk about all this. I want to run a gym; that's all," his eyes are sad as he looks down on the accounting and after hearing my investigation. "I'm broke. I get it, but there is enough to keep the gym going; right? I can keep doing the outside things I do though for money.

"I don't need much. I have my room upstairs. I have my Harley. I have enough clothes. I have friends like you. I'm fine. I don't want to mess anything up. What about if these criminals are still holding a contract over my last two uncles? My uncles…it sounds like they are far from righteous men, but…"

I think about his dead uncle.

192

"Look, you need something good to happen. You need a break. Let's get away for the weekend. I've had a few chances to get away with the kids, and it really helps; but two adults will make it better. Hold up. I'll be right back."

I trot over to my office and pull out my temperament changers from my desk; a couple of candles and some incense. I use them in my office to relax. I come back and light up. Then I go over and hit the light switch. No need to look at the paperwork anymore right now.

He chuckles when I sit down across from him in the candlelight.

"One of the parents of a kid I train, gave me a pair of tickets to a NBA game in Portland. We could catch the train. We could spend some time together," I put a little sexy in my voice and pursed my lips and bat my eyes being silly.

He has a look of he's not interested, or at least that is what I read in his face. I guess he didn't want to go. I guess going out of town with me is too much or...I don't know. My eyes focus center below his eyes. I'm trying to avoid the mirror of seeing myself in his eyes under the candlelight. His lips part. I anticipate it will take him a long time to tell me a convenient justification.

"Zelda, you always looked at me when I talk, so please look at me now. People avoid looking at me when I talk, and you never do...don't start now."

At this moment, I'm breathing deeply. I had made a move on this man, letting him know I wanted more from him than just a friendship. I felt nervous, but excited that I had stepped up and not waited for him to make a move. Now it feels like I should have sat my butt down and just chilled, and never put a fire to a candle, much less to my spoken desires.

"Aloy, I want to go away with you for a day, a night, and spend the next day with you. You don't have to sleep with me. Spend more than twenty-four hours with me, and I believe it will be nice. I have to believe.

"For months, we have seen each other almost every day as friends. We have been in the same space for hours. We shared coffee. I'm sharing my tuna fish sandwiches with you by candlelight, and you smiled, recognizing I'm being funny. But now, I ask you to go away with me."

He has an intense expression that I can't read, and I wonder, is my fantasizing and wanting too much. I put myself out there.

"Zelda, I can't afford the gym to be closed. I would go with you if it were different. You just showed me the money problems, I don't want to add to it. This gym keeps my soul afloat after what has happened. This place gives kids a place they can go to be safe, and the rest of the community, young and old, come here every day. We have had a few days we had to rearrange what goes on around here because of what happened. I'm not a cheap guy who doesn't want to go and have a good time with you, but…"

He told me the truth, and it sounded like he had no shame, but a sense of duty. He sounded proud of what he did and why.

"I don't think of you as cheap because you say you can't go. I can respect that, and it would never be a problem for me with you being honest. A cheap guy either doesn't want a woman to have a good time, or doesn't care that she has something special or does something special for her. A man with less who is working hard and being creative and giving in other ways, he is making a way for something special in his life and for those around him. I'm proud of you and all you stand for. I'll never turn my back on you over money."

The candlelight flickered and outlined his lips like two Indian summer half-moons. Wet like morning dew, they parted, and the universe was between. His tongue moved unhurriedly across from cheek to cheek like a falling star across the dark sky. I wanted him to stand up and lean over the table and kiss me. His teeth floated down onto his bottom half moon lip and he pulled it in, and he slowly, so slowly, released his bottom lip to meet up with his upper lip.

As if I summoned him, he stands up. He's coming around the table. I put my sandwich down. I stand and meet his arrival. He's moving inches closer. My skin feels like it's in a toaster and I need to pop-up; now. He's placing his hot lips onto my nervous smile. Shocks and eruptions; I feel electrifying. I place the back of my finger against his smooth cheek, feeling it rise. Our lips rest on each other's, and we inhale each other and let our noses have fun. Sweeping my finger gently down his handsome face, the softness of his lips is making me tingle below. Although he had just finished working out, his scent is rich in sweet manliness; it's a divine aroma. The slight moisture on my finger has me wanting to suck my own finger thinking I want to suck on him.

With my eyes closed, I want to experience his lips on my neck. He pulls back. "If we leave 3:00 PM on Saturday, will the train be able to get us there in time?" he asks.

"Yeah, yes…the game is at 8:00 PM, we can make it in time; and even if we are late, so what? And I can pack fry bread and tuna sandwiches in brown paper bags."

He is laughing. "Zelda, can the train have us back Sunday by 10:00 AM so I can open by noon?"

I happily nod. "Yes, I'll make sure we get back.

Chapter 28

JoBelle dropped us off at the train station, and from the time we got on the train, we knew how to be with each other instantly. The beautiful scenery outside couldn't compare to us. He is very affectionate, and I have no problem giving my version of being inside his warmth, and giving it right back. We're holding hands in silence as we view the world going by. Wish it never has to end. We're sharing my iPad and watching an old clip of Muhammad Ali and The Jackson Five on YouTube from one of The Jackson Five's variety shows.

He and I are kissing non-stop. I'm feeling high. He needs this. I need this. We put away the iPad and I pull out my Alexandré Cornet book, Quotes and Thoughts from a Poet. It makes my heart race when he says, "Yeah, and hmmm' as I turn pages. The feeling is, as if he was kissing me. I find it so sexy to know the man next to me is reading with me. We read several emotional erotic poems,

I'd walk in the shadows of the moons of every planet of the black hole to be in the glow of
the sun rays you cast on my soul
I'd walk naked in the hot sands of the hottest deserts to come be in your radiance
that is scorching and soothing to my soul
I'd be wrong to just feel your rightness
I'd be silent to hear you sigh or scream
I'd be blind in hope you can see the real me who loves
you in the dark or light
I'd cry to see you smile I'd take my last breath to know
you will breathe over me
I'd wait in one place never moving an inch for 1000 sunsets just to feel your kisses from
your soft cool lips
I'd die in the frozen waste land only to be thawed out and brought back to
life by the sunshine of your love...my soul wants to die with you in the cool
deep sea...but even then I'd feel

your radiance

Let Me Stand Next To Your Fire
fire images
You and I
Lightning and thunder
Crashing from the sky
Rising from the earth's core
Heat
Like the sun
Burn
Never burning up
Burning down
Like the planet Mercury
Too close to the sun, no one can live there
However, we make love there
Only you and I
I in you
As I come close to your core
Liquid boil
Organic orgasms
As I reach your core
Tails on fire
Friction
Feet walking on fire
Toes wrap around a burning ember log
Eyebrows noses, lips moisten in virginal oil
Leads to a beautiful burn
Black brown gold flames
Scent of exhausting sweat
Pulls us in to feed from the burnt forest floor
Erotic fires, visions that cannot be described
Scorching pleasures
Aches deep within the Inferno
Fanning in pleasures
Stoking, and stroking up flames A fire dance, the chief dances in the wild

village maiden's volcano
No controls
We scream we shout, we curse, it all says, I want to take
you higher
Up in emotional methane, we rise and float
Highly volatile, we explode
Emit hot but cooling affecting rain
Smoke, we smolder
I clean away un-burnt fuel
You spread to make room, for more fire images

It was the last thing we read together as I closed my eyes and floated along with train bumps and grinds until we arrived.

We are booked into the downtown Hilton. I love that Groupon thing; paying $55 instead of $150 dollars is making this date happen. We make it in time to eat a quick dinner before the game. He has on dark chocolate jeans with an olive green knit shirt with a long, bolder, darker brown stripe, and he's wearing it all well. He is what I might be scared of usually because he is so beautiful. He is so much man. I see women looking at him and I love it. The man opens doors and pulled out my seat. He's holding my hand; sometimes his hand is in the middle of my back guiding me. I have never been treated like a woman. I feel protected, I feel honored.

We watch Portland beat the Clippers. We go get a beer afterward and we're walking around. We are heading to the hotel. I'm anxious. We check in and now standing in our room, I start acting silly. I circle around him, punching him in the ass and in his rock-hard tummy. I stop. We stare. Nervous maybe? He? Me? We move around each other weirdly.

"Aloy, I'm going to get in the shower."

"Don't wash away…I like what I see."

"Hmm, really? Are you saying you like my tomboy ass? You like what you see; is that what you're really saying?"

"Always have liked."

"Really?"

"You normally have more words than that."

"I'll wash what needs to be cleaned, and let you put back the seasoning."

Closing the door behind me, I want him in the shower with me. Instead of the showerhead kissing me, I want his hands raining down on my breasts and sliding his finger in and out of my river. I want his body to lay me down, and for him to touch me from my hair down to my feet. Then I want his sweet tongue to taste, lick, and indulge in all I have, and I will do the same to him all over. I'm so ready to have him inside me. So damn ready. He doesn't have to be sweet about it, although I think he will at first; but then I need him to go rounds of pounding my ass. Let me get out of this shower.

We brush by each other as I come out and he goes in. Before he closes the door, I feel his lips on my collarbone. I'm ready to drop my towel and turn and jump him, but he closes the door. I stand in this nice hotel room staring at city lights filtering through sheer curtains. I would let the world see what I'm about feel. Never in my life have I had a man as a friend, and now he's about to become my lover. Oh-oh, I said lover. Could he love...me? Could we both...needing to be loved and know love...could we fall in love?

I stand next to the bed as I hear the shower cut off. I feel pleasure from him saying that he liked what he saw. Is that inside and out? I throw the towel off and lie down on the bed and love this moment before he comes out. I jump up and pull out some candles from my overnight bag and light them. I'm wondering if they will set off the smoke alarm. I crack open a window. With the candles on each side of the bed, I can see. I want to watch as he does me and I open myself up to him to do anything he wants.

The bathroom door opens; the light overshadows the candles. He appears. His silhouette looms. Naked brown perfection is walking my way. He is standing at the foot of the bed. He is using his forefinger to summon me to come to him. I sit up and move on fours crawling to him, deliberately taking my time. I place my head against him and circle my face and my hair over his navel. I sniff his skin.

My head keeps moving. I'm kissing his sides and now I'm moving up instead of down. I'll get there in time. I place my hands on his shoulder and I'm pulling my face up to his lips. He kisses my forehead, my nose, and we lip lock. The intensity has my legs jerking as our tongues have lost all patience. We kiss hard. Our hands roam. We are directing each other; I like that. He reached behind me and slapped my ass hard. My openings down there all tighten, and I squirm.

"Lie back down and let me see you," he directs." I do what I'm told.

"Stand there for a while for me, and I'll let you see something alright."

He smiles at my request. He keeps standing there looking as if he controls the world; and right now, yes…he does. I pull a couple of pillows and prop them up behind my head. I stare and admire him. My eyes can't help but look at his dick. It's pretty as it is so thick and plenty long resting against his muscled thigh. I think its drippin'. His thigh is wet with something in slow motion. I part my legs. I pull my feet back raising my knees. My toes stir and dig into the bed. I can't help it. I look at him with my tongue licking my lips. Teasing. He fists his dick and holds it. I put my finger in my mouth and suck on it, pulling it out slowly, and insert it into my pussy. My river is making the bed wet already. I slide my other hand under my ass and bring a finger from underneath.

Two for one, I slip my finger in and out of my pussy and my other finger circles my clit. I keep my eyes on my motivation. His eyes seem to grow wider while watching me play with myself. I let my two fingertips kiss; one from under my ass, and the other middle finger now. I'm inserting them in my pussy, spreading…getting ready for him. It's been a long while, so seeing his thickness I know it will feel tight; he'll be stretching me, filling me. I've been on empty way too long.

Aloy is coming to me. He puts his hands on the bed and lowers his face. Oh-oh, he is licking my toes. Oh-oh, all between each one. Now the

200

bottom of my feet, he is licking from heel to big toe. Now the other foot. He likes my feet. I'm grinding on my fingers as his lips move up my legs. He switches from one to the other. I spread wide when his nose pushes in my pussy. He is sipping and sniffing my scent and tasting as if he's trying to get drunk on me. I feel his face get wet now as his tongue licks my pussy.

Feelin' it, he muff-dives, and he yodels to the bottom of the ocean, making underwater sounds. His tongue is deep in my pussy, he slowly drags his tongue out and up to my clit. Damn it! I lost control and just squirted a bit. My head jerks as I feel a thrilling force of cumin'. I try to force a thought out my mind, he's way too experienced at what he is doing, but maybe he's a natural.

Tickling the edges of my short pubic hairs, he is moving his tongue around as if I he is swirling in sweet cream. I cum again, and still feel quakes as he licks my naval as if he knew he had to give me a break. I turn over and let him see my ass jerking, wanting to encourage his dick to command himself inside me. I want to hear his wild animal grunts and sounds. I'm ready to hear him get off. I want him riding me hard. I want him inside me. I want his sweat dripping down my spine and through the crease of my ass. The need has me feeling light headed – craving. I'm so ready for hot, sweaty, nasty sex.

He lies on his side and pulls me to be onto my side. Okay, I like it like that, too. But he throws his arm over me as if we already had a long session and we are done. He curls me into him. We spoon.

*****

It's been hours, I hear him lightly snoring. He never went inside me. He just held me and now he's out cold on his stomach. I'm staring at his muscled ass. I don't know what to make out of no intercourse, no penetration, no humpin', no different positions, no riding his hardness. Maybe he's holding back for another time and only wanted to go so far. I'm confused and trying not to feel slighted or selfish. But what he did do, I needed, and he is good.

The crack of dawn is just 100 more snoring exhales from him. We have to check out early to meet the train to be back in time. I'm lying here consumed with, *Did I do too much,* or *wasn't it enough? I'm not pretty enough, I'm too much of a tomboy to him...is that the problem? I did something wrong, or I don't turn him on? What's wrong with him*?

I'm tempted to start kissing his body and lick his lips, licking my pussy juice off of his lips. I was thinking maybe I should go down on him; suck his pretty dick, and then he might give me some before we leave. I have more questions than he has inhales left before I have to wake him. And then what? *Do I ask? Do I act like everything is cool?*

Chapter 29

On the train, I act like everything is cool. We are back to being lovers without having done the last part of loving physically. I am sitting next to him staring out the window. Again, I'm turning this ring around my finger like a like a merry-go-round going around without an operator to turn it off. Can a merry-go-round go in the wrong direction?

As we roll down these train tracks, we see Mount St. Helen; an active volcano which lost its top three decades ago. Like people, we go through life knowing life can blow up; it's a matter of time.

I sit quiet toward the end of the trip. I know holding onto feelings and questions is wrong. No good can come from it; never. I look at him when he's not looking at me. He is so peaceful. I flashback to when he stopped me from killing his uncle, and how he calls my name, controlling me. Even now, how he calls my name, I melt. This is from the man whose speech is troubled.

The train picks up speed, my mind races. I know he's like Superman, flying past this train with all my attention focused on him, but he can't stop my growing feelings for him. I realize I'm unrestrained. I'm feeling consumed by my desire. In the past, my desire was lust needing to fulfill the animal in me. What I'm feeling now as he smiles and kisses my forehead, is something I can't identify, but it arouses things in me I don't want to stop.

The trains come to a stop at the King Street Station. My mind is still moving on rails of could it be love, but what about what happened last night?

We catch a ride from his friend that picked me up the day Chevelle was beaten down. Sumlin had the tunes in his Cadillac Escalade bumpin' old school 80's Hip-Hop from back when Hip-Hop was fun.

He turned the music down. "Hey, Ms. Zelda, I take it your friend Chevelle is all good."

"Oh yeah, he's all good and all in love as he works on my house."

"That's cool; what kind of skills does he have?" "He can remodel a whole house, and he is very detailed and imaginative."

"Well, I'd like to meet him and see some of his work. Me and the wife are having a baby, and we…she wants a custom nursery."

I start laughing.

"What did I say funny?"

"Men have this thing of saying me and the wife are having a baby. But in reality, men get the pride of having their sperm travel, and a woman has the hurt and pain of having a baby."

We all laughed.

"Man, what? Why you smiling so much? You all must have had a good time." Sumlin hits Aloy in the arm while he's driving.

"Look at that pretty woman in your back seat. I like her."

"You like me, huh? And you like me so much that you tell your partner before you tell me? I wish I could punch you in your arm and make it hurt."

He turns his head halfway. "I did tell you, but you were asleep," he laughs.

"I'm not laughing, Mr. Snore in my ear. At least it's a cute snore, but…"

"Zelda, I like you…how about that, and I wasn't sleep all the time. I was just taking you."

"Me…you were taking me?"

"Ah, I don't want to hear all this. Should I take you guys someplace so you can get it on?" Sumlin acted like he was going to pull over.

"Aloy, you and I will talk about this later," I ran my finger on his neckline and he rolled his head enjoying me touching him, and then he nodded his head.

205

My phone had not rung, nor had anyone texted me since I was gone, but it was now showing that I have a restricted incoming text message.

Handled something for you. The gym will get its money from now on. I know you didn't want anything done, but I liked that kid when he was boxing, and he has suffered enough. Mr. Magoo.

"Shit!"

"Are you okay?" Aloy asked.

"I'm fine, just someone may have done too much."

Sumlin dropped Aloy off at the gym to open up on time, and now he's on the way to take me home. I had to talk. "Sumlin, I like your boy, he's a good man, but I'm not sure he really likes me in the way a woman would love to be."

"Why do you think that? And you must know I'll only say so much since he is my boy."

"I understand that. I want my friends to be on my side of never letting too much be known. My thing is, I have feelings for him, and I want him in my life. I wanted to see if we could have more without me losing him as a friend. That line is forever ever changing for man and woman and friends and lovers."

As I'm speaking, I see a young couple holding hands, but the man is on the wrong side of her as they walk down the street. Aloy would never let that happen.

"I know he is a loyal dude, and from what I know of you, he admires you. If you guys go there, or if you already have, and it's not good for both of you, he will still treat you as his best friend. I'm going to say too much right here, but he needs someone to give him a life. He and his ex G from another life…she had her own agenda and was not a team player to what he needed. End of that, I say no more."

"Got it, and thank you."

I throw my bag up on the porch and look for my spare key. When I travel, I don't like taking my keys. I fashioned a loose board on the porch to hide a key. The house is cold; it feels empty. Chevelle is down in the basement, I can feel it. I go upstairs to take a long hot bath. I don't feel dirty, but I need time to solve reservations in my mind, and figure out how to ask certain questions. I let the fragrance of the blended strawberries and olive oil with burning cinnamon scented candles, help me relax and drift.

Chapter 30

Iman and Chevelle invited me and the kids over for dinner on the weekend, and we are on our way over. Chevelle is cooking. He has been in better spirits lately, and spends time with Iman again at her place. A cleaner house, I'm sure is the reason. The kids always look forward to hanging out with me, even if they are quiet, which is the case now. Oceania stares out the window of my Caddy and it's a gray day in Seattle. She has her braids in her mouth and I can't stand that.

"Oceania, baby, please don't put your hair in your mouth."

"Ms. Zelda, I want to go back home."

"Home? Baby, we are headed over to Ms. Iman's apartment, and Chevelle is cooking for us." I glance over and her face is stone. I look in my rearview mirror and Skyler has his head craned with ears wanting to hear.

"No, I want to go home from where we came from. People here are the same kind of bad, I want to go back to my country. I can protect my brother. The kids at my school no good, they try to rule each other. Grown people look at us as pets to play with and then put us back in cages. Only you love us, and talk to me and my brother. You can come with us, then we all be happy."

I heard her clearly through her late-in-life learned English. Her feelings were written on her pretty pure African face. Her struggle was not the same for the common American child. She is a child who lived through it all, of many horrible adult circumstances; but now, in a strange land, she felt lost in a way only she and Skyler can grasp. I knew some of her pain from when I first went to a school away from the reservation. Me, a black child and part Native, I was a pet to the white kids and many of the teachers. I wanted to be with people like me even if there were bad surroundings. Under the guise I was getting education, I would run through mountain passes to be where I came from. My car rolls on streets with potholes; but Oceania and Skyler, their road has, and is, a minefield.

The world looks at a refugee child, now living in the richest country and living with clean materialistic means, and feels that the child is happy. Food in the belly is good, but is your soul being fed? Hospitals, doctors, medicines can't cure homesick.

Oceania can't understand she is living a lie. The world tells her the way it should be for her, and here it is. Her soul is retching. She has most every advantage, but that is a disadvantage. Man's blessings packaged as the only way to live, is a lie to them; it's a world they feel abandoned in. Forsaken is the mental country and state these children live in.

I just read this morning in Alexandré Cornet's book, Quotes and Thoughts from a Poet:

Pain is the greatest teacher - the ugly truth
Trying to sort the truth from the fiction
It is wrong to not try?
Because of the ugly truth
It is so very wrong to have never hollered and screamed at injections of insults of lies told
Instead you chose to keep trying and believe in waiting for everlasting embraces to replace cold damp places in your soul, and in their soul, too
Living with joy and pain
Like rain - some never understand what they do is shameful
Some never understand they did wrong...period
Yes, they do
And they will feel God
Fate is waiting for them
Closing eyes and eyes and mouth is not a bandage to bury wrong doing
Our eyes, our soul should never live to see being done wrong by the ones who claim to love us
And the excuse is?
The ugly truth
Words should never be spit, and drip down to the heart   Pain is a teacher of the bad for the sake of the good

"Honey, I know you have lived through a lot, and I would do anything to give you peace. It's just not that simple, and it's not up to me. If I could change this world, I'd change it for you and Skyler and me. And me, Zelda, I'm on an abnormal journey myself."

"Abnormal?" her face contorted.

"Different than most can be labeled as abnormal. I know you two have had to do and see so much at your ages. You have seen and done enough. Try to focus on growing into adults and then maybe you can go back. I have read about your homeland, and right now, it's not a nice place. It may even be worse than anything I have read."

I stopped at the bakery and picked up humus and Ethiopian flatbread – injera; it's seasoned with flavors and spices from the kids' homeland. They told me that sitting around with a huge plate of injera, and eating with their hands out of the same plate, symbolizes pure love and community.

I headed up Beacon Hill to Iman's apartment. I wondered about the kids' psyche as I watched their expressions as they looked out the windows. Passing by traditional houses, one may think them to be peaceful, when they may be engulfed in wars of the unthinkable.

Almost in harmony, Oceania and Skyler asked a question that sent chills through me. I'm sure in their heads and hearts, like the first question about going back to Africa, I'm sure they had given it their youthful buoyancy of hope.

"Can we live with you, Zelda?" Oceania took over, "We won't be any problem. We won't get in the way, and we'll clean our rooms and will help around the house," Oceana made it clear she will cook everyday if they could live with me.

I understood, since I spent a lot of time with them. I have become involved in their lives. I was taking them to Seward Park to ride bikes while I jogged. I was taking them to the movies and the library. I brought them to my home where we watched movies, but they seem to enjoy reading.

I have watched their expressions change from my house and going in the door of the peaceful, but somewhat cold, life at Pastor Shomer and Eneta's house. Their parents were busy with their own lives, and according to Aloy's opinion, he thought the kids were being treated as pets, or a sideshow of good works to be viewed by the church parishioners.

Having no children, it never really was a conflict inside me. Traditionally, I think, I would have a husband. I hoped for what my mother and my stepdad Eddie had provided for me, in order for me to provide that for children. I never felt that biological clock thing that women speak of. Maybe my soul fights with the fact that I've never been in love, but does that affect my child-bearing tick-tock? Although something is going on between me and Aloy, I'm not sure what that is. Maybe I'll feel a clock ticking if he and I…I'm tripping over my wants; let me stop.

I wrestle with the fact that he didn't go inside me. He touched me, tasted me. He made me feel good. Was it nervousness on his part? Or, is it me having stereotypical thoughts of what a man wants to do me, or was he being a gentleman in saying, no not the first time, and we'll only go partway. The train ride back, I wanted to ask. I didn't. We haven't talked about it since.

I have more on my plate than I think I can handle, and with the kids asking can they live with me…they have parents. Adoptive parents, yes; but they have a stable good home. Eneta has her flaws; she lies and lifts her skirt for a plaything, and buffers her wrongness behind her religion. I have no idea what Pastor Shomer is doing. He keeps pretty private, not saying too much. He may have female interests on the side. Women like a powerful man who walks and talks an influence game. Pastors and side chicks…some church women get hooked on a man standing above the crowd and telling them how to live. Power can be a spear in the eyes.

I pull over. "Oceana, as I spoke earlier, you need to let some natural progressions happen. You need to grow up more, and when you do, you'll be educated to understand more of the ways of the world. Skyler, you need to grow into a young man, and right now both of you are in a house with two parents. I just can't take you away and claim you. I do want you to know I do claim you as my best friends. I like to think I can be there for you

211

and help you. I'll keep spending a lot of time with you two. Now let's go to a good dinner. Chevelle and Iman are waiting on us.

I scanned over their faces; pain was evident. If I reached over and touch either one on their faces, I'd feel tears running inside them like a waterfall after a hard rain. Pieces of them were drowning in the American way. I'll need to keep them afloat and alive.

Maybe the children need a connection to their community to be happier. I had a conversation with Eneta about when a white family adopts Black children and how they have an obligation for them to be around parts of the Black community. Even though Black people are not a monolithic entity, as we are a variance in variety, a white adopter still needs to provide opportunity for their adored Black child, or whatever the ethnic background is, to assimilate with their history. Adopters need to provide a total view of the world for the child, or risk injuring the spirit of that child. A white mother should find Black women to associate with, so the children have aunties. White fathers need to know Black men, so that adopted Black children will have Black uncles.

I had proposed to Eneta that she should find people from the children's community to acquaint herself with. East African people are very community-based. I worked with a few at Boeings at the airplane plant. The children…now they're being raised in a Christian home, and there is nothing wrong with that; yet, missing their homeland's religion and their language may have them homesick. I'll bring it up to Eneta again in an effort to help these beautiful children stay beautiful.

As I pull into the parking lot of the apartment complex, trash is still spread like wild mushrooms on fertile ground near the dumpsters and other corners. The cars on big rims fill the parking lot. I checked my waistband in the back for my .22. I know it's there. I check anyway.

Change had come. As soon as I walked into Iman's apartment, it smelled clean. It looked organized with no clutter. The kids follow me to the bathroom to wash our hands, and the bathroom is fresh and spotless. It's decorated with arranged matching towels hung nicely along with paper towels to dry hands, and a wastepaper basket. I'm impressed there is some art hanging on the wall. The kitchen, I now have no problem eating anything made between these walls. I smelled the lemon pledge coming from the dining room table.

I knew when I challenged Iman to be better, I considered that I might offend her and she could go the opposite direction, but apparently she heard me. This beautiful Black young lady was showing that she was about something. She's walking through her apartment and no one would never notice that she is full-figured. She dresses very well, and her face is so pretty. She displays pride, she shows growth. I'm proud of Chevelle for sticking with her and helping her. They seem to be happy spending more time together.

Chevelle, as he does at the house, will break out a cookbook, or pull up a recipe from the Internet. He had prepared chicken and vegetables for dinner, in the fashion of Mediterranean African style. We let the kids eat in a communal manner sharing one plate as they do in their culture. Us three adults; we are eating on separate plates at the dining room table. I can tell the kids are enjoying dinner.

Chevelle brought the conversation up that he was interested in going to a fight club. I had to catch myself and not talk to him as if I was his mother, ruling him. I want to tell him to leave that thought alone, but I coolly listened to him instead. He's already made up his mind. He knew where the next fight club was going down. I knew I was going have to go with him to help protect him in the game of wolves. He will be new on the scene, and they will try to use him to get beat on. I knew he was a former highly-rated State wrestler in high school, but the virtual no rules fight club scene is another level of crazy.

I took the kids home after we played some board games. It was nice to see the kids laugh and smile. Walking in the house, Eneta is on the phone in the kitchen, and Pastor Shomer is in the front room watching TV, and cleaning a Taurus 4510 Revolver. He is often in the living room cleaning a gun from his collection. The gun is one I dream of owning. I visit the gun store often window shopping. I know about guns. The kids know to not go in the room with him when he has guns out.

I took the kids to their individual rooms. I read to each one their favorite story and let them know that life is going to be okay, and that I would never abandon them. I made that promise to both them and myself. Maybe I needed them in my life as a form of stability.

Chapter 31

I made a deal with Chevelle that he would train with me and Aloy to increase his boxing skills before participating in the fight club scene. Most of the fighters there are brawlers with some training in martial arts, but they lack boxing skill. Having boxing skills is still the best weapon; the art of hitting in combination with moving to avoid being hit in return, trumps most proponents.

Aloy was tough on Chevelle; he made him pay attention to detail as far seeing what an opponent was giving and how to counter attack, and then moving away within a defensive position. Some of the fighters Chevelle could encounter might kick in return after being hit in the face, and we worked on when fighters rush in head first. I, too, was tough on Chevelle; maybe tougher. Chevelle took it all in. I taught him how to kick proper pinpoint kicks to the body, and more head and footwork.

There was little attention coming from Aloy toward me. We talked small talk. He told me, more than a few times, that he enjoyed our trip. He hugged me often, and I felt intensity behind each embrace. He had this thing for kissing me on my forehead. I melted like hot Crisco grease on 600 degrees when a stove only goes to 400. He slapped my behind a few times, and I got wet with the sting. He whispered in my ear that he wanted to see me naked again.

I guess he has been paying attention to me, but I'm holding back; scarred of the next time we get naked in front of each other again. Will he get busy in me?

*****

Two weeks later, we are walking into a warehouse out in the Foothills of Seattle near a prison town named Monroe. I have been to this fight club before, and it got shut down; but now it's back up, and I see some folks I know. No one is a friend, accept JoBelle; she's with me and Chevelle. I didn't want Aloy to come. If a fight club is raided, they give tickets for trespassing and illegal gathering. It's a small slap on the butt, but if any well-known names are there, even if they are semi-known, it can draw more attention to them than it's worth.

Betting is going on and that is the major crime, but how to prove it? People in attendance are vetted in hopes of keeping cops from lying in the cut, but it can happen. There appears to be no money controller; nonetheless, the house does control the money on the slick by having a bunch of people appearing to be making personal bets, but they all work for the house. No drugs or drinking are allowed. Having someone drunk…that places the fight club on loose gravel.

"Hey, Zelda, did you come to fight?" is repeated at every turn.

"No. If you don't remember, there is no one on my level. I need to make money if I'm gonna fight."

"So, you just come to watch?" is repeated by admires and haters, and the women fighters I had beat badly in the past.

I go to the promoter who always calls me when he thinks he has a woman fighter to get in the square with me. Then those women find out about me and hurt themselves in training or just don't show up. They get cured of their ego crack when they hear of what I had done to other women before them. I was not kind in how I beat my opponents. It was me or them, and I made it all about always being me in control, being focused, and never getting angry while handing out a whoopin'. My step-dad, Eddie, taught me well.

"Mr. Waters, I see you're up and running. I haven't heard from you in a while."

"Your rep runs deep. Maybe if you wouldn't beat the living crap out of these wanna-be fighters, we'd make some money instead of just you winning the purse. You know, if you could make it look like you get hurt in a fight, and that someone is about to take you out, and then you knock someone the hell out, then maybe…just maybe, we could make some money. You know what they say, 'Fake it till you make it.'"

"Mr. Waters, faking ain't me. Going half speed is how one gets hurt."

"You're right."

"I got a friend. He can fight."

Chevelle is next to me stretching.

"What's his weight?"

"175," Chevelle says.

Mr. Waters glares at me as he has not looked at Chevelle straight on yet. "Zelda, you remember Bennie the Slammer?"

"Yeah, he was good with his brawler skills. If I remember right, he took a lot of punches to finally get in close enough to put someone into submission."

"Think your boy here can match up, or you need the pacifier-diaper level?"

From the two weeks of boxing training, I know Chevelle can hit like a mule kicks, and he knows the *how* and *when* within a game plan. Already knowing Chevelle's wrestling skills, I don't hesitate in responding, "Yeah, he can match up."

"Well good, the champ has needed a new challenge for a while now."

"Oh, he's the champ now?"

It's getting louder in the warehouse. A fight is going on, and it sounds like someone is taking a beating.

"Six months now, but tell me, Zelda...you're good; the best I've seen. I know you would knock the head off that Ronda Ra-Ra windbag chick if you were in the same weight class as her. So, with that being said, I know you must have walked in here with a kid that can fight. Do I bet the house on your boy here or not?"

Chevelle starts shadow-boxing, and his hands are fast. A few people start watching him, and not the fight going on in the square.

I stare down into the face of a man with no neck. He backs up. I slowly roll my neck as I keep my eyes locked to Mr. Waters. "My man wins and you pay him a champion's purse and ten percent of the house, like you paid me. He's with me, Mr. Waters, and he leaves with me and his money!"

He looked at Chevelle shadowboxing and knocking the air out with each punch. "Okay, he's up in an hour as our main feature. Could you chat up the match to increase the betting?"

"Yeah."

The bell is about to ring, and I go over the fight plan with Chevelle. He is sweating; not from being nervous, but he is warmed up and ready to go. The buzz in the fight club is on high. *Who is the kid that no one has seen before and he is fighting the champ?* A champion that has flaws, and we will expose them rather quickly, is what I'm betting. The betting line has Chevelle as a major underdog. People are not interested in an upset; they are simply blood thirty and want to see a major beat down. I bet $500 on Chevelle. JoBelle bets $1,500 on Chevelle.

The fight club rules are thin; no low blows, but they happen though when a fighter is full of rabid fear, wanting to survive. A fight lasts until someone is out cold or submits. If you submit, you don't get paid anything.

Ding.

Chevelle moves to the center of the ring and fakes a right hand and lands a left hook to the rib cage of Bennie the Slammer, then moves to reposition. Chevelle gets a look in his eyes of destruction. As I knew it would happen, after three minutes, Bennie has taken a lot of punches. Chevelle is hitting him hard, but not with all he has. However, he is doing a lot more than I told him to do. He's enjoying dismantling a man. At least he's holding back on an all-out assault of hard punches. We have even landed some hard kicks. Bennie finally bum rushes, head first. Chevelle side-steps, and nails Bennie on the temple with a cruel downward right hand. He follows with a thunderous left upper kick to the chin. Bennie lands face first on the ground. Lights out. Fight over.

I dropped off JoBelle at home. She is $9,000 richer. As I drive past my house on my way to the alley, I see Aloy leaning on his iron horse in front of my front porch in the rain.

Chapter 32

I pull around into the alley and park. Chevelle and I hug, and he heads into the basement with $7,000. I walk around to the front. Aloy is leaning on his motorcycle.

I walk into his space and stand between his parted legs. "We're back, and all much richer."

Our eyes locked as we felt rain on our faces.

"Let's go inside and get wet," his tone was assertive and oh my…I like it. We make it to the shower, and we are kissing with intense passion. I'm trembling all over. I'm excited. I'm high on his sweet, magical, tongue.

I turn on the shower. The room is steaming. I can't breathe. I'm loving this heat. As we step over the high rail of the claw-foot tub, he's behind me so close that I think I feel his whole body pushing through my skin. He's cupping my breasts as if he is molding me from wet clay. I feel his pubic hair softly abrading on my ass, and it seems to make my clit pleasurably ache. His thick, heavy, dick slides up and down the crease of my ass and I grind. I bend forward and hump into him. I feel him behind me jacking off and humping me. He makes grunting sounds that penetrate deeply past my ears, and it makes me say things in a nasty nature. He pulls me by my hair that I had in long braids. I love it. He's sucking on my neck. I'm washing between my thighs and playing. I feel his finger wash between my ass cheeks. I can't inhale enough air. I cut the shower off and take his hand, leading him to my room. I grab towels and spread them over my mattress on the floor. I don't want to dry off. I want us wet.

I lie down on my back, and my baby oil is near. He reaches and drips it on my cheeks, my neck, my nipples, and down to my naval. He is massaging my face as his tongues circles my lips. He massages me wherever he dipped oil on me with his strong hot hands. He pulls my nipples into hard sensitive mini-quarter-inch tootsie rolls, and keeps working them between his thumb and forefinger. He keeps doing that as his face eases down to my pussy. I lift my legs, reach for my feet and pull them back wide. I'm wide open. He doesn't waste time. His tongue is deep inside my wetness, dancing toward the star point of my pleasure. He licks me with his tongue, making its way to my clit. His mouth covers my whole pussy, but his tongue flips my clit like a humming bird flaps it wings. He stays at licking my clit or tonguing me. Damn…he's dragging his tongue through the crease of my ass, and all around. Now back at my clit, he put puts the work in and it starts my body is jerking out of control. I'm cumin'. I feel myself squirting on his chin. Glad I put a lot of towels down.

I need him inside me. I want it now. I put my hands on the sides of his face. I guide him to bring his lips to mine so I can lick me off his lips; as I do, I'm reaching for his dick to guide him in me. He's not hard. I avoid eye-to-eye as I stroke his thick, long, dick. No reaction. None. Is it me? I don't turn him on? What's going on?

His body is hard as a rock, but not his dick. It must be me. But he touches me as if he wants me. His tongue worships me, and it is so good. He made me cum harder than I could ever make myself cum; but I want him inside me. I moved to be on my side. He moves to his side and looks me in the face. I avoid the power of his eyes. I try to make sure my face is neutral.

"Zelda."

I don't react.

"Zelda, please look at me."

I take my time, letting my eyes gather in his face. The only light we have is the streetlight coming through the window, and it is more than enough. His eyes hold me as his hand on my back pulls me closer.

"I have a lot to say. You know it…it will take me some time. I see…you're upset…please… hear me out. Try lowering your guard. I won't hurt you."

I searched his eyes, I saw no deception.

"Hold still," his face is a bit puzzled. I put my hand over half of his face. I see beauty on that side. I'm putting my other hand over the other half of his face. I see the same beauty. He's not two-faced. Many people have two different looks. He is a beautiful man throughout, but something I see…I see pain. I nod my head.

"Talk to me, Aloy."

I turn away and spoon into him. "I want to see the sky, and lights and planes, while you talk to me."

I wanted stars; hoping they wouldn't fall, but rise.

"This thing, it rides back to the time a bullet entered my skull when I tried to save my friends. I guess my sexual dysfunction is tied to when I had to kill a man. My pain is deep seated in my head, not so much psychologically, but physically I'm told. The injury and the recovery left uncertainties. At first it was: can I think, eat, sleep, walk, and speak."

I had tears in my eyes already listening to him, as his hurt almost had an echo making me feel how deep his soul had sunk but he was sharing with me and I wanted to help lift him.

"I had relearned some basics. At first, my mind was scrambled; and once I came out of the hospital, my girlfriend, Parasol, was supportive. My memory, I had lapses, and for some time I felt the sting of people making fun of me."

I heard anger right at this point when he said that. He went silent for a while, and I was going to wait until God said I couldn't wait anymore.

"I had a turnaround. I got better. My Aunt Alanese helped me tremendously with rehab. The deepest sting…missing sex when you're eighteen years old and you're used to having all you want. The doctors wanted me to not be involved in any physicality of any type, including sex, for three months. When I went to bed, my head was supported by a cradle. Parasol was patient and sweet while I healed, but we were starting to creep towards almost having sex before I was supposed to. I would get headaches afterwards, but we were horny teenagers. He got hard just as I used to.

"I was raging sexually. I wanted her as we had been crazy in our prior times. She taught me how to go down on her in different ways, and I enjoyed giving her pleasure. But the first time we went buck wild again like we used to, which was a month before the doctor indicated would be safe for me to have intercourse, Parasol and I went at it like wolves tearing at fresh kill. It went on for days and everything was fine. The only thing wrong was the pounding headache that would double me over in pain. I assumed it would go away, and I was thinking with the wrong head.

"Two weeks later, and no hard-on. Nothing happened. I didn't get hard. I didn't even feel my testicles stirring. I felt the urge in my heart and head, but nothing happened. No hard-on, only a headache."

"Aloy let me get us some water and you can continue. You need a little break."

I reached over and rubbed his bald head, and as I got up, I leaned in and kissed his forehead. The electric cooler I kept in my room had a bright light that came on when I lifted the top. It highlighted the dry tear stains on Aloy's face. He stared out the window, and I gaze at a man right now and I know I'm in love with him. I'm trembling as I'm fighting from becoming emotional. I hurried to be next to him. I opened a bottled water and held it to his mouth for him to drink before I curled back into him. I grabbed his arm to hold me tight as he talked to me.

"Parasol acted like it was no big deal and that I was injured and just needed more time. A month later, I was feeling hard-ons in the morning, so we tried again. I wanted to be inside her, but something wasn't right once more. We were naked, and I was all over her kissing and touching and going down on her. Usually, she just had to lie there and I would be hard and ready to go inside of her, but that time, I didn't get hard. I stroked my dick, it didn't get hard. I rubbed the head on her pussy. I didn't get hard. She turned over and exposed her ass, and nothing happened. Seeing her pussy and ass from behind was something that made me rock hard in the past. She roused her ass in front of me and spread her cheeks as I rubbed my dick on her pussy and up to her ass; nothing happened.

225

"She turned around and screamed at me, 'What is wrong with you? I don't turn you on anymore?' I told her that I didn't know what was happening. She calmed down, but started keeping her distance from me. I went to a couple of doctors, and they told me that there was some nerve damage from the bullet fragments that could be affecting my sexual performance. They said that I may need more time to heal, and that maybe I would be continued to be impaired; period. Since then, I drip. I feel horny. Sometimes when I wake, I'm kind of hard; and even with you, I have seeped wetness from my dick on your ass and leg. I can jerk off by squeezing and stroking my dickhead, but I don't get hard."

I reached back and touched his face to let him know that I'm with him, and tuned into all he has said. I understand now what he meant when he said he had not had sex with any other woman since his first girlfriend. It made sense. I thought he was just stuck on her. He had said that he had tried to have sex with other women, but the same thing happened; but I took that to mean they just never had sex. Now he's lying next to me and can't perform.

"Zelda?"

"Yes."

"I understand if I'm not man enough for you. I've been told a couple of times that I'm not enough man for a woman's needs."

"Don't...don't say that to me."

I feel his non-hardness against my ass, and I'm feeling his soul enter into my soul. Right now, he's a lot more man than I have ever had wrapped around me.

"I'm feeling love for you, Zelda. I'm feeling I'm in love with you. I have wondered what it felt like, and I'm embracing it right now. I want to hold on; can I? Despite my situation?"

I took the deepest breath I had ever taken in my life when he said he believes he loves me. Aloy has me in his embrace, telling me he has deep feelings for me. The tears in my eyes burned. I hear a story that chars with lasting hurt.

"Aloy, I'm falling in love with you, too. I don't know what love is as I assume most others do, but I believe I am, and I don't know how that impacts our two bodies coming together. I do have desires and I want you inside me, so I don't know how this works from here on out. We'll have to talk. We'll have to grow through this, if we can."

At some point, we don't talk anymore. I last remember placing my head on his chest, and holding onto my fallen star. I want to catch him, if I knew which way he was falling, but it also leaves confusion inside of me. I've gone long periods of time without having sex, and I know for sure I have desires to have a relationship, and have intercourse within our love. I don't know how, but I want to try.

I awake facing the window. He's not curled in next to me, but I sense him standing over me and coming down to his knees. I pray, as I assume he may be doing the same; I hope, and I pray. At the end of my prayer, I feel his soft lips on my ear, and his warm breath voyaging near my face. It is the sweetest goodbye.

Chapter 33

I'm curled up wishing Aloy was still next to me. If I'm being a little girl, I love it. If I'm being a grown woman, let my head and heart be clear, and don't let me be an insecure adult.

I need coffee and I want a long hot shower. I check the front door to make sure Aloy locked it as he had forgotten to do so before. Once again, it's unlocked. I don't even care. I try not to be someone who sweats the small stuff. When I become perfect I'll care. Let me start some coffee.

"Who the in hell are you, and what are you doing in my kitchen?"

There are two women in my kitchen.

"Who are you?"

They are sitting at the kitchen table. One appears to be about the same age as me, and the other is older as I observe. They appear to be non-threatening, maybe even just the opposite.

"My name is Robin," the older appearing woman stuck her hand out for me to shake it. I didn't. There are two strangers sitting at my kitchen table uninvited, and I'm in a tank top. I can handle myself if this gets crazy, but I coolly walk over to the two coffee cans next to the percolator. One of the cans has coffee in it; the other has my .22. I take it out and sit at the other end of my table. The younger woman shows fear in her eyes; the older woman presses her lips tight and nods.

"We are not here to hurt or be hurt," Robin put her hands on the table.

"Excuse me, Robin. I don't know how you got into my house, and why you think we are about to have tea like queens of high society. Who in the hell are you?"

"Can we have coffee with you, me, and Shevon? We have things we want to share with you. We were able to come in because the locks have never been changed, we see. We would have knocked."

"Knocked? Really? That would have been mighty nice of you."

"I watched Aloy leave," Shevon starts crying with her first words. "He's so…so grown and handsome; and to think…he still walks in and out of this house."

I'm shook and confused. I get up and smell the scent in the air. I sense no danger. I can tell there is some history connected to the house. If they were going to try to hurt me, they could have ambushed me.

"I'm Zelda. I'm going to go put on some clothes, please make the coffee; this can has coffee in it," I say as I head out the room.

Upstairs, I put on my tights and sweats and tuck my gun in my waistband. I don't know them, but they know this house and Aloy from a long time ago it seems. I go back into the kitchen and the coffee is almost ready. I place cups on the table. My eyes scan their presence. I'm weary. I look out into the backyard and see my old Cadillac. The clear Seattle skies show glances of the Puget Sound and the Olympic Mountains from my house. It is a beautiful day. I'm hoping it stays that way.

I put brown and white sugar, as well as cream, on the table. I pick up the coffee pot and fill three cups. I sit, and I wait, to hear why they are here.

Robin bows her head and then looks up, seemingly looking past me as she talks. "Zelda, my story connects into Shevon's story. I'm Sadducy's much older sister from his father's first marriage to my mother. I have never met my brother, and I don't care to do so, as I'm aware he is a jerk. When I was ten, my mother had to fight my father to survive all too often.

"One day, my mother had taken all she could, and this gets creepy. My mother had her best friend from childhood pick me up from school, and drive me to Oakland, California, where she lived. Mom told me she would join me by driving down later in a day or two with our things. A week later,

229

no one heard from my mother. The family friend sent the police to our house, and my mother's car was gone. Mr. Cowen, my dad, said that his wife, and me – his daughter, had left him, and that he had no idea where we had gone. All my mother's things were gone; but no, my mother never made it to Oakland, as far as anyone could tell. I have never seen my mother again. I was blessed that the family friend raised me with love."

Robin asked to use my restroom.

With the second cups of coffee poured, Shevon started speaking as Robin constantly dabbed the corners of her eyes. "I'm the daughter of Mr. Cowen's second wife. I am not his daughter, but Duce and I are half-brother and half-sister because we have the same mother, but different fathers. I am older, and have a wonderful dad. I lived with my dad, but often visited my mother in this house while she was married to Mr. Cowen."

Aloy had told me about the history of this house. It matches the story of the two women sitting at my kitchen table in what they are telling me, but with more detail.

"Duce and I were cool as we grew up in the little brother and big sister roles; but as he became a teen, he made me very uncomfortable with his sexual conversations. One day, he exposed himself to me and tried to touch me. I stopped coming to the house after that, except for holidays; and even then, if I came, I insisted that my mother sleep with me in the spare bedroom. It got to the point that for a time, my mother took me on mini-vacations with just me and her."

"Shevon, I understand when we woman are put in tough situations a man can places us in. As a lack and Native woman, I have many stories that have been told to me. I now know stories." In my mind, I saw Sans' face. I got up to get some water as I kept talking. "I have heard from all races of women, stories from their pre-twenties days, as well as adult moments, of men and boys putting them in sad situations. It seems almost all women have had to deal with a man or boy making us feel nasty, and/or doing revolting things to us. Sadly, many women are affected in their adult lives because of what has happened to them years before."

"I went for counseling when I turned twenty. I didn't want to have a life controlled by his ugliness," Shevon added.

"Good for you, Shevon. Good for you. Some women affected become unable to have a healthy sexual existence, and only do it out of relationship obligation. The fix…boys to men must be taught from birth to respect girls, and women need to go get help when they have been molested, and stay with it until they recover their whole soul."

"My step-dad, Mr. Cowen, never treated me bad, but I knew my mother was not happy. My mother loved Aloy; he was always so nice to my mom, and my mom took me to see him fight when he was an early teen. I had a key when I visited my mother, and I never threw it away."

I thought, *Why haven't I thought to change the front door lock?* Duce had used a key to come in the basement, and I had a new door and lock down there now.

"Robin and Shevon, I'm torn inside with the suffering you ladies have experienced. I want a clock that I could turn back the hands of time for you. Yet, what brings you here now, and the way you chose to arrive?" I kind of smiled, but not because I was happy.

"We know it was wrong to enter as we have, but we couldn't take any chances on you letting us talk to you about our dilemma," Robin's face was twitching in agony.

Shevon stood and went to the back door and looked out. "Sans Delroy is dead," she didn't ask, she stated. My head swiveled hard in her direction. "He bothered my mother a lot. He looked at me, and it wasn't in a good way," she sat down and pointed to the basement. "When I was pre-teen, and before Duce exposed himself to me, he and I would play in the basement in the winter. One day, Duce was throwing his steel marbles off the side of the brick fireplace. Pieces of brick where chipping away. Eventually, Duce was able to pull out a whole brick. Duce's father came in through the outside basement door and yelled at Duce, 'Don't you ever touch that fireplace; you stay the hell away from it,' he kept repeating that. He pulled off his belt. I ran upstairs to my mom, and I heard Duce get an

231

awful beating. When Duce came upstairs, his face had welts on it, and his pants were bloody. My mom nursed her son, but something changed in him. He became a dark soul after that. I noticed the next week, the fireplace was bigger with a lot more bricks. It seemed my step-dad kept adding layers of brick to the fireplace."

As she is telling me this, I'm picturing the fireplace in the basement. It is way oversized.

Robin reached for my hands and I let her hold them. "Zelda, it may be the biggest reach of anyone's imagination, but I never saw my mother since she dropped me off at school that day." Tears dropped on my kitchen table. "If my father killed my mother because she was taking me away, and leaving him, she may be in this house buried. Maybe she's behind that fireplace."

I look at her trying to put all that together. It would be over forty-five years ago if her mother was put in a tomb in this house.

Shevon stared at me with almost dead eyes as she spoke. "If Robin's mother is here, there would be two women who have died in this house. My step-dad killed my mother's spirit and then cancer took over and finished the job. I know where my mother is buried, and I want to help Robin bury her mother."

"How did you two come together?"

"Alanese Delroy," Shevon said. "I won the house in a court battle against Duce, and he got the lot next door after his father died. I had a property manager rent the house out. I never wanted to come back to the house back then, and even now, it sends chills to my heart. I kept in touch with Alanese," she smiled wide, and her eyes lifted to the ceiling. "I was hoping my teenage crush on Aloy would grow old, but seeing him walk out of here this morning...boy, oh boy, he is still so fine. I know he has to have tons of women chasing him with his good looks." She came out of her, *Wonderful Wizard of Ozlittle gold brick road trip.* She became wide-eyed. "I'm sorry, are you and him..."

232

"Its fine; yes, women love to see him coming and going. But how did you, Robin, connect with Shevon?"

I found Shevon by public records and then on Facebook. I had questions to ask from the perplexing episode of what has happened. When Shevon told me about the fireplace and then added that to the mystery of my mother never showing up anywhere; we...I had to come here. And yes, I know we are disturbing your home, and I am sorry, but please understand."

"I forgive that, but I'm confused in how I can help you. I have spent a tremendous amount of time remolding the basement to accommodate my step-father coming to live with me, and I have a wonderful young man living down there. To tear the fireplace down to possibly find your mother buried in there, this would then turn this house into a murder scene. Police could possibly tear into my whole house, leaving us with...I can't imagine how bad it can get. I want to do the right thing, but you have to let me process all this, and how to go about this."

Robin trailed her fingers down my hand that held my coffee and released. "Zelda, I don't need a police case. I don't want your life invaded. You do what is best for you. Take your time. It can be a week or a year, but please find out if my mother is buried in this house. If she is, put her bones in a box, and I will come get her, so I can bury her in the Bay Area waters from where she came from. My husband has a boat, and my children and I can have our own ceremony at sea to give my mother her final resting place. No one has to know where, or how, her bones came to me. I'll leave you all my information and you contact me when...either way. You'll never hear from me until you contact me. If you choose not to look, I'll never bother you again," Robin bowed her head, and I knew she was praying.

I reached for her hand, and then I stretched out my other hand for Shevon to hold. She did, and she then took Robin's other hand. I prayed to my ancestors and God. We didn't say a word for minutes as our hands passed hope, while confronting fears, and giving promise to link us.

"Give me time; just give time to figure all this out."

I brewed more coffee. We had our fourth cups of coffee, and I learned other history and pains. I now had sisters linked together through coffee running through our bodies, and past unanswered questions. I reflected on never knowing who my father is, and whether he is buried or walking.

Chapter 34

The ladies left me with the weirdest encounter I had ever experienced, but it was also the realest pain that anyone could go through. I'm a part of their story now through front and back doors, windows, and time. I need to go to the gym and workout and write my weekly work schedule of events for my classes. I need to bust a sweat with so many things happening.

I'm not sure where I am in my relationship with Aloy, so it makes it difficult to ascertain whether I should share right now what has happened with me meeting those two ladies. I'll have to think about that. I need to talk to Chevelle. He's living down in the basement. He's been working all through this house. If by chance, someone is entombed behind that fireplace in the basement, I need to let him know.

I see Alanese as I'm going out the back door to my car. She has a knowing look on her face. She most likely saw the ladies leave my house, and she nods to me and I nod back. I know she is still going through the throes of emotions for the man that was blackmailing her for sex. The man that tried to rape me is now dead. *What part did she play in it I wonder?* Was it just emotional karma that killed that man, or could she have done the deed? If so, did she do it alone? I didn't ask Shevon anything about her having knowledge of Sans Delroy, but it all feels odd.

I'm parking in front of the Hob Nob Traven. I miss talking to my Uncle Don and seeing normal folk. I walk in and I hear folk saying things like, "Oh, you want to hang with us – you found your way here – what...you found better liquor?"

I sit at the bar and Uncle Don puts a beer in front of me. "You okay? His baritone meant it. He had a worried look on his face.

"Don, I'm good."

He stares. He walks away, and he has a slight limp. On a man 6'6" it's noticeable. He serves Purple Daddy his Crown Apple. I think about my history of being in tight spots, and the choices I made, and I tune into the music. A song I kind of remember feels good. I know the singer's voice; it's Teddy Pendergrass, and he is crooning, "*When Somebody Loves You Back.*"

I ask my uncle about his limp. He shrugs his shoulders and keeps moving. He comes back and I ask him, "Don, have seen my auntie? It has been over six months, and she has not returned my calls."

He shakes his head and turns to go toward the back.

"Uncle Don!"

He twists his head in the slowest, *How dare you speak to me firmly look.* My Uncle Don is someone that speaks an answer. He doesn't blow you off with nods and shrugs; maybe a stare down at best, but this. I don't like being chilled-out by anyone. If I can stand up to my auntie, and I do to a point, then no one is off limits.

I do lower my voice. "Don, this is some bullshit, please don't treat me as if I'm ignorant. Can I get answers instead of the blow of body language? I know you don't lie."

He walks over to me to tower on my space. "So, I'm telling you, don't ask me questions related to the questions you have asked, and then I don't have to lie."

He sucked the air out of my mind. I feel dead-numb and froze out by one of the men I trust. He didn't break a trust; I created one and got schooled.

"I won't ask."

I deflect being shut-down and head over to the tables to crack jokes or to be cracked on. I even ask Purple Daddy how he is doing.

"Baby, why don't cha come clean my house again? I'll pay you well, you know I do."

I'm glad I'm making some money and have housing, and don't have to do what I had to do before.

"How come you don't get a woman your age to come clean your house and take care of your needs?"

He runs his tongue over his false teeth, trying to entice me. "Women my age want me to take them pills, and they ain't doing anything in bed for me to do all that. Them old women, they just lay there anyway. They want me to jump up and down on their old bones like I'm a teenager."

I laugh inside, but it also makes me think. I wonder has Aloy tried erectile help like pills.

"Look Daddy-O, if you take the pills, you get your house cleaned, and most likely a good meal, too. You don't have to be alone at night. Go get yourself some pills to get it up."

Chapter 35

When I get to the gym, Aloy is leaving with his friend Sumlin. He runs over to my car and kisses me on my forehead nice and slow.

I tease him, "You gonna let your boy seeing you acting all soft over me?" "Why not over you? A pretty woman like you, accepting me as I am, I can do whatever I need to do for that."

He didn't hesitate with one word. My mouth is wide open. He has a way of making me do that. He slips his tongue in my mouth. I have never been pretty, as far as I'm concerned, but he thinks I am, so I am pretty.

His kisses my forehead and puts his lips close to my ear. "Can you clear next weekend, Friday evening until about noon Sunday?"

"For you, yes. Ahh, but what about the gym?"

"I have Sumlin to cover for me, and you're done teaching by the time we will take off," his golden eyes smile, and his lips spread their fullness into making me feel like a child with a new bike. He turns and trots over to his ride. I stand in the gym windows looking out over Lake Washington. It is a blustery day; there is slight white caps on the water. It has its own peace. A couple of hours later, I'm done with my schedule, and I clean up when Chevelle arrives to work out.

"I want to fight again real soon."

At the fight Club, everyone thought he was a white kid. He's worth a lot of money on the fight scene.

"I advise against it."

"Why?"

"Because you got high on beating down a man. I saw it in your eyes. You can only go so far before someone does to you what you just did. You have skills outside the fight game, and you are one of the most intelligent, creative, young men I have met. I'm glad you're my friend. I believe you came into my life for great reasons. I needed to have family. Between you and the kids, and the remodel of the house, I have become centered. You need to stay centered.

"See, once you get high on beating down another man, it will be your downfall if you don't break the lure earlier on. My step-dad made sure I understood that. Create a world with you and Iman; start your own business with her. Your hands are still swollen. I helped you, but now I remove myself from promoting you fighting anymore. I see something in you that's not good in the long run. Maybe your life of living behind the natural course of others has you wanting to get even with life by beating down on other humans. You can't fight blood-thirsty. You are good enough to kill a man in the square, and if you enjoy the high of beating another man down, you'll end up killing a man, or being killed. Is that what you want?"

"Zelda, I…no," his head slumped, and he turned to walk away as if he were ashamed.

"Come back, we need to talk."

I told him about the meeting with the ladies and the history of the house and that we might have to take apart the fireplace. He thought the fireplace had problems with size, and the foundation was weak in display as it was built up in layers. That made my skin crawl thinking the worse. We decided to take it apart next week, just to get the mystery out of the way, knowing that Robin did not want a police case, she just wants her mother.

Chapter 36

I'm boarding a four-seater plane with Aloy. JoBelle dropped us off at Boeing Field. It's Friday, and it's a clear night as we lift off. We are headed to Orcas Island in the San Juan Island of Washington State. Aloy is friends with the basketball coach at East Seattle University, Ayman Sparks and a couple of others guys Tylowe Dandridge and Psalms Black. Aloy wants me to know these guys as important people to know. They gave him a flight pass, and a two-night stay. They couldn't take advantage of the perk because of college rules.

This is my first flight in a small plane. I've only been on airliners a few times. Strange though, I worked on them and had sex in them. Our small commuter plane pilot is a white female who looks dangerous; even to me. She looks like Drew Barrymore, but she is physically fit, and she walks it. Suzy Q is what she goes by.

She keeps looking at me as if she knows me, and she sure looks like I know her from somewhere. As we clear Seattle and the bright light below us, I ask questions of our pilot, Suzy Q. She's a former Royal Canadian Mounted Policewoman who knocked out a fellow officer for homophobic comments. Then she came to the states, and she does private work now and works for a high-level security firm, One Safe Place Security. I let her know I have done a little of that myself. I tell her if she has any need for help, I like that kind of work.

"Well, let me tell you, some of my work can be dirty, dangerous, and sometimes people get hurt. Are you a warrior?"

"I've put in some work."

She seems to know what that means.

"I know you have. I watched you fight before, and I know Officer CC. I know your Uncle Don, and I know your aunt."

I'm almost put off, but then again, it's her job to know what people do.

"I see the look on your face. It's cool. It's my job to know who gets in my plane. I check out everyone to protect us both. Zelda, after I checked you out, it came to mind that I might have some work for you here and there. You game?"

"I like money, and I can handle myself. But what about if I need you to put in some work?" I cock my head and cut my eyes at her.

"I'll give you my numbers, and you call. My loyalty is unadulterated, and I assume yours is, too."

While Aloy was listening, I see he is puzzled; but as we climb higher in the sky, I see him relax. He looks out the window and he is smiling. I could only hope he is seeing me behind his eyes being naked later. Landing at night on Orcas Island was exciting. Suzy Q lets us know she will pick us up for a 9:00 AM flight going back Sunday morning. A hotel shuttle bus picks us up after we have been standing in the cold for a while. Waiting, it was perfect being inside Aloy's coat. I wish the shuttle had taken longer to come. He turned his phone music up loud, and we slow danced between the runway lights. This man gets me.

I have wanted to slow dance with a man ever since I used to watch my mom and Eddie slow dance. He used to let me step on his shoes and he would two-step me around the room, teaching me to dance. Most boxers can dance, and my step-dad could make my mom smile with his moves.

Our room overlooks the ocean. Something I have never done…I'm wearing something silky and sheer. We are slow dancing again on the deck of our room, it's on the top floor, and it is only him, the man who loves me, and the stars and God blessing me.

It's cold and so hot. I'm also doing something for me…I'm wearing some very pretty opentoe stilettos. I have to admit; my feet feel sexy, and look pretty. We walk in from the cold, and I sit on the bed and cross my legs. Aloy gets on all fours on the floor with a white bath towel wrapped around his sweet ass cheeks. His tongue is licking my arches and my toes, which are painted red. This is a first for me. My hair is in my loose afro style. I took out the long braids that went down my back. My Native and black DNA makes for a nice hairdo.

He is licking up my leg and then stands over me. He is slowly running his hands through my hair from the back of my neck. He combs his way through, and massages my temples, and rubs my cheeks. Then he kisses the tip of my nose. I look up at him and scan down his brown, perfect body; and to think, he wants me. I'm lean muscled, with small breasts and an ass that is round and protruding.

He is licking his way through my hair. My scalp is sexually sensitive, and I never knew this. Or is it just him, and everything about him? I feel a connection all through me. I'm squirming. I feel myself soaking between my thighs. He is sucking on my neck and leaning over me, licking my spine.

His hot hand lifts me to higher ground. I haven't done him like he has done me. I've been receiving each time we have been naked. I want to give him something.

"Aloy, sit down on the bed. Do it now!"

He looks stunned, but he complies. I take off my heels and sit on the floor in front of him, then I run my feet up and down his legs while I touch myself. I put on a freak show for him. I have two fingers going in and out of my openings. I lift his towel with my feet, and cup his balls with my toes. Stroking them, I make sure he can see me inserting my fingers inside me. I pull them out and hold them for him to do what he wants. He takes his hand and squeezes my feet around the shaft of his fat dick. Leaning forward, he sniffs my fingers than sucks them.

I get on all fours like he was before, and I lick his feet and legs, and I lick his inner thighs and suck. I make my way to his dick. I rub my face under it and all over it. I suck lightly on his balls while I stroke his dickhead. He groans. And I mean, he groans. He drips a lot of clear life in my hands. He even humped upwards. I suck his dick like I'm trying to suck it off his body. I let it go to the back of my throat and release. I take my hand and squeeze his whole length. I look up at him while I'm sucking him.

I turn around and reach back and spread my ass. I let him see my finger get nasty. "Aloy, stroke your dickhead. Do it now! I look back and he is putting lube on his hand and he starts jacking off. That shit is hot, even though his dick isn't hard. I stand and place my ass in his face and grind. I get on the bed and straddle over his bald head and grind my wet pussy on him. I put my finger on my clit and work and watch him stroke his dick while I rub my pussy on his head.

I throw my head back and grind, and try to cum on his head.

I look back down, and…he's hard. He stands and he's pushing me down on the bed. Like I was when I was on the floor, my breasts are down and my ass is high. I spread my ass so he can see ass and pussy. He's standing on the bed and squatting down with his hands on my lower back. I feel his hard dick slide slowly inside me.

The music player has changed to Color Me Bad's, *"I Wanna Sex You Up."* Aloy is humping to the rhythm of the song. His dick is good. Whatever got into him, I'm lost in it, and hope I have found the fix for him and for me.

He pulls out, and I was scared he would lose his hard-on, but he is still hard when I lay on my back. I pull my feet back behind my head, and take him in deep. He is hurting me, and I love it. He leans in and sends his tongue deep into my mouth. We are moaning and groaning into each other's mouth. My lover. My lover. My lover is sending me.

We talk in the morning after I had gotten him hard again. He lets me know no woman has set him off by trying to turn him on like I have. He had always been in charge, but he felt safe with me to let me control him, and it's not a little hard-on. Thick, and long, and strong. He now knows the problem was in his head. Maybe back then he was not healed, and maybe he had damaged himself when he had sex too early after the shooting. And whew'…he shoots a hot powerful thick load when he cums.

As we are flying back, I'm sitting with a very sore punany in the plane seat. Aloy was making up for lost time, and I was getting him hard whenever he wanted to get there.

Chapter 37

Glad to be home. Standing on my front porch, I've been looking for my key in my overnight bag. It's windy; clouds are moving over the city faster than the train I was on. I wonder if Chevelle is here, and if I can go to the back and have him let me in.

I'm wearing my stilettos and I'm in tight jeans. Hmm, it smells like Chevelle is cooking greens. Although he has a cooking station downstairs that he has put in, it's not big enough to have a big pot of greens on the small burners.

Damn, Chevelle, he has almost let the water boil out of the pot; he'd almost messed around and had a pot burning up in here. I open the basement door.

"Chevelle, boy you're gonna have the house full of burnt food with a burnt pot smell. You hear me?"

I'll have to talk to him about how he doesn't answer when a woman is talking to him. He'd rather give off body language answers, and I get it; but damn, if you're in the basement say something. He does that all the time. I'll be down in a while. Gotta use the bathroom now.

I head upstairs and drop off my bag, get out of my traveling clothes, and put on my baggy sweats. I look in the bathroom mirror and I think I see a woman. I think I see a woman in love, and who's feeling love come in. I see me being sensuous. After letting my behind feel stuck to the toilet seat from sitting too long, I decided to take a shower.

Now let me go have a conversation with Chevelle about taking down this fireplace. It's still early enough in the day to tear it down, and if there are skeleton bones in there, I want them out of here. I look in on the work going on in the first floor bathroom. It's almost complete, except for the finish work; the part where Chevelle's talent really shines.

Ever since I had the two ladies sit at my kitchen table unannounced—my sisters of pain, I keep checking my two coffee cans and what is in them. I have a question for Chevelle about the showerhead height. I call down into the basement. I hear him move about. I hear him call my name faintly. I made it down the stairs in one breath.

"What happened?" I scream. Chevelle is lying in blood. He lifts his hand in slow motion and points.

I turn and…

"Hello bitch."

I stare at a gun pointing at me. I see two faces, but the gun pointing at me has my attention. I know this is not going to be a threat whatever this about. Chevelle is hurt and laying in his blood. That asshole is holding a bat because he's not much of man; probably too scared to hold a gun, and can't swing his fists, so he's standing behind the gunman.

I move slowly toward Chevelle and motion that I'm going down to check on him.

"Stand your ass still!"

"You haven't killed him yet. You haven't killed me yet, so what is this?" I do the best I can to show I'm not scared. I'm frightened for Chevelle.

"Oh, your ass is going to die, and you're going to feel some pain before it ends. Both of you are gonna want to pull the trigger on your own asses."

"Would you share why?" my voice cracked this time. Trying to put my big gurl panties on ain't working. The light window curtains stir from air moving them. I know my house and what causes that.

"You know what time it is, and you know why," the second person, the one with the baseball bat, spoke with his nasally lisp. Sadducy Cowen talked shit standing behind the gunman. I did not want the gunman to shoot me or hit me. I had been hit by his now dead brother. Sargon Delroy looked at me with a hateful scowl. From the winkles in forehead, and down to lifted corners of his lips, told me I was going to die.

"You see, bitch…I know you had something to do with my brother's death, and I know that white boy piece of shit was near the house at the same time my brother was being beat to death." "You know all this how?"

My thought…*I did drop off Chevelle at the light rail station which is near the scene of the murder.*

"Oh, you standing there acting like it was a two for one. Besides killing my brother, you half-man-half-bitch, it's the money; that's the reason you're gonna have a hard, slow death."

"Money?"

It comes to mind quickly…the text a couple of weeks earlier from Mr. Magoo. I looked at nice new walls in the basement; some of them had blood splattered on them now.

"You move your ass in next door and shit starts happening? Of course, you take brain dead Aloy and make him a part of this somehow. He was fine all these years just being dumb and running the gym. But now, some men who kill for fun show up Friday night at my gambling house to talk to me and Duce. They tell us we won't get paid anymore; the loan is closed, and all the money now goes to the gym.

Now, it has to be you who's doing way too much. You've been stirring shit up, and I'm about need for you to use the bathroom one last time; but, you'll be shitting on yourself."

The curtains stir from air moving in the house.

I know I'll be talking to a lost cause, but I try. "Sargon, I didn't kill your brother, and I don't believe Chevelle did either."

"As if I care what you say. Hit that bitch."

Duce walked toward me and slapped me with a full round house backhand. Silly boy; a backhand is just silly. It barely stung, but I played along as if he did something.

"What about getting into our money biz? That money has taken care of me, my brother that you killed, and Duce, for a long time. Hit that bitch again."

"Ugh."

Duce took the bat and hit me with a full swing into my thigh. It hurts, but it didn't hit my thigh bone or knee. I drop to sit on the floor. I don't want to as it leaves my head wide open, but the pain. I grunt and breathe hard and fast to keep from screaming.

"Put- put the gun down." From atop of the stairs I hear my man. I hear Aloy. "Don't turn this way or I'll blow your head off, Unc."

Duce drops the bat.

Sargon keeps his gun trained on me.

"Put the gun down, I'm telling you. You and Duce, and his daddy and Sans, and maybe even Shomer, have been hurting people and using me for too long. It stops now," his speech was clear, flawless, and demanding.

"What you gonna do if I shoot your bitch? You gonna shoot me? You stupid mindless idiot, you can talk straight over this bitch, huh?" Sargon keeps the gun trained on me and never looks up the stairs as he laughs. "You like manly bitches, huh? Well, now you need to know yo' mama was a dike, and I watched ten men pinned her ass down and fucked her raw. Every drunk ass in the bar nutted in her one night, or on her dike ass or face, and nine months later, you popped out. Oh, and that would also include my daddy, too, but don't worry, he's not your daddy...he came in her mouth."

My mind swirled in hurt for Aloy to hear such evil and lack of human soul.

Sargon started to laugh a side-splitting laugh, as if it was really funny.

Boom.

I see blood squirt out of the side of Sargon's head. His body slumped to the floor.

A moment later, I see Aloy walking down the stairs with his eyes trained on Sargon's dead body. I get up; the pain in my thigh is making my head throb. I looked down at Chevelle. I see the bat. Duce has backed his coward ass over by the fireplace. I limp over to the bat and I hop over to Duce who has put his hands over his face. He is crying.

"I'm sorry, Duce, but you have this coming. I level the bat with full force on top of his head. He goes down, and I come down again on his head with the bat like I'm chopping wood. His body slumps. I know he is dead, or will be shortly.

I am keenly aware that time is important. When I saw the curtains moving, I knew someone was here. So glad it was him, but now he has killed the man who put a roof over his head, so to speak. My pain and puzzled look lets him know my questions.

"Alanese called me when she saw Sargon and Duce go in the house behind Chevelle and a gun was out. I rode over as fast as I could without knowing what was what. I'm glad you gave me a key. I was expecting the .22 in the coffee can, but the .38 was there."

Time, we need time. And Aloy's speech is bad again; it took a long time for him to say all of that. I start giving orders. We help Chevelle into the basement shower he put in. We can't call 911. I'm torn on my next decision. I go to my cell and make a call, and hope it's the right call.

Twenty minutes later in the basement, a doctor is tending to Chevelle. Plans are going down. First thing…we made Aloy leave; but first we made sure he was cleaned of all GSR. Gunshot residue may be found on the skin or clothing of a person after a gun is fired. He is wearing different clothes that he had left here from before, and he cleaned his body with chemicals Suzy Q brought with her. I'm queasy about all this, but I had to take a chance on who to call, and she is here in full charge. She brought a doctor, and he has Chevelle stable, but it will be a long recovery. He is clear minded, and knows he can never tell anyone, including the love of his life.

Suzy Q is good. She had two people wear clothes like the ones Sargon and Duce had on and sneak into my house from the other side of Alanese's view. I had wondered why she asked me what they wore. Then she had them leave for her view and any possible others. They got in Sargon's car and drove away. Before they left, they entered Duce's house and set it up to look like he packed to be gone a long time.

With Chevelle resting, and my thigh shot up with pain killer, Suzy Q and I get busy. The fireplace is dismantled in an hour, and yes, there is a dead woman's body buried inside. It is a huge hole, and Suzy Q had to crawl down way beyond the foundation of the house in order to pull up the bones, which were wrapped in what appeared to be wax paper. When I told Suzy Q about the ladies coming to the house, she said it has to be the first job we did. We had to rid the house of being a crime scene altogether. We put the bones in a plastic bin. Suzy Q brought many. She had me take the bones out to my trunk. I knew with the other bins, the bodies of Sargon and Duce would never be found.

Before I left, Suzy Q sat me down in the bloody basement with the fresh dead bodies on the floor. "I have sat in the Hob Nob Tavern in the corner, looking like another person, nondescript to you. I'm the old white lady in the corner playing chess. I know you've seen me put my big gun on the table before. I did that for you to see in order to see what your reaction would be since we both pack. Months ago, before your aunt gave you the keys to this house, she was worried about you."

"Why?"

"You have to ask her. I put myself in a position to know you without you knowing. I was hired for that. Plus, I upped my chess game."

I'm looking at her angrily in a, *What the hell are you talking about stare*. And damn, she really was that old lady in the Hob Nob. I've been sleeping on my awareness of what is going on around me.

"I do work," she is peering into me, and puts fear in me unlike anyone I have known before. I'm hired by your aunt through your Uncle Don who is good friends with the man named Psalms Black. I can't tell you that much."

The pain in my thigh has moved to my head. "Why?"

"She believed you could be in danger."

"Why?"

"You'll have to take that up with her. Aside from that, consider me a friend. I'm loyal."

I think about the fact that my Aunt Isiwata has not returned my texts or calls for nearly nine months now.

"Now I need you to leave. You call me if something don't feel right wherever you go."

I help Chevelle out to the car. The boy took a hell of a beating and is holding his own. He has proved to be a warrior a couple of times. I head out; a moving truck was coming to block the view of anyone seeing things coming out of the basement. I drive away with the one bin of once buried history. At the end of the alley, I open my car door and vomit. I drive to an Extended Stay hotel. The room is waiting, and the door is unlocked. I will stay here tonight until late tomorrow, and Chevelle will stay in the hotel for a week, or longer, if needed. A doctor will check in on him.

Chapter 38

I can't sleep. I get up and I head over to the gym. An hour later, Aloy and I are holding each other. We are lying down weeping in each other's arms in his loft bedroom. I can't know what he is feeling, and I won't try. I'll have to be whatever he needs. He has said that to me, he will be whatever I need.

We have blood on our hands. Our tears meet, puddle, and make love on the pillow we share. We cry ourselves to sleep.

The house. I stayed away for three days. I stood on the back porch and prayed to my ancestors and to God to ask for forgiveness if I need to be forgiven. The basement appeared to be a total rip out and redo, but with all the design work Chevelle had done before. The fireplace was gone, along with the old carpet. I could tell there was all new sheet rock walls, along with paint. There is no crime scene in this house.

I'm blowing up my auntie's phone with calls or texts; no response.

I meet with Mr. Magoo a week later. I tell him he put his desire to help ahead of the reality of what is real for the living. He nods. He knows what that means. I let him know that Duce's money needs to come to the gym as it should, but now I need money going to Alanese Delroy. She has no income coming in. He nods. He knows what that means. I assume he will take a cut to administer the funds.

I met with Robin who drove up from Oakland. She brought Shevon to the meeting. We are parked down at Lake Washington. The sun is out, although it is cold. I hand over the plastic tub that I have sealed with duct tape. We all don't say much. We hold hands for a long while and we separate.

Every night, Aloy and I sleep physically entangled in the safety of each other's arms. To be held by hurt, fear, trust, and love, is a mix of epic feelings; it either builds your character, or rips away your soul.

I was too emotional to sleep at the house the first week, so every night I slept up in the gym loft. I said my prayers to God, and then the man I love cradled my confusion next to his heart. Then like a king, he said we are going to stay at the house, and he will protect me. He stood tall for me in order for me to face my fear of what had been done under this roof. He is a warrior; much like the man I first saw riding his iron horse. He is the man who would have an Olympic gold medal. He is the man who would have been the world champ, and retired undefeated, and came home to me and his children.

The children…I had been away from them for too long, and Oceania was upset when I called. I still couldn't get by in a timely manner. I did not want them to come here to the house yet. I had taken the kids places with both me and Aloy, and they loved him. I told the kids I will get them soon, and I will bring Aloy. I know Skyler needed a male mentor. Oceania asked again could she come live with me. All I can do when she asks is listen to her, and say it will all work out.

The bruise on my thigh was so ugly. Ten shades of black and purple, and still pain kept me sleeping on one side. It was funny one night while spooning into Aloy, I felt him get hard. His confidence was in play. He apologized, and I laughed and told him to get hard all he wanted, and when my leg allowed, I was going to put his hardness to good use often.

Chevelle was nursing himself back to health. I told him not to lie to Iman, but to ask her to let him have this event in his life to himself. She told him she trusted him as he had trusted her.

I went over to see Alanese. I had no thought on how that would be. Her husband had now been away for ten days, as well as Duce, and I wouldn't know who would miss him. Alanese poured some coffee for me, and we had small talk. Then before I left, she showed me an envelope full of money.

"Pay your bills, Alanese. Pay them all," I said that in a way for her to clue in that life will never be the same again.

"I sent Aloy to save you."

"He did."

I turned and went home and cried in my bay window. Aloy saved me and he killed. He had saved before, and he had to kill. He has killed because he has been the most loving soul the Gods have created.

Chapter 39

My first night sleeping in the house alone. I'm in the bed early, 9:00 PM, and the phone rings before I drift off.

"Skyler, what's wrong?" his voice is hushed.

"Come get us." Oceania must have put him up to this because he never calls; it's always Oceania.

"Skyler, I'll come by tomorrow and take you guys out. Where is Oceania?" He puts her on the phone.

"They are fighting," Oceania says. I hear Skyler whimpering.

"I'll be there in the morning; you guys go to bed."

I try to go to sleep, and fifteen minutes later, I jump up and feel thigh pain. It's getting better, but still pains me. I put a lidocaine patch on my thigh, and hit the road to go check on the kids.

I head over to the Mont Baker area, and drive past the house because there is no parking available in the front, and Shomer and Eneta have their vehicles parked in the driveway. With my long car, I have to park several houses away. I use my key. They gave me one a long time ago because I pick up and drop off the kids, and they are coming and going all the time. I turn off the alarm and go in.

I figure if the husband and are wife are auguring, the kids got scared. When we got home late from an outing, or if their parents were gone and I stayed the night, we all piled in Oceania's bed, so I go there first. She's not in her bed, and it's still made up. Skyler pokes his head out of his room. I walk in and he grabs me like he going to tear my skin off, and she is in the corner trembling. I go to her and hug her.

"Where are your parents?"

They point downstairs, and at the same time, I hear some loud bumping and screaming.

"I want you and your brother to get a change of clothes, and go out to my car and wait for me." I hand her my keys. "It's a few houses down."

Their distress moves them along quickly.

Eneta and Pastor Shomer have scared these kids with the adult ignorance.

I see the kids out the door, and point them to my car. I make my way to the basement door, and I'm going to tell the Pastor and his wife that I have the kids. It dawns on me that Eneta was out of town at a conference; yeah, I now know that could be a lie. I hear low voices. It sounds like the sound system from the home theater. I turn the nob.

"You off playing with your boy toy in every city in America, paying his way with my money. So, I'm going to keep beating the shit out of you, and I'm going to poke you in every hole you got. Just like him."

"Shomer, I'm sorry; but please, I beg you, please don't."

Wham.

It sounds like a belt has hit skin.

I hear anger and I hear distress. I hear pain. I'm easing down the stairs; it hurts my thigh. There is a high wall that hides the stairs, so no one will see me until the last few stairs.

I just want to go down there and let them know their shit is scaring the kids. I'm hoping maybe if he is hitting his woman, he'll stop. If not, I take a deep breath and dislodge my .38. I'm just not going to let a man beat on his woman. Shit, I don't want to take my gun out. I have had enough of this.

I'm down the stairs. Shomer's back is to me. His shirt is off, and he is in his underwear. He has his Taurus 4510 Revolver aimed down to the floor. I hear Eneta. She's on the floor. My thigh hurts like hellfire. I aim my gun and move forward. I see Eneta is face down and naked. Eneta's back looks like something from slavery.

"Put your gun down! Don't turn around! If you do, I'll park a bulletin one of your eyes."

"You got a gun pointed at me? Well, I got one pointed at her."

"Yeah, but if I pull this trigger, you'll never take another breath, or be brain dead. If I unload on you, all your brain matter will be fertilizer for your garden."

Shomer puts his pretty gun down on the coach.

"Now turn around."

He does.

"What are you doing to your wife? And you're terrifying the hell out of your kids."

He doesn't respond. I see on his face he's weighing his options.

Eneta sits up. Her face had been beaten. Her breasts have welts, and her arms and legs have wounds and more welts.

"What is going on, Eneta?"

"I came home early from a conference and he found out I…"

I train my gun right into the eyes of Shomer. I breathe slowly as I'm in a fight and I can't lose my head. I need to stay focused. I can't kill again. I don't want to. I hope we all leave here living.

"Eneta, I doubt if you were at any conference. I saw you in Portland. Enough of the lies. You fake ass church folks. Pastor Shomer, there is special hell waiting for you for beating on a woman; no matter what she is doing, or not doing. I'm gonna make sure your 1,000 members find out what kind of man you are."

He flinches. He sees hell. The gun pointing at him might send him to hellfire and damnation. Eneta stands, beaten and naked.

My eyes are lodged on his. Eneta lurches for his gun on the coach, and she has it pointed at the back of his head. She is shielded from me.

"Eneta, you don't want to kill a man; it will stay with you forever. Let's just send him to jail."

"He has sexed me like a piece of crap for ten years. He humps on me for a minute and spews his hate-filled cum and goes off to watch porn." Porn is playing on the flat screen. "He hated me since his own brother, Sans, got me drunk and took advantage of me while I was passed out. I told him—my husband, trying to be the good wife, and he has despised me for it ever since. Now he screws half the women in the church. I found the videos, Shomer; you can't lie. You did women in our own bed, and then they smile in my face every Sunday. I only have a lover because I have needed to be made to feel like a woman."

Shomer turned in her direction. I kept my gun aimed on him. "Both you clowns can't prove anything," his pastor voice had pulpit power, but I wasn't a church girl as much as I prayed. His pimp a church woman sway wasn't working on me. "Eneta, you look guilty, too. You're in those videos, too. My dick is in every one of your holes in them same the videos recorded. I might lose my church, but I'm your income; you'll be known as a whore and a broke bitch."

Boom.

She shot her husband in the heart. The bullet exited through his back, and then whizzed by me. I ducked after the fact, but it would have hit me if I was one foot to the left. He sat down slowly on the couch then slumped over.

She dropped the gun as if she was frightened of it.

Time for concentration, as I see her going into shock.

"Eneta!" I scream. She looks at me. "I'm taking the kids, and they are coming to live with me. You will have a lot to deal with. These kids have dealt with a world of people taking advantage of them, including you. You never wanted the kids, it shows. In two minutes, call the police, don't clean yourself up. Don't even wipe the blood from your face. Don't even put on any clothes accept for a robe. Leave the gun right there, tell the police he was beating you. He got careless as he was beating you, and you were able to surprise him and rip the gun from his hand, and you pulled the trigger. Tell the truth of where you were standing. More than anything, let them know you are in pain, and let them take you to the hospital. Tell everything, even that you were having an affair. They can find out. They will find out. Leave the kids out of it. When asked, tell them they are with me. And this is very important...if asked did you make a call to my cell phone tonight, say yes." I pull my phone out, and the kids had called me an hour ago. I give her the time. "Tell them you were checking on the kids because you had missed them when you got back, and you wanted to say goodnight. Get it right, Eneta, or you're going to prison for a long time."

I made her repeat all. She got it right. I had her attention.

Chapter 40

I use the burner phone that Suzy Q left with me, and I called her, and told her everything. Her response is that she's proud of me that I didn't kill, and that I did the best I could out of a funky situation. She said her people will locate the videos and make sure all of the videos with Eneta wouldn't be found, as that could lead to an assumption that she had vengeance in mind. I let the kids sleep next to me when we got to my house.

In the morning I watched the local ambulance chasing news was all over the homicide or self–defense death of a prominent preacher. Church members were on the news praying and lighting candles outside the church. Very pretty women were showing how much they were upset on camera, as if it would bring back Pastor Shomer. Others spoke highly of First Lady Eneta, and how she could never take a life unless she was forced to.

It's few days later, I get a hold of Eneta's lawyer to get permission to get the kids' beds and clothes and other items from the house. She has signed over temporary custody to me, and she will do all she has to do in order for me to have full-time custody, regardless of the outcome of her legalities. The lawyer passed a message on to me from her that she is thankful for all my help.

I go see my step-dad, Eddie, and I tell him I have kids not of my own but they are mine, and much like him, I will take good care of them as he did with me. I tell him I have a man in my life and he is good to me.

As I leave, he grabs my hand. "Zelda, are you my daughter?" It has been over a year since he has said my name, and asked that same question. "Zelda, you are my daughter; right?"

"Eddie, you're the only daddy I know of. I may not be your blood, but you are my family. I love you, and you're coming to live with me soon."

He smiles like a drunken sailor. I hug him and let him feel my tears roll down his cheek.

Auntie Isiwata called, she finally wants to meet. I tell her I need a few days.

Chevelle came back to the house. He's healthier and he likes his space as well as spending time with Iman. He loves the kids, and it has allowed me to leave the house. He has helped set up their rooms on the first floor. They are small rooms, but its home, and they are adjusting. We have talked about what has happened to a point. I'm glad they were out of the house when the shot rang out. Neither has had much to say, but if I think they need counseling, and I will seek it.

Chevelle and Iman had the kids spend the night and now I'm leaving the loft Sunday morning. Last night was the first time, in a long while, that Aloy and I made love. It's getting easier for him as I enjoy making him excited. We made slow grinding love.

I'm headed to meet with my auntie at a lakefront restaurant. She is sitting in a booth. My auntie is pretty. She must be on one of her diets again. I wish she and I were closer.

"Zelda, I am aware of the three men who are dead." No small talk from her. "I know those men. I knew those men."

I don't ask questions; I'm going to listen.

She has a glass of wine and I have coffee. I waited for her to talk.

She has made very little eye contact. She's staring out on the water.

"I was seventeen, and you know my sister was two years younger. I protected her all the time. I would beat up other girls over her if they looked at her wrong, or teased her. She was shy and reserved, and the homemaker type. Me, I was into school and partying.

"I had met a guy at a party near the naval base one weekend, and he wanted to see me the next weekend. He said he had a shy friend to double date, and I thought it would be a great thing to take my baby sister.

"We meet at his apartment, and then we were going out to go dancing. These guys were nice. Shomer and Sargon…I really thought they were nice. Another guy came by. They were all brothers; Shomer, Sargon, and Sans. They tortured and raped us. They hurt us badly. They seemed to enjoy it. They held us until the morning and told us they would kill us if we said anything, and we believed them."

I had not seen tears of hurt from my Auntie since her and my mom shared holding me. She was barely able to talk at some points. I'm stunned. I'm putting it together that my mother was the victim of rape, and all three of her rapists are dead in association with me in some form or another.

I want to curse at my auntie, but she is melting in shame. But why did she put me near them. One tried to rape me, and he is dead. Who did it? I don't know. Another of the brothers tried to kill me, and hurt Chevelle. Then the last one is dead because he was an ass to his wife, and I witnessed him taking his last breath. Least not I forget, I killed Sadducy Cowen.

"Back then, I wanted to keep track of those brothers to make sure they didn't come after us. I forged a distant relationship with Alanese. She was the girlfriend of Sargon. She never knew my connection, but I was able to track the brothers and where they moved. People wrote post cards and letters before email. I was almost seven months pregnant before I understood I was having a baby."

"What?"

"I was smart with numbers and words, but dumb to many other things. I had graduated from high school early, and had academic scholarships to colleges. They didn't let girls come to college with a baby in tow back then. My baby sister stepped in and became my baby's mother. Your mother. Our mother agreed it would be the best thing to do."

I'm staring at what I can't believe.

"No!"

"Yes, Zelda, I am your birth mother, and my sister gave the biggest gift to you that I was not able to do. Yes, I'm your birth mother, but my sister is your God sent mother."

"Ah, ah, I...I...I need to go outside for a moment."

I almost ran. I make it to the edge of a dock, and there is a couple nearby, but I lose what I had in my stomach in the water below. I go in the bathroom; my bowels are making me sit.

I pull out my phone and turn the voice recorder on.

"Who am I?
I'm born on a date and I'm here in the present.
Who am I?
A child of God, yes.
Who am I?
A sinner, lover, thinker.
Am I a forgiver?
Who am I?
A woman who is not sure whose blood runs through me. Who am I?
A woman who wants love, and surely wishes the love I have to give is needed and wanted.
Who am I?
A woman of creative thoughts; a mastermind of my own desires.
Who am I?
A mastermind often controlled by my un-mastered necessities.
Who am I?
A bleeder who absorbs hurt, who in return, kills the mind's deceivers and bodies.
Who am I?
Challenged and challenging.
Who am I?
Who am I?
A woman expressing joy and pain.
Who am I?
Days come, and I have no clue
Who am I?

267

Well, according to a twisted history, I am…

Who am I?

I'll get back to myself to find who I am."

I didn't care that there was someone in the other stall when I asked, *Who am I*. I come back and stare at the womb I came out of. I try to talk, but nothing comes out. We sit in silence.

After Isiwata had another glass of wine, I learned more.

"Il tried several times to come claim you as my child, but my sister would not have it. If I took you away, I felt bad and brought you back. I had hoped when she got sick that she and I would sit down with you, and tell you the truth. I believe she never came up here for better medical attention that might have saved her life, because she never wanted to tell you and hurt you. I learned later from your grandmother that she was damaged in the rape and was unable to have children herself, and that is the reason she and your step-dad never had children and you were her soul to keep.

"Who, which one of them is your father, there is no way to know. I'm sure there is a medical test that can be done, but they were awful men. I'm not in your shoes, but maybe it's best not to know; and for the fact that you, me, and others helped put them to rest for their sins."

"You…Me…and others!"

"Now, Zelda, I must face my shortcomings. Will you accept me still into your life, in the life I have left?"

"What are saying, Auntie?"

"You have not seen me since I last dropped you of at your house, and it is your house. It's paid for, and your name is on the deed. You have not seen me even though you have asked. You have called and texted me often. I've been in treatment for pancreatic cancer. It's going give me some life but not for a long time."

With what she has told me, all the tons of questions I had of what and who and when, don't matter. I look out the window at the lake and see, in the shadows, the kids I now have to take care of. I see Aloy, and he and I found each other and need each other. He is talking to me about marrying me in time, and we both raise the kids. I see new and lasting friends in Chevelle, Iman, JoBelle, Alanese, and Suzy Q. How will I enjoy life with so much death? I must help others live to keep the living in me going, and to know who am I.

"Isiwata, I'm here, and I'll help you live until there is no more life to live. I have many questions, and you are my blood. My mother would want me to take care of her sister."

I look outside toward the parking lot and I see my old Cadillac. I see other cars looking wet from drizzle. I had parked by my auntie's classic Pontiac. Our two cars seem dry, and every other car seems to be grasped in a drizzle when ours are dry. My eyes are wet, so maybe I'm seeing things the way I want them to be. I look down at my mother's ring on my finger. I would be spinning it around as if it was a windmill in the wind. I'm not. I see the beauty. I look at my auntie, my birth mama, and she is pretty like my mother. I smile thinking about what Aloy sees in me when he looks at me. I'm pretty now, I believe, because I look like the two women who loved me in their own way. I understand now through all I have been through, and why my stepdad would say often, "There is, bad before good and those in between."

ABOUTTHEAUTHOR

Alvin Lloyd Alexander Horn has lived, breathed the Northwest air, and floated in all the nearby rivers and streams leading to the Pacific Ocean. As in the stories of Hemingway, the poetry of Langston Hughes, and the novels of Walter Mosley, their writings – as well as Alvin's – are all byproducts of their childhood environments and their subsequent travels. Alvin's African-American experiences in his Emerald City background, shines through in his poetry, short stories, and novels.

Growing up in the "liberal on the surface" Seattle lifestyle, Alvin's childrearing was grounded by interactions with Black people who had jobs, who could go most places they desired, and who were not residents of stereotypical ghettos. He feels that his passion for writing was triggered by his mother sending him to the library when she placed him on restriction; often for daydreaming while in school. He also credits the little gray-haired white lady – the librarian for introducing him to the likes of Richard Wright and Zora Neale Hurston. Upon reading the work of Nikki Giovanni, Alvin knew he wanted to be a writer of love stories and poetry.

"Some of my erotic writing imagination came from my dad leaving Playboy magazines in a not-so-secret place. My friends were fixated on the pictures; but me, I just read the stories...most of the time."

Alvin also had a storied athletic career as an athlete, a coach, and as a musician; the skill, talent, and knowledge gained from those backgrounds often shows up in his writings. Alvin played sports at the University of New Mexico in the mid-70s, and had a short sports career after college. Prior to launching his writing career, Alvin had a fifteen-year stint in the aerospace industry. For the last fifteen years, Alvin has worked in the field of education teaching life-skills, poetry and creative writing, and working with at-risk youth.

Alvin is a highly acclaimed spoken word artist which allows him to travel and promote his art of words. He has balanced his writing career alongside doing voice-overs for radio and TV, music, video, and movie productions, as well as acting. His writings have appeared in many periodicals ranging in genres from fiction to erotica. He can often be found all over the Northwest reciting poetry and playing stand-up bass at different venues, but he has a fond admiration for Houston, Hot-Atlanta, Vegas, Vancouver, B.C., and most parts of California and New York. Most of all, Alvin loves being on the back deck of his houseboat writing love poetry and stories.

Alvin L.A. Horn is the author of:

The World That fell into My Dresser Drawer; a book of poetry, 2001
BRUSH STROKES; a novel, 2005
PERFECT CIRCLE; a novel published by Zane and Simon and Schuster, 2012
ONE SAFE PLACE; a novel published by Zane and Simon and Schuster, 2014
BRUSH STROKES; the re-release, with an added short Story, 2016
All in available in paperback and e-book.
To read more about names mentioned in this book, Tylowe Dandrige, Ayman Sparks Psalms Black, read these books.

Maybe he thought he could read her mind with her head next to his because he sure wanted her to know his thoughts. He wanted her to understand the world might be breaking apart; but no matter what, he knew in his heart and mind, she was his one safe place to lay his burdens down."
~ONE SAFE PLACE~

"A woman is a King maker, a man is a Queen keeper; the sun rises, the moon never sets on their kingdom. The Queen is rich; the King protects her heart of gold. Her King leaves his legacy. His Queen is his authentication."
    ~PERFECT CIRCLE~

A man may admire what a woman does for a living; he may admire her education and social circle. He may be enamored with her physical beauty; but he only truly falls in love with the softest and warmest part of her – her soul."
    ~BRUSH STROKES~

Alvin L.A. Horn is also a contributing author in the anthologies: *Pillow Talk in the Heat of the Night*, and *The Soul of a Man 2*, and a writer for the *Inner City News*, and a feature writer for *Real Life Real Faith Magazine*, as well as several other publications.

Youmayvisittheauthorat:
www.alvinhorn.com
https://www.facebook.com/alvinhorn
https://twitter.com/alvinlahorn

Alvin L.A. Horn was also voted the 2012 Billboard Best Erotic Romantic Spoken Word Artist of the year. You can hear his voice audio art and leave feedback at https://soundcloud.com/alvinhorn.

Additional video art by Alvin L.A. Horn available at:
AM THAT MAN
https://www.youtube.com/watch?v=UNTdcurtrHg
The Lonely Sun
https://www.youtube.com/watch?v=Np8Qo4z9LUQ
Mountain Top
https://www.youtube.com/watch?v=hCenJLmXyhc
Armorist from the Galaxy
https://www.youtube.com/watch?v=dqA53TxlZbg&feature=plc
p
Book cover models;
Toyia Taylor, founder of Young Artists Academy -
https://www.facebook.com/toyia.taylor.9
Alvin L.A. Horn
John Harding aka whizzy whizzer, the artist, and rights to the drawing of 1950 Cadillac
See some great art at, http://www.hardingsart.com/

Back cover photo rights: Allison Pickens aka Allison TennyPick. Ms. Pickens requests that you support the American Cancer Society

BAD BEFORE GOOD & *THOSE IN BETWEEN*

Questions

#1: The scene the bar could you see the people from different walks of life all searching or not wanting to be found? An old-school bar/tavern have you been there, maybe your family member had their favorite place, their own "Cheers Bars" in their hood?

#2: Zelda had her own kind of blues in life what did you feel and what here they? Can love and hurt live as one in one's soul?

#3: Zelda seems to have been pushed to the limit in more than one way from her experiences. What about her behavior did it show and it humbled her of how much she could take and now how to live another way. What were the limits?

#4: A lifestyle that most women run from, she embraced a level of violence without being thuggish or even criminal, she did what she felt she had to do or was it over the top as she was willing to take a life if pushed in that direction.

#5: For sure Zelda had sex was on her mind, do you think most women feel and think as she does? Remember you read her inner feeling and as in everyone, no one knows but you, so could it be?

#6: Chevelle turned out to be a trusted friend because his life he too did not know who he was in many ways as in with Zelda. She needed him and he needed her. Ever met someone like that in your life, but it could be dangerous?

#7: What was the meaning of the passage, "Zelda, it is no fairytale for us women. Men have dropped their drawls mentally at some time for less desirable women than the woman he has in his life supporting him. We, women, want to believe in the fairytale of *Never, Never Land*, shall my man stray. Somehow, we say things like, *Just don't let me hear about it*, and he *bet not make some baby out there*, or even, *Don't bring anything home.*

"We have been thinking and saying those types of things for a very long time, to which men feel it's a license to spread his seed just as long as it doesn't sprout, and just as long as we don't find out what other fields he tends to."

#8: Was Zelda comfortable in who she is or not. Did she have a weakness(s), and what were her strengths?

#9: Aloy is a tortured soul. Why beyond his speech? How did Zelda break his sexual dysfunction?

#10: Could you feel the Northwest and some history throughout the story?

#11 Zelda hated to depend on others, but for sure needed people she could trust. Beyond Aloy and Chevelle who else did she trust?

#12: Did the book make you think that anyone from any part of life?

#13: Who would play each part in a movie?

#14: Zelda Killed Sudducy. Aloy killed his Uncle Sargon Delroy-the man who lived next door and was married to Aloy's Aunt Alanese. Pastor's wife Eneta killed her husband Pastor Shomer Delroy, Who do you think killed Sans Delroy the third brother??????